I0539316

THE HIGHLANDER'S FRENCH BRIDE

The Highlander's Bride series (book 5)

By Cathy MacRae

www.cathymacraeauthor.com

PRINT EDITION

Published by Short Dog Press
Copyright 2015

Copyright Notice

Dedication

To love which only
grows stronger
and never gives up.

THE HIGHLANDER'S FRENCH BRIDE

Heir to a lairdshsip, Kinnon Macrory is driven to prove himself fighting the English on the battlefields of France. His dreams of heroic valor are destroyed by his inability to come to grips with the atrocities visited on the very people he is sworn to protect, and three years in a French prison for a crime he did not commit leave Kinnon longing for the one thing of beauty in his war-torn life—a young woman of great kindness and wisdom named Melisende.

Melisende de la Roche struggles to stay one step ahead of soldiers who would imprison her for helping an injured Scotsman accused of treason. She finds refuge in her uncle's shop—until a chance encounter sends her fleeing into the unknown once again, always haunted by the beguiling friendship with the troubled young Scotsman she is certain she will never see again. Determined to find the woman of his dreams, Kinnon returns to France, only to discover a trail of clues to Melisende's whereabouts. Their reunion will open the doors to passion, but half-truths and lies from the past could destroy the one thing they both are willing to fight for—each other.

Books in The Highlander's Bride series

The Highlander's Accidental Bride (book 1)
The Highlander's Reluctant Bride (book 2)
The Highlander's Tempestuous Bride (book 3)
The Highlander's Outlaw Bride (book 4)
The Highlander's French Bride (book 5)

A note about this book:

As I began my research for this book, I discovered I needed to tweak history just a bit. It was clear from earlier books in the series that the setting for this book was France during the Hundred Years War. However, during the particular year this book was set, France and England were in an uneasy truce. But another storyline began to intertwine with Kinnon's as I discovered a man named Bertran du Guesclin, Constable of France. He was a resourceful figure, a man who had risen from somewhat less-than-noble beginnings to become the champion of the king, and the hero of the people. His story became integral to that of my hero.

Bertran du Guesclin died in 1380 as described in this story, though my timeline has him passing several years earlier. My most sincere apologies to this great man for cutting his life shorter than it already was. May he rest in peace.

CHAPTER ONE

1374, Châteauneuf-de-Randon, France

Kinnon Macrory stared into the face of death.

`Tis nae fair. After all the battles I have survived, to arrive at this.* He would have sighed at the injustice of it, but he was, quite frankly, afraid to make an unnecessary move.

The black mask surrounded dark topaz eyes, a burnished coat, and a fine set of strong, glistening white teeth revealing themselves from beneath snarling black jowls. The Alaunt's ears lay flat against his skull in warning, and his hair stood up along his neck and shoulders. As did Kinnon's.

Shite.

He lifted his eyes carefully from the reddened hand laid across the dog's neck. The slender fingers could have belonged to a nobleman's daughter, but the nails were short and the skin rough. *Amazing what the mind registers when death is imminent.* Kinnon's gaze wandered further. The owner of the hand wore a serviceable gown, patched areas meticulously sewn, sleeve cuff turned back on itself, almost hiding the frayed edges of her struggling circumstances. A smudged apron covered the front of the gown, the bucket of milk at her feet announcing her job before he arrived—and came face-to-face with death.

"Do ye mind calling off yer beast?" He offered a winsome smile, splaying his hands at his side, a small bag of coins in his left palm. The young woman stared at him, giving the bag only a brief glance.

He tried again. "*Chien?*"

The young woman's gaze did not waver—clear, cold blue eyes bore into his. Wisps of dark hair curled damply against her temple, attesting to her work ethic and the warmth of the day. Her thin nose sat atop full, red lips that neither smiled nor frowned at him, her thoughts inscrutable.

The dog growled, a deep menacing sound originating from his enormous chest that warned Kinnon from making a further move—if he wanted to keep his throat intact.

Kinnon did.

His heartbeat kicked up. The impressive muscles in the dog's forelegs rippled, his claws gripped the ground, his hindquarters bunched, ready to launch himself at the least provocation. Savage power quivered beneath the thin hand of a milkmaid Kinnon could have easily tossed over his shoulder without so much as a grunt of effort. Endless moments passed as he roundly cursed the man who sent him to this farm on an errand better suited to one of the camp lackeys.

"*Se calmer*, Jean-Baptiste," the young woman murmured as the dog leaned forward.

"Jean-Baptiste?" Kinnon couldn't help himself. "Ye call this beast John the Baptizer?"

The woman gave him a curious look, but the edge of her lips quivered, threatened to smile. "He has changed *la religion* of more than one man."

Kinnon's eyebrows shot upward and he shifted his weight against an alarmed ache in his loins. "Aye. I can believe that."

He took measure of the enormous beast, its shoulder almost even with the woman's waist, his possessiveness clear. With his mistress's soft command, the dog settled, but his eyes did not waver, his threat remained unmistakable. No pampered pet, Jean-Baptiste was all business. And today his business included eating soldiers.

"I was sent to ask ye for what supplies I could buy." Kinnon gently flipped the small bag in his hand. The movement and clink of coin drew the woman's attention.

"You brought coin?" She snorted and hefted the milk bucket in one slender hand. "Most simply take what they want."

Kinnon moved automatically to take the burden from her but froze at the snarled response from the dog. His startled gaze darted to the milkmaid, gaging her next action. Cool blue eyes met his, and this time, the young woman smiled.

"*Merci*, but I can manage. If you would like to keep your *virilité* intact, please take a step back. Jean-Baptiste and I do not like to be crowded."

Kinnon let out his breath and took the required step back. "Aye. And I thank ye."

She raised her eyebrows. "For what?"

"For not letting yer beast change my religion."

The young woman jerked her chin, indicating him to follow. Keeping a respectful distance, Kinnon trailed her.

"What is it you wish to purchase?" Her voice hitched as she swung the bucket onto the back of the small cart against the edge of the stone stable. Moss grew over the crumbling edges, softening the façade. Hay spilled into the yard, fresh and clean, its odor mingling with the sharp tang of manure.

"My commander sent me for chickens, eggs, beef—whatever ye can spare." He gave her a sideways glance. "The coin would purchase material for a pretty gown for ye, or mayhap a bit of ribbon."

The woman gave him a stern look. "I have no use for such fripperies. The English soldiers care nothing for our welfare, and our cupboards bear the brunt of their greed."

Kinnon shook his head. "Bertran wouldnae condone such behavior."

Her face darkened. "His is not the only army in these parts, *monsieur*. The English have garrisoned here many years."

"That would explain ye speaking English, though yer accent is quite lovely." He gifted her a winsome grin.

"Your *accentuer* is strange. Neither *Anglais* nor *Français*. It is not one I recognize."

"Nae English. Scots."

She lifted fine eyebrows. "You are Scottish? Fighting here, on French soil? Have you no battles to fight in Scotland?"

Kinnon's grin broadened.

"Och, aye. There are always skirmishes to whet one's appetite. But as part of the Auld Alliance, we Scots are grateful for any chance to fight the bluidy English."

Wiping her hands in her apron, the young woman nodded. "Do you have a wagon?"

"Aye. `Tis in that copse of trees. Bluidy rocks around here make driving it a bit of a nuisance."

"We will pick out what you need and load the cart. Jean-Baptiste can pull it to your wagon." She led him into the stable.

Kinnon eyed the beast's beefy shoulders. "A good use for his muscles."

"He can take down an angry bull with a mere tug of his head. His ancestors were bred in the mountains and came with the Romans as war dogs. He fears nothing, yet cares for us with gentleness."

"Us?"

She nodded. "My sister lives here as well. She is gathering eggs."

Kinnon paused. "Mademoiselle, I have been too long at war, but even so, my ma would say my manners need polish. If we are to do business, I should introduce myself. My name is Kinnon Macrory." He held out his hand.

"My name is Melisende. Let me see the color of your coin."

* * *

"So, you met the lovely Melisende and Jean-Baptiste?" Bertran chuckled and shoved a chunk of meat into his mouth.

"St. Andrew-on-a-spit, ye could have warned me about the beast. For a moment I thought I wouldnae live to tell the tale." His gaze stole downward. "Or return in one piece."

"Do not be alarmed, *mon ami*. You have nothing to fear as long as you keep your hands to yourself and do not irritate *la mademoiselle*. It is why I sent you and not some camp provisioner. Her farm is remote and mayhap less ravaged than others nearer the English garrison. It would behoove us to keep it that way."

"Not kill the goose with the eggs, aye?"

"*Exactement*. I have neither time nor inclination to take up farming. Nor the men to spare." Bertran wiped his hands on a linen square and an aide hurried to clear the table. "*Merci*." He waved to his empty trencher. "This is as good a meal as I have had in a time. Are you certain you do not care for any?"

"Thank ye, no. I only wished to see if there was anything else before I turned in. How is the garrison holding up?"

"I have not had conversation with De Ros in several days. He still believes we will tire of this and go away."

"Even after yesterday's skirmish?" Kinnon rubbed his chin, eying the boxes of provisions stacked to one side of the commander's enormous tent. "Mayhap he will reconsider on an empty stomach."

"We can wait him out, do not fear. After our losses in Poitiers, it became clear pitched battles with the English are not our best option." He nodded his thanks to the aide who placed a small plate of cheeses at his elbow. Picking a soft white lump, he popped it in his mouth, clearly relishing the rich flavor. "I, on the other hand, have the means to enjoy the surrounding countryside as well as the delicacies De Ros tries to slip past us."

"We Scots have been known to favor small skirmishes over large battles. Especially when it harries the English."

Bertran du Guesclin's smile turned grim. "We lost several men in yesterday's skirmish. And the mercenaries grow bored with lack of activity and plunder. But I feel something decisive will happen soon, *mon ami*. We must remain patient."

Taking his leave of the commander, Kinnon stepped from the tent into the fading evening twilight. On the hillside stood the village, an English garrison on the border between French and English territory, ceded to Edward III by the Treaty of Brétigny. It was to reclaim French land for Charles V that Bertran du Guesclin, *L'aigle de la Bretagne,* had been recalled from Castile ten years earlier and made Constable of France.

L'aigle de la Bretagne. The Eagle of Brittany. Kinnon cast his gaze at the extravagant tent, the interior lamps lit against the fading light, Bertran's figure a soft blur against the heavy fabric. Such an enigma, this man, his commander. Kinnon made his way through the guard and along the paths between tents, placed to provide no direct route to the commander's pavilion. Entering his own tent, Kinnon scattered a few rocks and broken twigs at the entrance to alert him should anyone approach.

He placed his sword on the ground beside his pallet, then removed his sporran and unrolled his plaide from his waist, tossing the heavy fabric atop the bundle of furs. He reached into his sporran and began his nightly ritual. A bit of dented metal with the Macrory crest etched into its surface. *Brody was a braw fighter.* Laying it on the plaide, he reached for his next treasure. *Jamie, my lad, may ye have a thousand drinks on my account.* He sniffed the wine plug, but the deep aroma had faded. Frowning, he placed it beside the scrap of metal.

Gently he withdrew a tiny wooden carving. He lifted it to the final rays of sunlight casting their golden lines through the opening in his tent. The wood glowed umber and gold, giving the wee horse a mischievous glint to his eyes. One dainty leg was snapped at the knee, and its flowing tail had been abbreviated long ago. *How fare ye, wee sister? I miss ye more than I could have imagined when I left home two years ago. With God's grace, I will see ye again soon.*

He set the statue amid the others, feeling the burning tug of loss deep in his chest. *Three of us set out looking for a grand adventure.* He touched each relic. *Two found foreign graves, God rest yer souls.* His hand lingered on the tiny horse. *What will be my fate?*

CHAPTER TWO

Clucking encouragingly to the two horses hitched to the wagon, Kinnon settled in for the long haul up the rugged mountainside. Would De Ros hold out against the French forces in this heat? Kinnon supposed not since Bertran's army had successfully waylaid every bit of stores the British garrison tried to slip past them. But there was one very interesting reason to hope the English commander lingered a bit longer. A lovely French *mademoiselle* named Melisende.

The wagon creaked and groaned as the team dragged it around boulders scattered randomly across the grassy hillside. *Ye would think a man would at least have a respectable path to his home*, Kinnon groused as a particularly hard bump tossed him on his seat. *Bluidy rocks!* He stared at the landscape around him, looking like a giant had dropped an armload of stones—and forgotten to pick them up.

Up ahead—or at least it would be as soon as the wagon maneuvered around a particularly large boulder—lay Melisende's home. Kinnon sat up straighter, looking forward to seeing the prickly woman again. It would be his third trip to her farm, and he was glad Bertran insisted he make the trek each time.

Jean-Baptiste greeted him at the wooden gate as Kinnon leapt down from his seat and secured the horses in the shade of a sprawling tree. The enormous dog growled.

"*Se calmer*, Jean-Baptiste." The rich, melodic voice rose over the dog's warning. Rounding the corner of the ramshackle shed, Melisende wiped the back of her hand across her brow. Her nod of welcome made Kinnon's heart soar.

"He wagged his tail at me!" Kinnon declared, a broad grin on his face. He reached a hand toward the dog, eager to test their friendship.

"*Monsieur!*" Melisende's voice rose in horror.

Kinnon eyed the glistening white fangs and weighed them against the slow wag of the dog's tail. Thinking better of his actions, he shoved both hands behind his back. "Och, the wee laddie knows I mean no harm."

"Knowing it and accepting friendship are two different concepts, *monsieur*," Melisende observed dryly. She released the latch and opened the gate. Poking his head through the gap, Jean-Baptiste nosed Kinnon about, then licked his arm once.

"See? He likes me."

A half-grin tilted her lips. "More likely he simply tastes you for future reference."

"Och, then 'tis official. I am a tough lad and he has no wish to overly exert his jaws on my behalf. We will be friends."

Melisende motioned him through the gate, latching it firmly behind him. "What is it you wish for today, *monsieur*? We have eggs and milk and cheese, and a few early vegetables from the garden." She strode toward a stone building on the other side of the small yard, Jean-Baptiste at her heels.

Kinnon hurried to catch up, eying the swish of Melisende's skirts as he ignored her question. "What about us, *mademoiselle*? Are we friends?"

She stopped and turned, her bewitching blue eyes piercing his soul. Kinnon slid to a halt.

"I mean no disrespect. I am not looking for a woman to toss. Merely a friend to talk to."

"Why me?" One fine brow stretched upward. "And why not?"

Kinnon gave her a startled look. "I wouldnae show ye such disrespect. Ye are not a camp follower or a loose woman who shows herself to be looking for such a liaison. Ye are bonnie and smart. I may like what I see, but it doesnae mean I will touch ye."

"Surely you have friends among the soldiers to talk with, *oui?*"

"*Oui,* but they talk only of war and killing, and I tire of it."

"*Vérité?*" Her clear blue eyes perused him. "I would think such a man as yourself would be committed to war."

Kinnon felt warmth steal up his neck and settle low in his stomach. *St. Andrew's spare balls! The lass has made me blush!* He rubbed his jaw vigorously with his thumb, hoping the flush did not show on his face. Part of him wanted to flex the muscles in his arms, suck in his belly made lean and firm from constant activity. But the military actions that had fleshed him from brash lad to hardened man were ever on his mind. He paused.

Melisende tilted her head. "Is something wrong?" She stepped close and placed a hand on his forearm. "What has happened?"

There was a pull in her touch, an element that held them together. *Do I need a woman this much?* Kinnon shook his head. His cock was interested, but not demanding. She touched him in a way he could not define. He decided to trust her.

"I am not sure I was meant to be a soldier."

Her hand fell away and her half-smile returned. "You appear to be one very much."

"Knowing how to use a sword and dagger is verra important. Knowing how to take a life to save one, even more so. Making a profession of it? I dinnae know any more."

She picked up her skirts and motioned him to follow with a jerk of her head. "Come with me, *monsieur.*"

Surprised, Kinnon followed her from the yard. She wound past the eastern side of the old stone manor house to a small copse of trees. Only a few yards distant, the draping limbs provided a sense of privacy. Two large rocks lolled at the base of the tree trunks, and the land fell away beneath them in a startling manner.

Melisende stepped gingerly onto one of the rocks. A dark line in the stone writhed slowly. Kinnon's belly tensed in revulsion.

"Wait!" He darted forward, but she was faster.

"It is only a *couleuvre lisse,* Kinnon. A smooth grass snake," she said as she swept the snake off the rock and took her seat. She patted the stone beside her in invitation.

He cautiously surveyed the second large rock, a shudder rippling his shoulders. "I dinnae care how smooth the beastie is, I dinnae like it."

"Do you not have snakes in Scotland?" She tilted her head, interest rounding the cat-like slant to her eyes.

Kinnon shrugged. "There is the wee adder. They are verra difficult to find, but can cause a nasty wound if ye handle it." He gave Melisende a pointed look.

"I did not pick it up. I merely pushed it on its way." She waved him closer with her hand. "Come and sit. The *couleuvre lisse* will not hurt you and often eats very young snakes. Possibly even vipers. For this I will tolerate his presence."

Jean-Baptiste nosed about the clumps of tall grass then settled beside Melisende with a sigh. She rubbed the base of the dog's ears and he leaned into the caress, tongue lolling

12

comically from one side of his massive jowls.

Kinnon took a last cautionary glance around, then sat on the rock. Warmed by the early summer sun, it was a comforting place to be. He stared into the distance at the trees and rocks that dotted the grassy hillside. "I dinnae like the snakes I have found here."

"Somehow I do not think you refer only to the slithering kind."

"Man or beast, there is a darkness to their soul."

"A deep thought, *mon ami*."

Kinnon dropped his gaze. "I dinnae mean to sound so morbid."

"Mayhap more *mélancolie* than morbid. It seems there is much on your mind."

"How do I explain to you the horror of war from my viewpoint? You have seen first-hand the predations of the conquering force. As terrible as it may seem, starvation is a lesser evil."

Melisende nodded. "It is true. They have, for the most part, left us alone here. But it was not always such."

"What do you mean?"

"We lived in a large town where *m'pere* was a goldsmith. It is there I learned to speak *Anglais*—as well as Spanish and Latin. I had no gift for creating beautiful things, but I was quick with numbers and did his accounting."

She paused, but Kinnon instinctively knew the rest of her story. It was all too common, and part of the reason his faith in his commander had become shaky.

"Ye dinnae have to tell me," he reassured her softly. "I believe I understand."

"*Non*, you do not. But I will make it brief. My father was Jewish, and we belonged to that community. Soldiers, one of the Free Companies, came to our town. They swaggered in, offering 'protection' for all who would pay them. My father would not."

Her eyes narrowed, and Kinnon saw the pain lurking in their depths. He wanted to comfort her, but even a chaste, well-meant pat to her hand could be misconstrued by her ever-vigilant protector. Jean-Baptiste yawned, showing strong, white teeth. Kinnon let the moment pass.

"Predictably, we were harassed. Small things at first, but the actions quickly became violent when it became clear my father would not bend. Others counselled he strike a bargain with them, but he would not."

Melisende's hands clenched, then she spread her palms flat against the stone, fingers stretched toward Kinnon as though seeking solace, and this time he did not hesitate. With an eye to Jean-Baptiste, Kinnon gently curled his fingers around hers. With a slow, deliberate move, he edged close, the folds of his kilt touching the shadow of her skirt. Jean-Baptiste lowered his massive jowls to his paws, topaz eyes glittering with warning.

Melisende's voice lowered. "We were warned, Lucienne and I. Warned to stay strictly at home, to not admit strange men to the shop. But we ran a business and saw many strange men every day, and as careful as we were, Lucienne was taken. She was only fourteen."

Melisende gave Kinnon's hand a squeeze. "Father caught them before they got too far. His rage startled them, and Lucienne escaped and ran home. We huddled together, waiting for the outcome. *M'mere* ran about the house flinging belongings into *valises*, Lucienne shook in my arms, crying—I was terrified."

"How long ago, lass?"

"Three years. Father did not return that night, and *m'mere* did not wait past morning. We stole away before dawn and made our way here."

"Why here?"

"*Mon grand-père* owned this farm. It was once famous for its cheese, though much of the secret of it died with him."

Kinnon glanced around at the tumble-down buildings. Three cows grazed nearby, their clothes-rack hip bones tenting russet hide, their pendulous udders dangling beneath. A small herd of goats scampered over the rocks, their peculiar scent mingling with that of the fresh grass. Kinnon's shoulder tilted toward Melisende. A low growl rumbled from Jean-Baptiste. Kinnon resumed a respectful distance.

"Ye dinnae have yon protector then?"

Melisende gave the dog a fond smile. "*Non.* He was born here a few weeks after we arrived. I was terribly lonely and spent much of my time with the animals. It was easier than watching *m'mere* slowly kill herself as she grieved *m'pere.* I missed him very much, also."

"How long has it been just ye and yer sister?"

"A couple of years. *Grand-père* passed not long after we arrived and m'mere did not live to see the anniversary of his death. We have struggled but managed to survive despite the English garrison in the village. Keeping the farm going is hard work, and feeding extra mouths who pass through the farm and contribute neither coin nor effort has beggared us."

"Do ye ever think to leave here?"

Melisende shook her head decisively. "*Non.* The city was fascinating for me, but I can never take Lucienne back. To even mention it sends her into tears."

"A braw young man and a passel of bairns would help."

Melisende laughed. Kinnon watched, fascinated, as her clear blue eyes danced with merriment. She tossed her head, red-gold lights winking in her nearly black hair. "Spoken like a man! What need do I have of a man who will demand I fix his meals, clean his clothes and dance to his tune? Lucienne and I manage to keep our bellies fed and the house warm in the winter. We have need of no one else in our lives."

"Is that so? Ye dinnae want a man's arms around ye when nights are long? When ye have something in yer heart ye wish to share? Someone who cares for ye more than himself?"

Lines of weariness returned to her face, and Kinnon knew an emptiness dwelt deep in her soul whether she denied it or not. A similar pang of loss echoed in his gut. He turned his attention back to grass and cows, pastoral and mundane—as far from heartbreak as he could get in a land torn with violence and pain.

CHAPTER THREE

Melisende stole a glance at the man beside her. His dark brown hair sparkled with gold in the afternoon sun, and his broad shoulders and muscular frame bespoke his rigorous lifestyle. As a soldier, she had been prepared to hate him on sight, but his manners and accent both attracted and amused her. Ever the gallant, his winsome ways even threatened to put Jean-Baptiste at ease.

He appeared every inch the dedicated soldier, from his well-muscled poise and grace, to his array of bristling armaments—yet he had doubts. A curious combination.

"You said you came to fight the *Anglais*—and yet?" She allowed her question to dangle, luring him to answer.

Kinnon's head ducked and his gaze drifted to a blade of grass he twirled between his thumb and forefinger. "'Tis only fair I say my piece, aye?"

She shrugged. "That is something only you can decide."

He gave her one of his heart-shattering grins. "I like ye, Melisende. Ye are a rare woman."

"*Vérité?*" She would rather hear his story, but his declaration piqued her interest.

"Och, most women would be dying of curiosity to hear a soldier's quandary. Most women seem to have a yen for talking and gossip. But ye allow me my own time." His midnight blue eyes narrowed as he perused her and her heart fluttered. "I like the way yer hair is neither black nor brown, and how yer eyes pierce my heart."

Her brows lifted in amusement at his clumsy wordage. "And what do my eyes perceive now, *monsieur?*"

His gaze fell and he tossed the piece of grass away. "They see my lack of words to tell ye how much I admire ye."

She allowed a small smile. "Would you care to try again?"

"Mayhap yer first question would be easier."

Acknowledging his discomfort with an accepting nod, she felt a tug at her heart as he changed the subject. *Do I wish to hear more from him? What can he say that will not one day break my heart? That my hair is like an autumn night, rich with hidden ambers and gold? Or my eyes are the blue of a clear spring morning? It would be foolishness beyond measure to listen to such—oh, so foolish.* She stared at him, surprised at herself, aware of his closeness—equally aware of how far away he would soon be, through either travel or death. Either just as final, just as distant.

He drew his legs up, dangling his hands over his knees. "There were three of us at Scaurness, my home—Brody, Jamie and me. Brody was ever spoiling for a fight, and a more loyal friend there never was. We were inseparable as lads growing up and got into our share of scraps and trouble. And then there was Jamie. He showed up one day almost three years ago and never left. He could best us on the practice field, then drink us under the table with never an ache nor complaint the next day."

Kinnon's voice faded and he stared into the distance, lost in thought. Melisende allowed him his reflection, then nudged him gently. "The three of you came to France together?"

"Aye. 'Twill be two years ago this summer. We were eighteen to twenty summers old, and between the three of us, we thought we knew everything. We had won a few skirmishes against pirates along the coast at home and wanted real adventure."

Melisende smiled indulgently. "And you wanted to fight the *Anglais?*"

He flashed her a dazzling grin. "Of course we did. I believe 'tis one of the more notable pastimes for many Scots."

"But the Treaty of Brétigny was signed more than twenty years ago. We are not officially at war with England."

Kinnon snorted. "France is always at war with England. And the Auld Alliance is older than yer treaty with England." He waved a hand dismissively in the air. "The treaty left many soldiers without a means to make a living, and they prey upon the villages and countryside. Many of them are English."

"And you wish to right this terrible wrong?"

His eyes glittered as he met her gaze. "Do ye not? After what ye and yer family endured, would ye not fight to end this?"

Melisende shook her head. "I have done what I can to give Lucienne a good life away from the predations of such men. We accommodate their demands for food and go about our business of living."

"Would ye not fight? What if they demanded Lucienne instead of food?"

Her chest tightened. "It is for that reason I do not allow her to show herself when others are here. It is enough for her to have endured the rough handling, the terror of abduction. Today she is a sweet young woman of seventeen who has not aged emotionally much beyond that day three years ago. But she is my sister and I love her dearly. She is my life. I do what I can to protect her."

"Ye cannae close yerselves off from the rest of the world," Kinnon argued. "What if one day men decide to visit this remote hillside and demand its best wares? Ye cannae depend on yer rock-strewn path to keep people away forever. 'Tis an arse-beater, but not impassable. How will ye protect yerself? How can two women alone survive the realities of war?"

A black curtain fell, shutting out the scenes her mind could not see again. Wave after wave of noise struck her as forcibly as blows from a fist and she fought her rising panic. Slowly the screams faded and the darkness lifted. Bright sunlight rippled through the undulating leaves and birdsong chirped its summer song.

She spoke slowly. "I know what we have here is a façade, that there are those who could tear our lives apart. I know how fragile life is, how careful we must be. But believe me, if danger travels up that trail, I will not hesitate. I would kill again."

* * *

Kinnon fingered the supple leather reins as the horses wound their way down the hillside. A barrel rattled against the wood of the wagon as the wheels jarred against scattered stones.

I would kill—again.

Conversation had pretty much wound down after that, a cloud of unease settling between them. Kinnon didn't blame her for any actions she'd been forced to commit by arrogant, randy soldiers. Outrage at Melisende's and Lucienne's treatment, however, had him even more at odds with the life he currently led than ever before.

What gives a man the right to take what doesnae belong to him? Food, clothing or another person's life—to take things without recompense, to brutally disregard another's rights—the reality of it ate away at his soul.

The wagon settled from the rock-strewn path onto the main road and Kinnon clucked his tongue, encouraging the horses to greater speed. Their harness jingled as they picked up the pace, hooves beating a tattoo on the packed dirt. Kinnon nodded at the guard on the edge of the camp and drove past without challenge. Skillfully, he maneuvered his team around the sea of tents scattered across the field. All about him lay the spoils of war—horses, weapons, food, clothing— not to mention the items tucked away in the soldiers' tents. Items they had neither bought nor bartered for.

A woman darted across the narrow space between the tents in front of him. Stifling a curse, Kinnon hauled on the reins, sending the wagon wheels into a slide that bit into the soft soil. She glanced up at him, her eyes wide and startled beneath the shawl she wore over her hair. Kinnon shook his head. She was young, too young. Yet he recognized her as one of the women who serviced the tents, moving from protector to protector, scarcely lingering beyond a few days in any one place.

Shite-in-a-basket! This time he didn't bother muffling his words. Sure, the men took what was offered, but what calamity had befallen her that this was her only option to survive? He thought about Melisende and Lucienne. Victims of the actions of men who decided a young girl's life was of no consequence beyond their immediate pleasure, they now resided in near-poverty, one overworked, the other unlikely to lead a normal life.

He dragged the team to a halt near his commander's tent and a page ran to the wagon, a hand on the horses' reins. Two others hurried to unload the eggs, milk and vegetables destined for Bertran's table.

"A nice haul, Scot," Bertran's aide-de-camp noted, quill and parchment in hand as he watched the items being unloaded. "It appears you made it beneath her skirts this time."

Kinnon's arm cocked back and he let his fist fly. It landed with a satisfying crack along the man's jaw, dropping him to the ground. The sting radiated along Kinnon's knuckles, but he ignored the throb as he stepped over the man and stalked to his own tent.

Rage roiled through his veins as he quickly shoved his belongings into his bag. There was very little to pack beyond an extra leine, a shaving kit he used when the mood struck him, a small square of linen with a leather box of needles and thread tucked inside, a flint and steel, and a wooden bowl he had carved months earlier. His possessions were few. Only his glaive and axe were stored with his horse's tack. The rest of his weapons never left his presence.

He pulled the neck of the pack closed and tied it with a piece of leather. *I must speak to Bertran. I willnae desert, but I cannae stay.* With one last glance around the tiny tent, he stepped outside.

The aide he'd cold-cocked stood rigidly before him, flanked by two armed soldiers. Already his jaw bore a dark red mark, purpling nicely and beginning to swell.

"Bertran commands your presence," he said, rolling his mouth uncomfortably around the words.

"Aye. I wish to speak with him as well." Kinnon eyed the man who cast a surly look his way. With a shrug, he tossed his bag over his shoulder and strolled across camp to meet with The Eagle of Brittany.

CHAPTER FOUR

The bucket slipped from her grasp and bounced once on the cobblestone path. Melisende scrambled to keep the pail upright as frothy milk splashed over the worn edge, spattering in lacy trails between the stones.

"*Merde!*" she muttered under her breath. She carefully placed both buckets on the ground and wiped her palms down the rough fabric of her apron. Flexing her tired fingers, she glanced up, meeting Lucienne's gaze.

"I am sorry, *petite soeur*. I should not say such things." She kept her voice carefully neutral, not revealing how much her sister's sudden appearance startled her.

"You should use the yoke to carry the heavy buckets." Placing her hands on her hips, Lucienne smiled sweetly. Pulling her shoulders back, she stretched, flattening her hands as she slowly slid them down her hips. Shocked, Melisende noted the sensual movements and the way the fabric of Lucienne's dress pulled taut across the bodice, accentuating breasts Melisende had not noticed before. But the movements were gone in an instant and her sister's angelic face lit with excitement. "We had a visitor?"

Melisende motioned for her sister to assist with the buckets. With eager compliance, Lucienne grabbed a wooden handle and hefted the bucket before her, bracing it against her legs with all the grace of a child. Melisende let the question pass.

"Jean-Baptiste seems to like him." Walking backward, Lucienne grinned, her eyes alight. "Why will you not tell me about *le bel homme*?" She tilted her head slyly. "Do you like him?"

"Oh, Lucienne, you are such a goose. I do not know why you would think such a thing. He is merely a soldier purchasing supplies for his commander, nothing more." To her consternation, Melisende felt heat creep into her cheeks. She ducked her head. "Take that bucket to the house. Pour it into the crocks so the cream will rise. I will be inside shortly."

Lucienne pealed with laughter. "You like him! I knew it!"

Melisende glared at her sister. "Hush! You do not understand."

Lucienne halted, the bucket swinging carelessly from one hand. "What do I not understand? Does he not think you are pretty? Does he not make you want to touch him?"

"You are too young to ask such questions, Lucienne," Melisende scolded. "Your time is better spent considering how to make the cheese we sell in the village."

For a long moment Lucienne regarded her with a puzzled gaze. Then she shrugged. "If you do not want him, mayhap I do."

Alone in the cheese room, Melisende shoved her cuffs to her elbows, still reeling from her sister's matter-of-fact statement an hour earlier. *What am I to do? She has been fearful of men—of other people—for so long, I did not consider such a change. Her body does not care that her mind does not age apace with it. I see the child she was—and the woman she is becoming.*

She poured the milk from her bucket into two smaller pots set within a basin of heated water. Adding just the right amount of goat's milk to each pot, she stirred carefully.

Picking up a broad wooden spoon, she moved to the next step. A line of pots whose contents had been curdling for nearly two days sat on the next table, the clear whey glistening on the surface. She broke the curd into smaller pieces, releasing more of the whey.

How to talk with her? I scarcely know what happens between a man and a woman—how do I explain what I do not know. To a child? She reached for a clean crock and ladled the curds into it, placing it over another pot to collect the whey as it drained through small holes in the bottom of the crock. She repeated the process until all the curds were in their forms then checked the cheeses she'd moved to molds the day before. With a sigh, she noted everything was proceeding as normal, oblivious to the chaos in the region, uninterested in the upheavals in her own life.

Hands on her hips, she stretched her back, gazing about the stone-walled room. Here in the front, where the warm summer breezes kept the area at the perfect temperature to start the cheese-making process, mis-matched pots and crocks filled every available surface. The hut was built against a large stone outcrop, and in the dark depths of the room the temperature fell, and it was there her grandfather's secrets came to life.

Mentally, she checked the bottles and jars lining the shelves. Coarse salt for brining, herbs, ash, dried berries and paprika to create flavor for the rinds. She frowned. *We are getting low on a few of these. I must make a list for the market.* A frown crossed her face. *How can I leave Lucienne alone, knowing she is no longer a child at heart? What if soldiers come whilst I am gone?*

She removed the apron she'd donned for the cheese-house and replaced it with the one she usually wore, then gathered the empty milk pails for scouring. *And what will she ask me to bring home this time? Lucienne-the-child wanted candy. Lucienne-the-woman-child will likely want velvets and ribbons and perfume.* Crossing the yard, she hurried to the house.

Intent on her inner unrest, she marched through the door, her voice unintentionally sharp. "Lucienne, take these and wash them." She halted as odors of supper cooking assailed her. "It smells very good in here. What are you cooking?"

Lucienne's face lit with happiness as she turned from the hearth. "I am sorry I teased you earlier. We had extra eggs today and I made an omelet with some fresh herbs from the garden."

Melisende couldn't help smiling at her sister's obvious eagerness to please. "You did what any annoying little sister would do," she quipped, tweaking Lucienne's nose to soften her words. "And you have made a nice choice in apology." She set the buckets by the door. "I will help you wash up after dinner. I certainly do not want our supper to get cold."

With childish exuberance, Lucienne poured them each a mug of milk, rich with froth, as Melisende scooped the eggs onto a trencher. They sat together and ate their simple meal, finishing it with sharp cheese and bread left from the morning.

Melisende perused her sister. Lucienne licked her fingers unselfconsciously, as though her earlier foray into young womanhood had merely been a dream. *Ma petite soeur will be fine alone for a day. Deep inside she still carries her scars. They will protect her for now.* She touched the golden curls, and Lucienne glanced up, question in her eyes.

"I need to make a trip to the market in the village, Lucienne. If I leave this evening, mayhap I can return before dark tomorrow. Will you be comfortable here alone?"

Lucienne bobbed her head, curls bouncing, as she wiped her fingers on her skirt. "Jean-Baptiste will stay with me?"

"Of course he will."

Lucienne waved her finger airily. "Then I will be fine." Her tone turned wheedling. "Would you bring me some sweets?"

* * *

Kinnon shuffled his feet impatiently as he waited for Bertran to finish reading a dispatch. Tension in the tent choked the air, making his nerves tingle. Or was it his imagination? He glanced at the two impassive guards facing the tent opening. Backs straight, their shoulders were, however, relaxed. Kinnon felt some of his apprehension fade.

Bertran wiped his face and Kinnon caught the movement from the corner of his eye. A fine sheen of sweat marked the man's brow, and though the tent warm and sweat dampened Kinnon's leine, he felt a stirring of curiosity. *Bad news, or is he ailing?* But his commander's stern gaze as he lifted troubled eyes from the document before him, doused Kinnon's concern for his health.

"De Ros has refused me for the last time." Bertran's normally pugnacious face crumpled into a snarl, startling Kinnon.

"I thought the English commander—"

Bertran cut off his words with an agitated wave of his hand. Shoving back his chair, he rose. He laid a palm on his stomach as if in pain, but the gesture was quickly gone. "*Damné* De Ros! I have fought the length and breadth of France, chasing down the *free companies*, the merciless swine, as they plunder *les gens*, leaving them starving and beaten." His step pounded the carpet-strewn dirt floor and he ran stubby fingers through his cropped, already abused hair. "De Ros should have emptied the area of brigands, but seems to find them useful to keep the citizenry in order."

"Paying for protection," Kinnon scoffed.

Bertran narrowed his gaze. "It is *inacceptable*. And it is time to end it. You will help."

Kinnon's chin jerked backward in surprise. "Me? Ye have loyal commanders to call upon."

Bertran snorted. "Are you not loyal? You and Herve will take two score men, search out the *bâtard* brigands and make sure they do not interfere with me again."

Herve? The hair on the back of Kinnon's neck bristled and the tent flap billowed as the man in question entered the already crowded chamber. Stepping past Kinnon, Herve halted before his leader. His shoulders jutted backward as he came to attention, and dread pooled in Kinnon's gut.

I have lost my chance to leave, and he pairs me with this arse? St. Andrew preserve my hide for a carpet, for there willnae be aught else left if Herve gets his hand in this pot. Kinnon took a step forward, ignoring Herve's bristle.

"Bertran? Might I have a word with ye?" Kinnon sighed heavily. "Alone?"

Again Bertran's hand drifted to his abdomen as he leaned across his desk. Fisting his scarred hands, he propped himself on whitened knuckles, his brows bunched together furiously. "I do not have time for disagreements among my staff. I entrust you with leading this venture." He cast a quelling look at Herve's sputter of protest. "But your French is not perfect, and Herve will go as your second."

Stab me in the back now and be done with it! Kinnon winced as he regretted taking a moment too long to pack his bag.

"I have the higher rank, Commander!" Herve's nose quivered in protest.

20

Bertran motioned around the room. "In case it escaped your notice, *mon ami*, the advancements in this army have little to do with rank. The nobles have largely ignored my commands, and yet the king rewards my efforts."

Herve sniffed, his tone aggrieved. "The last time Scots were entrusted with French command, they turned tail and ran."

Kinnon longed to wipe the arrogant sneer from Herve's face, but controlled his temper, bringing his weight to bear on the balls of his feet, his fingers flexing as they anticipated the grip of his sword. It wouldn't take much more to entice him to put an end to the man's insufferable attitude—or the man either, for that matter. He wondered if he would be rewarded for his forbearance or for his decisiveness.

Bertran scowled. "That was four-and-twenty years ago. The Scots did not abandon the field until all was lost, and I do not recall Kinnon Macrory's name on the roster in any case." He shook a forefinger once at Herve. "Do not continue to try my patience, for it is at an end. I have other matters to discuss." He seated himself carefully and Kinnon again wondered if he was the only one who noticed the commander's hesitancy, the hint of pain in his movements.

Bertran assured himself of everyone's full attention and continued. "As I said, De Ros has again declined my request for the English garrison's surrender—however courteously worded—and he must be dealt with. The men are being readied for an assault, and we depart just after dusk, before the moon is up." He turned his gaze to Kinnon. "You must locate the brigands' camp and destroy it. Doing so will divide De Ros's men, denying him the unprincipled louts he relies on for their force of arms. Can I count on you?"

Once free of this siege, `twill be easier to seek severance from the army. To do so with Bertran's blessing will likely be a boon. The weight of Kinnon's bag suddenly increased and he absently shifted it to the opposite shoulder. He gave his commander a decisive nod.

"Aye. We will track down their camp. They will be either dead or too busy to answer De Ros's call. They will not bother ye."

Bertran gave a short nod. "Good man. You will not regret your success."

CHAPTER FIVE

Melisende patted her pocket, reassuring herself of the coins she'd placed there. A dagger, small but with a honed blade, hung heavy beside the coins. With a final glance about the room, she shouldered the battered leather satchel. "I will return tomorrow, *ma petite*. Remember to check the cheeses."

"And milk the goats and cows and tend the garden . . ." Lucienne's voice trailed into long-suffering silence. She hugged her sister. "Do not worry about me. Jean-Baptiste and I will be fine. It is you who needs be careful."

Melisende smoothed the curve of Lucienne's cheek with her palm. "I know these hills and paths well and expect to reach the village quickly. But I must leave now—you know 'tis safer before dark."

"If we only still had our pony, Pierre . . ." Lucienne's voice faded and her face grew sad.

"The road is too rocky. I would spend half my time repairing the wagon. I am sure Pierre has a good home." She refused to chide herself for the lie. The soldier who had stolen the sturdy pony had likely ridden him into battle, and who knew his fate now? At least it was unlikely he met his end spitted over a campfire.

Giving the enormous dog a stern admonition to guard, Melisende slipped out the door, resisting the impulse to remind Lucienne to latch the door. Within a few steps, she heard the firm snick of wood as the bolt slid home, and Melisende nodded. `*Tis good she remembers such things. Ma petite soeur is growing up. We must have a talk when I return.*

Her hurried steps made little sound on the thick layer of last winter's leaves that clogged the wooded trail. The sun's long afternoon rays pierced the tree branches, marking her way among the rocks. It was well-known brigands had a camp not far from town, far enough away from the village to stay out of De Ros' way, close enough to maintain their reign of terror over the villagers. It was equally well-known that De Ros received a monthly stipend from the brigands to turn a blind eye on their activities.

As if the English soldiery is not problem enough, she groused, keeping a sharp eye on the shifting shadows around her. She worried the citizenry grew weary of the two-sided assault. Memory of her father's defiance and death rose to the surface.

Out of work since the Peace of Brétigny, mercenaries and French soldiers alike had formed bands of *free companies*—free from law and order—to make their living from the citizens they once fought for, claiming food, rights and loot as they willed. Particularly beset by these brigands, the people had petitioned the Constable of France, the great Bertran du Guesclin himself, to rid the countryside of the free companies invading the Languedoc region, and the village of *Chateauneuf-De-Randon* where the English, led by De Ros, held the garrison.

It is only by the Grace of God Lucienne and I have not been overly beset by the brigands. A matter of time, only, before they decide confronting a large dog, no matter how fierce, is worth the effort to exploit more from our small farm. The care I have taken to show our poverty will not protect us forever.

She frowned and pulled her cloak about her more closely, casting a sharper look around. *I must find someone trustworthy to sell our cheeses, or Lucienne and I will be forced to travel together when I go to market.* Suddenly, she regretted leaving her sister behind. The garden would have survived the loss of a day's care. But the daily milking of the goats and cows was another matter. *I cannot leave the farm unattended—the village is too far to travel and return the same day. Add the chores at home and sales and shopping in town . . .* Weariness settled over her with the weight of indecision.

Mayhap Kinnon had the right of things. *Even if Bertran drives the brigands and the English out, our remote farm is no place for two lone women.* A glimpse of life with a man—or men should Lucienne ever marry—flashed through her mind. Curiously, the man boasted the dark hair and powerful physique of a particular Scotsman she had come to know. In her mind, he turned his fathomless blue eyes on her, and heat rushed beneath her skin.

Melisende gasped and shook her head, dispelling the intriguing thought. *What an impossible dream that would be! Though he seems to enjoy his trips to the farm, he is only a soldier with time on his hands, not a man looking to marry so far from home. And I know so little of him. He likely has a family and duty waiting for him in Scotland.*

But for a moment, she let her imagination wander, recalling the pull of cloth across his broad shoulders, his impertinent comments softened by a smile that would charm the very angels down to earth to bask in its warmth.

Will I ever find such a man as he? Someone who listens to me, who admires me. She twisted a fold of her cloak between her fingers as a smile played across her lips. *Marrying only to bring help to the farm would be a far cry from sharing my life with someone like Kinnon. And my body.*

A rush of warmth infused her with a happiness she had never felt before. Her heart seemed lighter as anticipation of Kinnon's next visit welled up inside. She quickened her step. Ahead, lights twinkled in the darkness.

* * *

Cold mist shrouded the camp, torches a dull red glow that afforded no real light beyond a strangled circle. But even on a night like this, the faint glimmer would be enough to catch the eye of an alert guard.

"Have the men douse their lights," Kinnon murmured to Herve.

"But, they cannot see—"

Kinnon's fierce look effectively severed Herve's complaint and he spoke a low command to the gathered troops. "*Éteindre les torches.*"

Around them the lights extinguished one by one, eliminating the wink of metal on the horses's harnesses.

"Have them mount and remain close together until we approach the brigands' campsite. I will tolerate no talking or unnecessary noise. There will be complete silence."

The creak of leather answered Herve's command, and the soldiers moved forward, fading into the shadows of the trees. All understood the importance of their mission, and Kinnon approved the forty men assigned to him for the task. Mercenaries, they would answer to him without question, all well-experienced in the Fabian strategy of attack and fade Bertran often favored.

'Tis a good thing we will rid the area of these brigands. Melisende and her sister shouldnae have to worry about such. And yet, would they not be replaced by others? Mayhap not for a year or two, but how long could two young women live in peace, alone and unprotected?

Kinnon dragged his attention back to the mission at hand. There was no time to worry about Melisende and her sister. At least they were safely tucked away at the farm with Jean-Baptiste to guard them.

The clop of hooves on the packed earth whispered through the leaves covering the ground. The soldiers moved wraith-like through the trees, their passage a mere hiss of sound. Kinnon's leine soon became soaked with the night moisture and his own sweat. Accustomed to such discomforts, he ignored the clinging fabric but regretted the increased squeak of leather as the mist permeated the well-oiled saddles and harnesses.

Ahead a light glowed, then winked out abruptly, only to repeat the pattern again. Lifting his hand in a silent gesture, he reined his horse to a halt. Around him, his men did likewise, and the phantom sounds of their advance faded away.

A few moments later, two of Bertran's scouts appeared from the deepest shadows. The moon's first glow slid over the double-headed eagle on the standard borne by the young man mounted next to Kinnon, and the men made their way to Kinnon's side.

After a hushed conference, Kinnon directed his soldiers' moves. Without a sound, they fanned out through the woods, encircling the camp Bertran's spies had led him to. Kinnon watched silently as first one torch then another flared around the perimeter, indicating his men were in position.

A guard apparently noticed the flares, for a hoarse cry went up. "*Éteindre les torches, vous fous!*" Grumbles from the makeshift tents and bedding rose and subsided at the nighttime interruption.

With a blood-curdling war cry, Kinnon led the charge into the camp.

Chaos erupted as men scrambled for weapons, shouting as Kinnon's men overran the scattered tents and huts. This was the home of the renegades De Ros would not allow to live inside the village, men who had no regard for law beyond what they made themselves. They were adept at keeping the citizenry in a constant state of fear and submission, and they paid De Ros well for the privilege.

Kinnon aimed the tip of his sword at a half-dressed man running barefoot through the camp and pierced the blackguard's heart. His weapon ran black with blood in the moonlit night, glistening with the stain of fallen men.

He reached the far edge of camp and reined his horse in from his charge. Setting him on his haunches, he wheeled him about and sent him back into the middle of the fray. The air filled with the shouts and cries, the clang of metal. Kinnon smelt the coppery tang of blood, freshly churned mud, and the stench of death. He saw two of his soldiers engaged with a stout man wielding a sword in each hand. Another catapulted from his horse as it crashed to its knees. Others were a blur of movement, but he saw them all, one sprawled next to his charger with a spear through his neck, another spinning through the air as a spiked mace splintered his helm.

His horse screamed, jolted forward, one rear leg dragging as it struggled to stay on its feet. Caught off-guard, Kinnon lurched sideways in the saddle. His left foot slid forward, his hands, encumbered with sword and axe, grabbed at his horse's mane, but the heavy strands slid from his grasp. With a curse, Kinnon fell, one foot still caught in the stirrup. His horse squealed again as an arrow pierced his meaty shoulder. He spun his heavy body away from the source of the pain, lurching through the melee of battle, dragging his master behind. Dropping his weapons, Kinnon pulled himself upward, reaching for his trapped foot, unable to yank it free. His body bounced across the ground and he wrapped his arms about his head for protection.

Another arrow found its mark and the beast crashed to the ground. Shaken, Kinnon struggled to his feet and freed his glaive from his dead mount's saddle. Bracing his feet in the soft ground, he hefted the pole arm in both hands and faced the enemy.

* * *

Pushing thoughts of Kinnon from her mind, Melisende entered the village gates just as dusk fell. Amid the last of the people hurrying home from a day in the fields, she passed the guards without question and was soon on the market street.

The tall building on the right housed the butcher and his family. She routinely did business with him and could count on his wife for hospitality for the night. Traveling alone was something of a necessity, but spending the night unaccompanied at a local tavern was unthinkable. Raucous noise from the inn at the corner of the lane reinforced her decision as candlelight spilled from the open door, three obviously drunken soldiers stumbling into the street.

Melisende adjusted the collar of her cloak about her throat and stepped into the doorway of the butcher's shop. The sign on the window read '*ferme*' and the curtains were drawn, but she could see the glow of lights in the back room, and she knocked briskly on the door.

Booted feet sounded on the wooden floor. "*Je suis entrée*," a baritone voice grumbled. Suddenly a pair of dark eyes peered at her through the small glass in the door. The butcher gave a grunt of recognition and the latch rattled.

"*Bonsoir, monsieur*," Melisende murmured as the door opened. "I have arrived for tomorrow's market. I have no cheeses to sell today, but could offer coin for a night's lodging."

A feminine voice floated through the door. "*Qui est-il, Piers?*"

"It is Melisende, the cheese-maker—."

Piers' wife bustled into the room and nudged him aside. "Come in, my dear. Quickly! Do not let those loutish soldiers see you." She took Melisende's arm and tucked it beneath her own, drawing her into the room. "Have you come to stay the night with us? Mariette has just cleaned the kitchen, but the lazy girl can find you a bit of supper." She held up a hand as Melisende opened her mouth to protest. "You will be hungry after your long walk down from your farm. When will you replace that pony, hm? You should marry and have your man bring you to market."

She handed her husband Melisende's cloak and seated her at the freshly scrubbed wooden table, sending the maid scurrying with a flick of her wrist. Pouring water from a steaming pot on the cook hearth, she added a bundle of herbs and set it before Melisende. "Warm your hands for a moment whilst this steeps. We do not wish you to catch a chill this late in the evening."

"Madame—," Melisende began, but the woman patted her hand with a laugh.

"I have told you before to call me *Cateline*. 'Madame' will not do between us."

Melisende ducked her head, the memory of her own mother awash in the words and actions of the butcher's wife. Suddenly, she was seventeen again and a paralyzing fear crept coldly beneath her skin. Muffled shouts rose in the streets, the flares of torches glared through the windows, and Cateline half-rose from her chair.

"*Que se passe-t-il?*" she whispered, her voice tight and frightened, her eyes on her husband. Melisende shook her head, but the feelings of urgency and fear did not dissipate.

Piers slipped across the room and stood to one side of a window. He peered cautiously through the thick glass as shadows and flames rushed past. "Soldiers. They are armed." His gaze swiveled to Melisende. "Did you see anything when you came in?"

Fear descended through her like ice, numbing her mind, her tongue. Her body began to tremble. "*Non.* I saw nothing unusual." She cast frantically through her memory. Were there more soldiers than normal at the wall, at the gate, in the streets? She thought of Kinnon, of Bertran's army just beyond the wall. *Are we under attack?*

Panic exploded behind her eyes in a white-hot flash of light. *Lucienne!* "I must get to her!" She pushed away from the table, but Cateline's hand caught her arm.

"Who, Melisende?"

"My sister! She is alone at the farm." Shaking off the woman's grip, Melisende darted for the door and wrenched it open, pulling against Pier's attempt to stop her. The door flew open and she pulled up short as the bloody form of a man crashed through the opening. His sword clattered to the flagstone floor from his lax fingers and his sightless eyes bored into hers.

CHAPTER SIX

Piers shoved Melisende aside and grabbed the dead man's shoulders. With a great heave, he tossed him past the stoop and slammed the door shut. The whoosh and click as the bolt slid home echoed in her head.

"No! I must get back!" She dove for the door, but he held her back.

"You would not make it, *ma petite*," Cateline said soothingly. "The soldiers are too many in the street." She glanced at her husband. "Piers will find out what is happening, and we will make a plan."

Melisende trembled, her heart a huge fist knotted in her chest. Shouting continued beyond the safety of the bolted door as torchlight threw frightening shadows on the white walls of the butcher shop, and she was forced to agree. "Thank you, *madame, monsieur*. You are very kind to help me."

Cateline's hand gently cupped her chin. "Do not worry. There is likely a brawl down the street, nothing more."

Melisende managed a small smile, accepting Cateline's words they both knew were placatory at best. Men did not fall dead into the doorway because of a fracas nearby. Too many booted feet pounded the dirt, too many torches lit the air, and the shouts bordered on panic, reverberating through the narrow streets.

"Come, let us see to your room." Cateline tugged gently on her arm and Melisende turned to follow. Picking up a candle, she led the way up the stair to the small room beneath the eaves Melisende had used before. Cateline placed the lit taper in a holder on a table near the bed. "I will have Mariette bring up a pitcher of fresh water and a cloth to wash your face. You will feel better once you are refreshed. As soon as Piers hears anything, I will let you know. Please try to get some rest."

"Thank you. I am sure things will be better in the morning," Melisende replied, doing her best to keep her voice from shaking.

Cateline beamed at her, obviously relieved she showed no more signs of hysteria. The spare room's window overlooked the small courtyard behind the shop where farmers brought their beasts, and all was quiet and dark. Only the occasional muffled shout could be heard through the thick walls. With a last fond pat on Melisende's shoulder, Cateline turned and made her way from the room.

Mariette soon arrived as promised, sparing Melisende the need to worry as the young girl's chatter spiraled about the room. She knew nothing more than Melisende did, but had no difficulty embellishing with stories she recalled from her *grand-mère* years ago. When she got to the part where the town was over-run by soldiers who set fire to buildings, empty of their owners or not, Melisende threw her hands into the air.

"Stop! I implore you. It does no good to think on these things. There will be a market as usual in the morning, and I will make my purchases and go home."

Mariette's brows lifted. "You may of course believe that. I think Bertran, the Eagle of Brittany, has come at last to save us all." Delivering her pronouncement, she spun on her heel and acquitted the room.

Melisende sank down on the bed, her hands clasped tight in her lap. *Then I pray he is quick about it and successful.*

* * *

Kinnon opened his eyes to the night sky. Black clouds rushed overhead, alternately obscuring the moon's weak light. Voices rang in hushed tones across the clearing. A light bobbed in the darkness.

"*Il n'est pas ici.*"

"Then look again. The dead do not go far."

Is that what I am? Dead? He tried to move, but his mind did not seem able to command his body. He blinked his eyes. Slowly, he turned his head to one side. The sleeve of his leine fluttered in a light breeze, tattered and spotted with black stains. Blood. And yet, he felt no pain.

I am not yet dead, but 'tis not far. Is this how Jamie and Brody felt before they died? He tried to remember their passing, but his mind drifted far away into darkness.

When he opened his eyes again, the moon's light was brighter, the two voices louder.

"We must find him. Bertran will want to know what happened."

"Bertran will be too busy to care beyond the fact his Scottish *militaire* let brigands escape."

A light shone bright in Kinnon's face and his eyes blinked in surprise.

"*Le voici!*" the first voice exclaimed. Both men bent over him and he recognized Herve as the second voice.

Aye, here I am, he wanted to say, but his mouth was too dry and his lips would not form the words.

Herve scowled. He wrenched Kinnon's plaide away with an unkind flick of his hand. Coldness he never believed existed washed through Kinnon, and he began to shake. Herve's scathing glance took in Kinnon's form. He reached for something at Kinnon's side, then straightened.

"He will be dead soon whether we move him or not. His leg is all but hacked away and there is little blood left in him." He turned to the man next to him. "We will send for his body later."

"But—"

Herve cut the man's protest short with a wave. "We must join Bertran and tell him of this night's venture." He cast a scathing look at Kinnon. "He will not be so eager to retrieve his dead Scot."

Motioning for the man to follow, Herve strode away. Kinnon followed with his gaze until they left his view. *Do not leave me!* he implored silently. His tremors increased and he again faded into blackness.

Something warm roused him, pushing at his cheek. The pain of a thousand knives shrieked through his left side and his eyes flew open. Large topaz eyes stared at him, and a rhythmic heat pulsed in his face. Kinnon's focus widened. The pale pink sky cast the dog in dark relief. No sounds other than a soft panting reached his ears. The pain in his side became an intolerable agony radiating from his thigh. He ground his teeth.

The dog whined anxiously and licked Kinnon's face.

"Jean-Baptiste?" The words slid thickly from his tongue. The dog whined again. Nearby a goat bleated. Jean-Baptiste bounded from his side with a bark.

No! Shite. Even the damn dog has left me. But he felt stronger, and he fisted his right hand. It closed on empty air. He lifted his head a scant inch from the ground and glanced at his arm and the area around it. *Damn Herve took my glaive.*

He sighed and turned his attention to inventorying the rest of his body, ignoring the searing pain in his left leg. It took an effort, but he raised his right arm. Other than a few scrapes and bruised areas, it appeared intact. His left arm was in a similar condition, and he slowly lifted himself to his elbows. Herve had ripped his plaide away the night before, and his words drifted back.

"His leg is all but hacked away . . ."

Though scraped and bloodied, his right leg appeared to have come to little harm. His left leg, however, was crusted in dried blood with a large area of glistening, still-damp blood pooled mid-thigh. Suddenly dizzy, Kinnon sank back to the ground.

He left me to die. Why have I not died? The thought of living with only one leg horrified him, but there was a stubbornness inside that refused to give up. Taking a deep breath, Kinnon rose on his elbows. Agony ripped through his leg again, and this time he cried out.

Suddenly, gentle hands were on his shoulders, pushing him back. The dog's whine pierced the fog of pain and for an instant he wanted to tell the beast to cease his caterwauling. Until he realized it was his own voice making the unmanly racket. He clamped his mouth shut and opened his eyes.

Soft lavender eyes stared back at him. Wispy curls framed a sweetly oval face like a shimmering golden halo. *I am in the hands of an angel. Why do I still hurt in Heaven?*

"You are the soldier who has come to our farm, no?"

Kinnon searched his mind for the correct answer, but could not make the connection. The dog whined again and the girl shushed him with a nervous glance over her shoulder.

"Who are ye?" he gasped.

"I am Lucienne. Melisende's sister. I have seen you before."

Of course. Now he remembered. Though he had never seen her, she obviously recognized him. "Where is Melisende?"

"She went to market. She will be back tonight."

Kinnon shook his head. Even if Bertran's attack was successful, they would likely allow no one in or out of the village for several days.

"You are injured, *monsieur*. You must let me help you."

The offer both relieved and repulsed him. "I am hurt—too bad. You should leave. Men will be here." Talking drained his energy, and he closed his eyes, his breathing ragged. As if to prove him correct, a murmur of sound drifted toward them. "Go."

"I cannot leave you here. They are heartless, cruel. You will come with me."

Kinnon would have laughed at her, but it required effort and a certain amount of caring, and he was beyond both.

Determined, Lucienne grasped his arm. "Take Jean-Baptiste's collar. He is strong."

"He cannae carry me, lass." Kinnon protested weakly, but found it easier to go with her insistence rather than oppose it. He found himself tugged to a seated position, staring bleakly at his left leg. A fresh wash of bright red blood rose through the darker clots. "My leg—" He gestured numbly at the wound.

Lucienne shifted her skirts and tugged at the hem. The fabric did not tear and she frowned. "Melisende makes it look so easy," she huffed. Setting the cloth between her teeth, she gave it a good jerk, and tore a long strip from the bottom of her gown. She reached for his leg, and Kinnon set his teeth, but her touch was gentle as she wrapped the makeshift bandage about his thigh. "This may hurt," she warned as she pulled it tight and knotted it.

Kinnon's head swam, and he swallowed hard. "Nae so bad," he murmured as nausea swamped his stomach.

Lucienne grabbed his arm again and half-rose, using her weight to pull him to his feet. "Come on!"

He loomed over her and stumbled forward, but the enormous dog stepped between them, and Kinnon braced against the sturdy body. He found the dog's thick leather collar and gripped it tightly. Squaring his jaw, he gave a small nod. "Lead on, fair lady."

She beamed at him. "I will get the goat."

CHAPTER SEVEN

"The town is under siege. No one is allowed in or out—by De Ros' command." Melisende heard the butcher's words, the sympathy in his voice. She saw the empty look in his eyes. "Many men and women lay dead in the streets. Bertran has attacked using all his forces, but De Ros is determined to resist. I have never seen its like."

"Is there no one you trust to smuggle me through the gates? A hidden path? Or a window from a house on the wall?" Urgency gripped her and she paced the floor.

Cateline wrung her hands. "Melisende, it is madness to consider leaving. Alone in the streets—you would be murdered, or worse."

Melisende recognized their apologetic sympathy to her plight, though she disagreed with their plan of action. To them, the brigands and the English occupation of Châteauneuf-de-Randon was an inconvenience—albeit an occasionally frightening one—best dealt with by acquiescence, money and a blind eye. As with the occupation, they would stoically wait out the siege and pray for the best. For now, Melisende could see no other option. "I appreciate your wisdom, and ask you inform me as things change."

A hopeful smile lit Cateline's face. "Of course, *cherie*. We understand how upset you must be to think of your sister alone. But you must see the danger is in town, now."

Piers nodded vigorously. "All of the fighting is here, not in the fields. We are in the most danger, no matter which army takes the city. There will be looting and burning. Your sister is much safer where she is."

Melisende frowned. If he hoped to reassure her, his tactics were faulty at best. Instead of standing beside her husband, agreeing with his assessment her home could be overrun at any time by an invading force, Cateline should be packing her bags. And urging Piers to find both herself and Melisende a way out of the beleaguered town.

"Perhaps I could help around the shop—try to keep the place as normal as possible," she said, needing some activity to keep her busy. Not that they could expect sales today. But, it would help create an outlet for her building anxiety.

"You could assist Mariette with her duties," Cateline suggested.

Not Melisende's first choice, as she hardly wished to find herself closeted with the excitable maid. "Mayhap we could divide the duties. I would be happy to sweep and dust the shop, and she could attend the household chores."

Cateline clapped her hands. "A wonderful idea! We should at least try to be as normal as possible. Only God knows how long this will last." She picked up her skirts and turned to the door. "Come. I will get you started."

Melisende followed, learning where the broom and dust cloths were kept. With a word of reassurance that she was managing to not worry too much, she took the broom and dust pan to the front room of the shop and closed the door behind her.

In the morning light, the white-walled room appeared large and almost hauntingly empty.

Piers had not changed the sign on the door to indicate they were open, and Melisende assumed it did not matter. Few, if any, people would be about the town today.

She leaned against the wall at the edge of one of the two large windows at the front of the shop. Sometime during the night, Piers had secured the heavy wooden shutters against the possibility of damage, but the slats were old and time and weather had caused them to shrink, allowing her to see between the cracks. A group of soldiers hurried past, their boots thudding on the packed earth, the metal on their weapons glinting in the sun. Over the rooftops she could see a spiral of smoke, though she could not tell if the fire was deliberate or not. The dead soldier from the night before was gone, but a dark stain remained on the edge of the dusty street, though the stoop appeared to have been washed clean.

Her ears carefully sorted through the noises fouling the air. Orders shouted authoritatively. Curses flew about in a staccato manner. The neighs of horses, and the occasional squeal of a pig from the yard behind the shop. Thudding sounds she could not identify, but could imagine as stones or other heavy items colliding with the walls of the village.

Mayhap I can find some way of escape while all attention is elsewhere. Leaving Lucienne to an unknown fate gnawed at her, leaving her restless and uneasy. She peered across the narrow street, but saw no clear path to the outskirts of town. Soldiers appeared to cluster at every corner, and certainly they would not allow her to pass unchallenged. *I will find a way. Things will quieten at dusk when hungry men care more for their stomachs than for someone such as myself, seeking a way out.*

She chewed her lower lip, trying to remember if there was a way past the soldier's watchful eyes, and if, once beyond the walls, she could circle Bertran's encampment unseen. *At least the house should be quiet once Piers and his wife have gone to bed. Mayhap I could leave before the moon is up.* She glanced around the dimly lit, silent room. *They will surely be abed early with no customers and naught else to do.*

She returned to her vigil. A pall of smoke lowered over the town, and the sun's rays faded behind the thin curtain. Melisende pulled her shawl closer. Though it was early July and the summer's heat already apparent, fear's chill carried all the way to her bones.

Men hurried to the door, beating on the portal with force. "*Ouvrir là-dedans!* You are ordered to open the door!"

Her body jerked in startled reaction as men, blackened with soot and dried blood, hammered on the stout door. Glaives and pole axes bristled from the tight group, but across their shoulders draped men who dangled helplessly, faces and bodies marked by the battle.

The butcher appeared beside her, peering through the small glass in the door. With a muttered curse, he worked the bolt on the door and allowed it to open a few inches. "What do you want? The shop is closed today."

"We will be using your shop as a *fermery* for our injured. Stand aside."

A fermery? Oh, Sweet Mother of Jesus, please no!

In horror, Melisende watched as soldiers filed through the door, depositing wounded men on hastily tossed cloaks and blankets on the floor. A table was pulled to the center of the room and a severely wounded man laid upon it.

The leader turned to Piers. "You are the butcher, *oui*?"

Piers nodded reluctantly.

"You will help treat these men. Our *cirurgian* will be here to tend the worst cases." He regarded Piers sternly. "There will be guards posted. You will send word if more help is needed."

Eyes wide with disbelief, Melisende watched as the quiet shop became the guarded headquarters for the hated English wounded, and her chances of slipping away unnoticed dropped to near impossible.

* * *

Gentle hands pushed his shoulders forward and Kinnon felt a cool liquid against his parched lips. Water, sweet as ambrosia, touched his tongue, and he gulped it eagerly.

"Do not drink so fast, *monsieur*. The last time, it came right back up. Go easy."

To his dismay, the water was taken away, and he was lowered to the pillow. *The last time? God's teeth—how long have I been here?* He opened his eyes, but everything around him appeared dim, hazy. A movement in one corner of the room caught his attention. Tall and slender, the form moved with a simple, almost child-like grace. A darker form, reaching her waist, padded beside her, and Kinnon's memory began to return.

He was at Melisende's farm, but the young woman in the room with him had golden hair tumbling to her waist, while Melisende's dark hair was forever escaping from a tight braid or kerchief covering her head. *Lucienne?*

He must have spoken aloud, for the figure turned toward him. She slipped to his side and knelt. "Do you need anything, *monsieur*?"

"Water?" he croaked. At least, he intended to ask for water, but the sound that came from his throat was similar to the rasp of a dying crow. Lucienne must have understood, for she ran a cool palm over his forehead, then patted his cheek.

"*Oui*, but do not gulp it. Drink slowly." She picked up a mug from the low table beside the bed and held it to his lips, again cradling his head as he leaned forward.

He tried to do as she instructed, but he was too parched, and he sucked the water down as fast as he could, coughing as he stopped for air. She laughed lightly and he stared at her, her face now so near his own, and he was again struck by her delicate features, her lavender eyes, and the hair that billowed about her head like a golden aura.

"Ye are an angel," he murmured, and meant it. Not only for her beauty, but for the care she showed him.

"And *ye* are still quite delirious," she mocked him with a delighted smile.

He considered the likelihood she was correct, and gave a mental shrug. "How long have I been here?"

"Jean-Baptiste and I brought you here yesterday morning. 'Tis now mid-afternoon. Do you not remember?"

Kinnon remembered. Perhaps too much he'd rather forget. The battle, though a surprise attack, was against seasoned, hardened troops with nothing to lose. They had fought back with a ferocity that surprised him, though his soldiers responded with a fierceness that had left few alive. This much he knew before a well-aimed blow to the back of his head had felled him like an oak tree. That and the blood-loss from the wound to his thigh.

He shifted on the bed and was rewarded with a shooting pain in his leg that exploded white-hot behind his eyes. He gasped, but grudgingly appreciated the knowledge he kept his leg—for now at least.

"Your leg!" Lucienne exclaimed, leaning over him as she pulled back the coverlet to examine his wound. Air touched his skin and he realized he was naked beneath the thin covering.

"Saints-in-a-cave, lass! Have a care for my sensibilities and give me back my kilt—or at least my leine!" Heat flooded him to realize this mere lass had unclothed and cared for him as he lay unconscious.

Lucienne giggled. "Your 'sensibilities' were covered in blood and muck and needed cleaning. As was your leine and kilt, though I have washed and mended them and they will soon be dry." She eyed his groin, and her eyebrows shot skyward. "I must say, you were much softer and smaller yesterday. I wondered how a man could mate with such a thing as that. But look at how it has grown!"

"Shite!" Kinnon grabbed the coverlet and snatched it over himself, damning his cock for taking this opportunity to be interested in a pretty lass. The thin covering tented upward and he grabbed the pillow from beneath his head and plopped it over his straining cock. "Can ye find something better to do than stare at a man?" His voice was sharper than he intended, but Lucienne did not seem to take offense.

"I am happy you are so much better, though fever could still take you. You are not out of the woods yet, and will likely be rather weak for several days." She gave his pillow a pat and rose to her feet. "Do not fear. I will care for you until you are mended."

Her fingertips trailed lightly down the length of the pillow and Kinnon swallowed a groan, wondering how he could have thought her an angel.

It was some time before he drifted off to sleep, unsure if the pain in his leg or his groin was the culprit. When he next opened his eyes, his sight was clearer and candles lit the room. Lucienne must have been waiting for him to wake, for she laid her sewing aside and slipped from her chair beside the bed. She placed a cool palm on his brow and her look of concern blossomed into a smile.

"You are doing well, *monsieur*. Would you like something to eat?"

"I could eat the bark off a tree, my stomach is that empty, lass. But I would sell my soul for another cup of water."

Her laugh tinkled merrily. "I will fetch a mug and then be about a bit of dinner."

The gurgle of water as she poured it into the mug had him licking his cracked lips in anticipation. He struggled into a half-seated position, scarcely noticing his pillow had been replaced behind his head while he slept, and took the mug from her. She gave him a questioning glance, but he hid the tremble in his hands and managed to down the water with nary a drop spilled.

The cool liquid sloshed around inside him and nausea took a short lap around his stomach, but settled nicely as savory smells began to permeate the room. His interest was high as she returned with a large, two-handled mug wrapped in a cloth against the heat steaming from the surface. Kinnon reached for it, taking it gingerly between his hands. Pulling it to his nose, he sniffed the contents.

"I made a vegetable broth," Lucienne announced.

Kinnon gave her a puzzled look. "A what?"

"A broth. Made from vegetables."

He quirked an eyebrow at the liquid. "And meat."

"Oh, no, *monsieur*. No meat."

"Ye expect me to get well eating plants?"

She giggled, and he decided to try a sip—just to make her giggle again. He rolled the broth around in his mouth and found it flavorful, though not quite what he was used to. "It isnae bad, lass. I thank ye for yer help."

She waited patiently, hands folded in her lap, until he drank it down, then set the empty mug aside. "I must clean your wound, *monsieur*."

Kinnon frowned, not liking the thought of her slender hands mere inches from his cock. Or, perhaps his cock liked the idea far too much. "I can see to myself," he told her firmly.

"We can keep your mating parts covered if you wish." She pursed her lips in a forlorn moue of disappointment, eyeing the area in question. "But I really would like to see it get big again."

Kinnon choked and she quickly helped him lean forward, pounding on his back to help clear his chest. "Give me the bloody bandage and hie yerself off!" He scowled at her, but she fisted her hands on her hips.

"'Tis a large wound and you cannot care for it yourself."

"Are ye a healer?" he challenged her.

"No."

"A mid-wife?"

She began to look unsure. "No."

"A married woman?"

She stomped a foot. "Of course not."

"Then, I will thank ye to keep yer hands to yerself. My sincere thanks for yer help so far, but I will treat my own wound."

Lucienne wrinkled her nose at him and threw her hands in the air. "Fine. I will cook and clean and slave for you, and not lift a finger when your wound reopens and your life's blood pours onto the bedlinens—which I will uncomplainingly clean. Again"

Kinnon ignored her and leaned forward as far as he could, reaching for the bandage on his leg. To his consternation, he could not grasp the knot tied behind his knee. "Where is my damned dagger?"

Without a word, Lucienne let it slip from her fingers to the bed beside him where it landed with a soft *thump*. He swept it up and picked at the bandage at the top of his thigh, trying to find a loose enough spot to slide the tip of the dagger.

"Let me know if you cut yourself."

"Insolent wench," he muttered, refusing to give in. Four minutes and three minor cuts later, he threw the dagger across the room, burying the tip into the doorframe with a decidedly louder thump. He clamped the bed linens firmly across his groin.

"Fine. Ye may remove the bandage, but I will rewrap it."

With a sassy toss of her head, Lucienne leaned over him, her nimble fingers making short work of the heavy knot. Kinnon held his breath as her fingertips skimmed his leg as she unwrapped the layers of bandaging. He peeked around her as she lightly touched the flesh around the wound. Even, black stitches marked the long trailing wound that traveled from the top of his thigh near his knee, around behind the thickest part of his leg near his groin.

Much higher and we wouldnae be having this conversation or this problem. He gave a wry, pained grin at his injury, then jerked to attention as Lucienne prodded his thigh with a forefinger.

"I believe the sword, or whatever weapon it was, struck deepest here, then slid down your leg as you turned away." Her finger followed the curve of the gash, and he tensed at the prickling sensation that rushed straight to his groin. He felt himself grow heavy, pulsing with need.

"Oh! Is that how it works?" Before he realized what she was about, Lucienne reached beneath the edge of the thin blanket and cupped his balls in one hand. "They are much harder now. This morning, they were quite soft."

Kinnon swatted her hand away. "Leave me some dignity, aye? 'Tis quite a normal reaction to having a hand near my private parts."

"Any hand? Even yours?"

Kinnon broke out in a sweat. "Damn, lass. Dinnae ye know not to be so bold around a man who isnae yer husband? Ye could be in a world of trouble with yer forward ways."

She nodded, a solemn look on her face. "I know. Men stole me once when I was a child, but *mon père* saved me before they did more than drag me away." She tilted her head. "But you are too weak to do more than answer my questions. I have had a lot of questions lately. And I am no longer a child."

CHAPTER EIGHT

Kinnon stared at the woman-child before him, the images blurred between the sweet girl who had brought him literally back from the dead, and the willowy siren who dared inflame his blood with her touch and words.

Her words. *Hell's afire! I willnae sate her curiosity!* He glared at her, feeling at once like an auld man, not a tried youth eager for an easy toss. "'Tis unseemly for us to discuss this. Ye should take this up with yer husband on yer wedding night." *Lord help the poor bastard. He will be unable to walk for a fortnight.*

Lucienne cocked her head to the side. "I have seen the cows and goats mated, and everything seems to go well. But why do men seem to crave it? That is why the bad men kidnapped me, though I was only fourteen at the time. I heard *Maman* whisper of it, and she cried over me for a long time. And the next day, we came here." She shrugged. "But none of them hurt me except where their grip left marks on my arms." Absently, she rubbed her upper arms, as though to erase a persistent memory.

Kinnon's heart jolted to be reminded of the reason for this confusing young woman. "Poor lass. I will reassure ye things work quite well if both parties are full-willing. And 'tis fine for the *wife* to enjoy it, too," he added, to be sure she understood the marital issue.

Lucienne gave a satisfied nod. "That is good. I hate not knowing things. Here is your bandage and a pot of a healing salve. Knot the cloth tightly."

With that abrupt change of topic, she dropped a length of clean fabric on the bed beside him and turned away. She grabbed a cloak from a peg by the door and spoke to him over her shoulder as she draped the worn fabric about her. "I must feed and milk the animals and check on the goat that strayed yesterday. Jean-Baptiste will be with me, but we will not be far. Please rest."

The door snicked shut behind her. Still reeling from the conversation he'd just had with the lass, Kinnon stared at the portal for long moments before turning his gaze to the small pot beside him. He propped himself on one elbow and removed the lid. A not-unpleasant aroma drifted out and he glanced at his long, neatly-stitched wound.

Evenly-spaced black thread held the edges together. *She may not be a healer, but she is a mighty fine seamstress. But I am glad I wasnae awake when she plied her needle*—he began counting—*thirty-five times! And the cleaning of it!* He shuddered. *No wonder Herve thought my leg had been almost hacked off. Ruthless bastard.*

His mind wandered to the battle. The last memory he had of it, he was unsure if they had routed the brigands or not. The fighting had been fierce, and by now, nearly two days had passed. Time did not sit still, even to allow someone to recuperate from a vicious wound. Had Bertran been successful in taking the town from De Ros? Did the battle still rage? Would the English be scouring the area for enemy soldiers? Kinnon felt the urge to be up and about, discovering information that could potentially save his—and Lucienne's—lives.

He quickly slathered some of the unguent on his leg, pleased to note no redness and very little pain at the site, though moving the leg was troublesome. He wrapped his leg with the clean linen strips, knotting them firmly. Swinging his legs to the side of the bed, he paused as dizziness rocked through him and a roaring filled his ears. He grabbed at the bedframe, the coverlet, the small table—anything to keep from pitching forward into the black hole that opened to receive him. Pain exploded in his head and he crumpled to the floor.

* * *

Melisende drew a weary hand across her forehead, pushing damp tendrils of hair away from her face. Around her feet lay the detritus of war—bloody bandages, ruined clothing, dirt and other nameless muck. She shoved at the pile with her broom, pushing it into a dust bin before carting it off to a larger container to be taken away later by one of the soldiers.

Wounded men lay on every available surface. Their low moans tore at her heart. She had learned much herb lore in the year before her grandfather died, but had no desire to come under closer scrutiny by the English than she already was by offering her healing services. Even with the guards at every entrance, she had not given up on her plan to escape. It was just the formulation of it that defied her at every turn. She had made tentative friends with the grizzled warrior who kept watch at the back door at dusk. Perhaps because he reminded her of her grandfather, possibly because he did not eye her like so much feminine flesh to be consumed as the others did. But most likely because it seemed she reminded him of his granddaughter and her newest plan hinged on his sympathy.

The past two evenings, she stood at the door, partly hidden in the shadows, until it was time to lock up for the night. Each time, she dragged reluctantly inside, a wistful, partly worried look on her face that she'd practiced only hours before. The second night, he had asked whom she waited for. Surprised at her own talent for story-telling, Melisende spun a sad tale of the weaver's son, to whom she was engaged and had not seen since the siege began.

The soldier, whom she'd discovered was named Edward, had listened then shooed her inside with a sympathetic smile and encouraging word. Today, she had scoured the butcher's pantry for a small flask and poured a measure of whisky into it. A few hours remained until she could put her plan into effect.

The guards changed shifts and Edward took his accustomed seat at the rear door of the butcher's shop. Melisende watched anxiously as another soldier seated himself next to the older man, leaning his weapon against the doorframe as though he intended to remain there indefinitely.

The moon rose, and the two men remained deep in talk. *Merde! If I do not start soon, I will not make it far before sunrise.* The second man rose abruptly, gathered his weapon and strolled through the small yard, disappearing into the shadows. Long, agonizing minutes stretched before Melisende decided he had moved to another post. Picking up the flask, she crept down the dark stairs.

Edward jerked to his feet, his sword *en garde*. "Who is it?" he challenged.

Melisende hurried the last few steps through the door. "It is I, Melisende. I trust I did not startle you?"

Edward's roughened skin flushed unevenly around a knotted scar on his cheek. "No, *mademoiselle*. Your presence is a vision of an angel to these old eyes. 'Haps you hope to see your *beau* tonight?"

Melisende ambled closer, trailing a finger over the doorframe. Edward's gaze followed the caressing movements of her hand, his old eyes widening.

"I miss him *beaucoup*, and I am fearful something *terrible* has happened to him. Would you be so kind as to let me go to his home and see? It is not far, and I would not think to be gone long. But my heart pounds in my chest to know nothing all these days!"

She gently placed her palm on her bosom in emphasis. Edward swallowed hard as his eyes followed her hand's movement. He stared as her deep breaths moved her chest up and down. Suddenly he cleared his throat.

"I am under orders to allow no one to leave without permission from the captain." He shrugged. "I can do nothing."

"That is a shame, for I brought you a gift to keep you warm tonight whilst you waited for me." With the hint of a seductive smile, she pulled the flask from her skirt pocket. Glancing about her, she offered it to him. "It is fine whisky from my master's own stock. Guaranteed to warm your belly."

Edward laughed. "Cheeky girl! I thought you wanted to seduce me, but this is more to an old man's liking!"

Melisende waved a hand airily. "A simple toss is but a moment of fleeting pleasure. *Pouf*! and it is gone. But a full flask—ah, that is another thing, surely."

"Your *beau* is a lucky man. I am too old to appreciate more than what these eyes can see, but the whisky is much prized."

"Then we are agreed? I may look for him?"

"You may go to the end of the walkway, but no further. I cannot allow you to go further. It is against orders."

How long before he is more attentive to the whisky than to me? She fumed silently, but it was a chance she could not forfeit. "Thank you for your understanding. I will stay within sight."

With a nod, Edward stepped aside, allowing her to pass. She slipped silently down the path to the end of the walkway and stared at a scene she scarcely recognized. Overturned wagons piled haphazardly in the street. A man who would never seek the services of the *cirurgian* sprawled across a pile of broken wooden crates. Here, the smoke seemed heavier and Melisende pulled a corner of her cloak over her nose. The normal night sounds of laughter and of neighbors calling to one another were replaced by coarse shouting, punctuated by an occasional scream. She shuddered to realize she placed the *cirugian's* whereabouts by the source of the agonized cries.

She chanced a glance over her shoulder. Edward's attention fell directly on her, the flask of whisky apparently untouched at his side. She turned back to the street, stealing a look at Edward from time to time, hoping, praying for a moment of inattention that would allow her to slip away. Each time, she caught his speculative gaze. Finally, she made her way to the shop.

Edward eyed her over the flask as he took a deep swig. He downed the contents in three large gulps then handed it to her, wiping the back of his hand across his moist mouth. "'Tis not bad. Mayhap another round would be in order any time you wish to catch sight of your *beau*."

Insolent swine! He thinks to make me pay for the privilege of merely walking to the end of the way? No wonder he did not allow me out of his sight. No doubt he thinks this an easy way to procure a nightly draught of whisky.

Blinking quickly to cover the anger she knew showed on her face, she smoothed her scowl into a pout. "I worry about him so much. Thank you for your kindness. Mayhap I will see him one day soon. It is all this heart longs for."

"An agreement, then," the old soldier noted, a smirk on his face as Melisende passed him into the butcher's shop.

With a touch of black henbane, opium poppy and hemlock if any can be found, she vowed. *The cirurgian is not the only one who can mix herbs, mon ami.*

CHAPTER NINE

Battle raged in the village. Injured men poured into the make-shift infirmary set up in the butcher shop's front and storage rooms, even spilling into the small barn behind the building. Soldiers came and went, the surgeon did what he could to treat the terrible wounds, and Edward was replaced as the night guard for the rear door.

Be damned! Melisende eyed the eager young man at Edward's old station. Spine stiff and eyes averted from her, he appeared anxious to carry out his job with the utmost precision. He also looked scarcely old enough to shave.

Melisende stormed up the stairs and slammed the flask of whisky down on the small table in her room. *Milk would be a more appropriate bribe for le jeune homme.* Frustration knotted her chest. Fatigue made her head swim and she bit her lip to keep tears at bay. With a thump she collapsed onto the edge of the bed, head in her hands as she scrounged furiously for a new plan. She discarded one after the other before she lay back on the coverlet, beseeching God to care for her little sister.

Her mind somewhat eased, or at least temporarily resigned, her thoughts turned to Kinnon. *I wonder where he is. Would he have been with the main attack four days ago? He seemed to be part of the Eagle's close command. Would he serve at the rear, closer to Bertran?* It seemed safer to hope he was not part of the common soldiery pounding the village walls. She sighed.

Where will he go when this is over? Will he return to Scotland or remain with Bertran's army? Again she wondered if he was bound to a woman back home. A stab of jealousy surprised her. *I have no rights to him*, she admonished herself. A curiosity came over her. *But if I did, what would that be like?*

Her lids closed, she imagined his eyes, the way they crinkled at the corners when he laughed. Only a bit lower, his lips, chiseled and manly, a day's growth of whiskers framing them, moved as he spoke. The memory of his voice warmed her and she smiled.

I am not sure I was meant to be a soldier, he had told her.

She recalled his friends who had boldly sailed to France to rid the countryside of soldiers—mostly English—who preyed upon the helpless. Kinnon was the only one left. The life of a soldier. So short, so unpredictable. She gripped the bedclothes in her fists, fighting a surge of despair.

Why must there be war? Why must good men die? Tears leaked from the corners of her eyes and she shook her head, denying the emotion. *I am tired, nothing more. There have always been wars. Large ones, small ones, diseases, accidental death. I have experienced all of it and more. Why should it matter now?*

But his last words burned in her heart and she shook to remember them.

Do ye not want a man's arms around ye when nights are long? When ye have something in yer heart ye wish to share? Someone who cares for ye more than himself?

God help me, I am so lonely. I love my sister, but you have opened something in me I had wished to keep closed. Damn you, Kinnon-Macrory-from-Scotland! Damn, damn, damn!

* * *

"You are a foolish man, *monsieur*." The soft voice chided and Kinnon struggled to open his eyes. He wasn't sure he disagreed with her. Light burst before him, but a head moved in front of the source, blocking the glare. Lavender eyes glowed in a sweet face framed in golden curls.

"I am a lucky man," he replied, his voice hoarse and scarcely above a whisper.

"*Oui*. You are lucky you did not cause your wound to reopen when you crashed to the floor." A soothing hand stroked his cheek.

"Nae, I am lucky to be cared for by an angel."

Tinkling laughter filled his ears. "*Monsieur*, I believe you injured your head when you fell. Can you tell me your name?"

Kinnon closed his eyes, screwing his forehead in concentration. "I am Kinnon."

"*Très bien*. And who am I?"

He had to open his eyes again, and this time the lavender eyes sparkled, her pink lips tilted in merriment. For a moment he basked in her smile. "You are Lucienne."

"*Oui*. And now you need rest. Would you care for a drink before I leave you to your dreams?"

He reached for her, surprised at the tremor in his arm. "Dinnae leave me. Tell me what happened."

"I am no healer, but I know you lost a lot of blood the other day. I would guess you jumped to your feet to prove you are not injured as much as you really are, and your body is not yet ready for such actions."

Kinnon scowled. Of course. He had been impatient to be about his business and blacked out as soon as his feet hit the floor. "My leg . . ." He silently begged her reassurance.

"Again, you are in luck, *monsieur*. For if you had reopened the wound, I am not sure I would have been able to help you."

He sobered. Like it or not, it looked as though he would be taking orders from this wee lass for at least the next several days. The necessity to rest and heal warred with the need to discover the outcome of the battle, report to his commander, and protect this young woman from harm. He stifled a growl of discontent.

Her delicate hand again stroked his cheek and he sighed. Perhaps a day or two of her care would not go amiss.

For two days he submitted to Lucienne's ministrations as she fed him and included him in her conversations as she went about her work inside the house. He drew the line at her help with changing the bandage and personal care, though he had to admit to the need for assistance with the chamber pot. To his relief, she treated him benignly, with no hint of her earlier fascination with his body or its responses. Responses he tried somewhat unsuccessfully to keep at bay, for her gentle touch laid unbidden heat beneath his skin, and her fragrance raised his cock to attention.

He sought the mundane to keep his wayward body under control. He couldn't help but worry about her, but Jean-Baptiste followed her when she went outside to tend the animals and garden or check on the cheeses, then curled unconcernedly on a rug beside the hearth when inside, apparently accepting Kinnon's presence—or perhaps simply ignoring him as being no threat in his present condition.

Slowly, his strength returned and after the fourth day he was able to move about the little house with the aid of a stout branch Lucienne cut for him. He spent endless hours stripping the bark and carving designs in the wood, as well as smoothing the fork in one end to fit beneath his arm for extra support.

"What is in the pot, lass?" he asked, leaning on the staff as he peered into the simmering crock Lucienne stirred with a wooden spoon.

"A lot of those green things from the garden you say you do not like," Lucienne replied sassily. She waved the spoon under his nose. "That *potage* you turn that oh-so-cute nose at, is the very food that brought you back from the brink of death."

An eyebrow shot upward. *I have a cute nose?* The audacity of the chit! "I thought `twas ye who rescued me from an early meeting with Auld Cluitie."

"With whom?" She set the spoon down and wiped her hands on her apron, puzzlement on her face.

"Auld Cluitie—auld Nick." He searched for the translation. "Auld Satan."

Lucienne's eyes widened. "*Le Satan?* Oh, *non, monsieur.* You have been very honorable to my sister and me. You are *un saint.*"

Kinnon chortled. "I can think of no one who shares your kind opinion of myself. But I will show a wee bit of saintliness by not arguing with ye." He hobbled to the table and sank heavily onto a chair. "Come sit with me and tell me something."

She perched on the edge of the chair next to his, hands folded in her lap, eyeing him expectantly. "What is it you wish me to tell you? A story?" She canted her head and leaned toward him eagerly.

"Nae. I wish to know what is happening in the village. Have ye seen or heard anything?"

Worry banished Lucienne's sunny smile and her eyes darkened. "I have neither heard nor seen anything, *monsieur.* It is my hope Melisende made it to the village before the fighting began, but I have no way of knowing. It has been almost five days since I heard from her." Her voice hiccupped. "I miss her."

"Och, dinnae fash." Kinnon patted her knee awkwardly as she dipped her head. "I am sure she is simply waiting for the best, safest time to return home."

Lucienne hunched her shoulders and gave a short nod. "She always stays with the butcher and his wife. She says it is safer there, and they are well-known to her."

"There! You see? They will take good care of her." He chucked her under the chin with a curved forefinger. "What will she bring ye from the market? A bit of lace? A pretty bauble?" Her head came up reluctantly, and Kinnon saw the sheen of tears on her face. "Och, lass. I dinnae mean to upset ye." He started to pull her onto his lap, but thought better of it when a twinge of discomfort brought his attention to his wounded leg. Instead, he dragged her chair against his and allowed her to rest her head on his shoulder.

Shudders racked her slender body, and he tightened his hold, stroking her golden head sympathetically.

"She—she always brings me sweets from—from the market," Lucienne at last managed, her breath hitching with remnants of tears.

"She is a grand sister, aye?"

Her plaintive voice tore at his heart. "What if she never comes back?"

What if Melisende doesnae return? What will happen to Lucienne? A fierce wave of protectiveness surged over him. *She has no other family, no protector other than that misbegotten son of a devil and a pony. Where do I take her?* Suddenly overwhelmed by the possibilities and implications, he absently continued to stroke her head while his mind sorted through his jumbled thoughts.

I planned to return home after this mission. I still can—with Lucienne? I cannae bring her with me like a puppy. An idea struck. *Would the butcher and his wife take her in?* His shoulders dropped. *If they live?*

He shook his head. *I dinnae have an answer for a question that is not yet real. I must see what I can discover about the village and the battle and Melisende.* He glanced at his injured leg and the staff leaned against the table. *Shite. I can barely hobble about this small room and take care of my own needs.* He felt Lucienne's body relax against his in sleep and he ached to be able to tell her all was well when she woke.

How can I possibly take care of her?

CHAPTER TEN

Kinnon shifted in his seat, trying to relieve some of the growing pain in his leg. Lucienne's weight, though slight, seemed to have increased in the hour or so since she fell asleep against him. Shards of sharp pain mingled with the fuzziness of impending loss of feeling in the leg and he needed to move about to allay the sensation.

With a sigh, Lucienne slid to wakefulness and drew away from him, uncoiling her body in a fluid movement as she slowly stretched her arms over her head. Her gown pulled tight across her lush breasts, and Kinnon hardened in response. *Shite!*

He scowled, twisting away from her line of sight as he rose from the chair. Peering over his shoulder, he took in her tousled, slightly bewildered look. Her eyes rounded, dark purple with widened centers, as she stared at him.

"You smell good." Her voice, raspy with lingering sleep, tugged at his groin.

"Ye need to be up and about," he muttered, annoyed at her words and his lack of control where she was concerned. Lucienne's face fell, and he instantly regretted his rudeness.

"I felt safe. I have not slept well lately," she murmured, averting her gaze. Her fingers twitched in her lap, a helpless gesture that compounded Kinnon's remorse. "But you are right. There are still chores to be done, and they will not get done on their own." She rose and bolted for the door.

Her words, reminiscent of Melisende's pragmatic approach, brought her sister to mind and Kinnon's agitation grew. "I am sorry, Lucienne. This injury has me befuddled. I wish to be back with my unit and my words arenae kind. I dinnae mean to bark at ye."

She gathered a bucket, her hand on the door latch. "I will return shortly."

Jean-Baptiste lifted his head, ears pricked in her direction. Kinnon motioned to the beast. "Take the dog."

Lucienne slammed the door behind her and Jean-Baptiste whined, casting a worried look at Kinnon.

"Dinnae look at me like that. Women are unpredictable. Ye best get used to it."

Not sure if the advice was for himself or the dog, Kinnon grabbed his walking staff and stomped over to the hearth. He prodded the embers back to life and set a pot of water to boil. A basket of eggs sat on the shelf by the door, and he hooked the handle over the end of his staff and slid the basket neatly over to him, guilt tugging relentlessly at him.

"I could at least help by cooking a wee bit of supper whilst she attends the outside chores. Something other than that green soup." He eyed the nearly-empty shelves doubtfully. "Not even a bag of oats for a nice batch of bannocks." He shrugged. "At least the hens are laying, though I am a wee bit tired of eggs and have no way to add a nice, fat hare to the meal." He glanced at the dog who gazed at him mournfully from his spot by the hearth. *Ye are of no help.*

Looking about, he found a large bowl and began cracking eggs into it. *Five? Six?* He eyed the bright yellow globes, then glanced in the basket. *One more ought to be enough, aye?* He added another egg, then stirred the mass vigorously. Placing a pan in a corner of the hearth, he let it warm a few moments, then dumped the eggs inside. They firmed quickly, and he stirred the resulting mass, turning the mixture as it cooked.

With a triumphant chortle, he dumped the pile of steaming yellow eggs onto a platter, eying the results. "Mayhap that last egg was one too many," he murmured. "I hope she is famished."

He divided the eggs, placing half on a second plate for Lucienne. He dragged the chairs back to their proper positions at the table and sat before his dinner, waiting for her return.

Jean-Baptiste rose from his blanket, a low growl in his chest. Before Kinnon could do more than look at him in surprise, the dog launched himself at the door with a snarl, teeth and nails tearing at the ancient wood.

* * *

Melisende stirred groggily, glancing at the small window beneath the beamed ceiling. The light was faint, though she was disoriented, unsure if it was late evening or very early morning. She rose and splashed water from a pitcher on her face, relishing the coolness. Patting her skin dry with a piece of linen, she cautiously opened her door and peered out. Quiet darkness filled the hallway. *It must be night—the patients are not stirring.*

Her stomach rumbled and she frowned. *Mayhap there is something in the larder left from supper I can nibble on.* She lit a candle and slipped noiselessly down the stair and into the kitchen. The embers on the hearth bathed the room in a warm glow, and she quickly discovered a basket of biscuits covered by a damp cloth and a chunk of cheese on a platter. Slicing a wedge of the yellow cheese, she popped it in her mouth, savoring the sharp, peppery flavor.

In no particular hurry, her gaze traveled over the contents of the room. Dry goods lined the cabinets, but empty spaces bore witness to the inability to replace the goods while the battle raged. *At least we are not responsible for feeding the wounded soldiers!*

A locked cabinet in the far corner of the room caught her eye. Picking up the candle, she crossed the floor and ran her fingers searchingly across the paneled doors. The hinges moved. Intrigued, she set the candle on the long table and pushed on one door, surprised when it opened to her touch. *Someone must have forgotten to lock it.* Curious, she eased the double doors open and gaped at the treasures inside.

Her eyes quickly scanned the delicate writing on each small box. Chamomile, fennel, feverfew. Garlic, hensbane, lavender. Her eyebrows rose. *Saffron? That is expensive—and unexpected. Few people risk the wrath of the church to have anything from the East these days.* Oils in slender bottles also lined the shelves, standing shoulder-to-shoulder with a mortar and pestle, a sieve and a set of measuring spoons.

Yarrow, wormwood, spiderwort. She drew a fingertip across the list. *Poppy!* A tremor ran through her at the find. Opium, as well as all things from the East, had all but disappeared, as many people remembered only too well the impact of the Inquisition that charged these items as being from the devil—and, by association, the owner of such goods.

But in some circles, its uses were remembered, and Melisende knew its power. She pulled open the drawer and the tiny black seeds gleamed in the candlelight. Fingers flying, she scooped a measure of the poppy seeds into the mortar and ground them into a fine powder. Tearing a small square of cloth from her underskirt, she bound the powder and wiped the residue from the mortar and pestle. *If I can discover what the baby soldier likes, I can tempt him to drink this. It should not take long to put him asleep at his post.*

Not bothering to hide her satisfied smile, she closed the cabinet and crept up the stairs to her room. Hiding the square of fabric with the poppy seed powder beneath her pillow, she drifted off to sleep.

Pounding on her door jarred her to wakefulness. Her hand darted beneath her pillow, reassuring herself the small packet was still there. She swung her legs over the side of the narrow bed and reached for the door, opening it to the reddened face of Piers the butcher.

Alarm rushed over her, but her gaze slid to the faces behind him. Cateline and Mariette bounced up and down, excitement rolling off them in palpable waves. Cateline tugged at her husband's arm and he took a step back. She slipped in front of him, her face beaming.

"De Ros has agreed to a surrender!" She clasped her hands over her breast. "Can you believe it?"

Melisende darted her look back to Piers. "Are we free to exit the village?"

"*Non*, but as soon as the surrender is complete, you will be free to go."

"I must get home." She ran across the room and yanked her cloak from the peg next to the bed.

Cateline grabbed her hands, forcing her to lower them. "You must not try to leave now! There will be chaos at the gates and soldiers looting what they can in the town before they are forced to leave. A young woman such as yourself would be in great danger!"

Her eyes glowed, brimming with tears as she pleaded with Melisende. Seeing the woman's distress, Melisende relented and placed her cloak back on the peg. "I will wait," she reassured her. "A few more hours will make little difference."

Cateline eyed her doubtfully, then gave a slow nod. "You are a sweet girl. I could not bear to think of you harmed in any way." She hugged Melisende then shooed the others from the room. Their voices and footsteps clattered down the stairs.

Melisende stared at the empty doorway. *What she says is true. Soldiers will be fleeing the village into the countryside. It is only a matter of time—mayhap hours—before they stumble across the farm—and Lucienne. I cannot wait. I must leave now.*

She pulled her cloak from its peg and rolled it tightly into a small bundle, which she tied with a short strip of cloth from her underskirt. Stepping to the bed, she retrieved the packet of ground poppy seeds from its hiding place beneath her pillow, and shoved it inside her worn leather satchel. She slipped the strap over her head, the pouch snug against her side, and crept down the stairs. Pausing at the bottom, she peeked into the main room. Men hurried everywhere, strewing bandages and other filth as they went. Orders were shouted, the wounded cried out as their beds were exchanged for litters. Those who could walk in any form were shoved about, left to their own devices.

Melisende edged into the room, but the disorganized evacuation continued unabated. She inched forward. An aide's head swiveled in her direction.

"You! Gather up this mess and put it in that box." With a jerk of his head, he indicated a chest lying open on the floor, small packets strewn about and in danger of being trampled.

Merde! I have no time for this. She made no move to do as she was commanded, cutting her wary gaze back to the aide.

Tired, angry eyes met hers. "Do it, or I will see to it you meet your new master with stripes on your back."

Melisende bristled, but dared not reply. She glowered at the man and moved toward the chest, collecting packets in a fold of her skirt as she went. With a defiant gesture, she dumped the load into the chest, not bothering to sort them into the smaller open boxes inside. The aide shot her a disgusted look and a muttered curse and continued with his own business.

Keeping an eye on him as she worked, her attention drifted to the packets in her hands. Chamomile, comfrey, feverfew, hensbane—HEMLOCK! Casting a quick glance over her shoulder to the busy aide, she stuffed several packets within her leather pouch and hastily returned the remainder to the chest. With a heave, she righted the box and latched the lid.

Just then, a pair of orderlies hustled by, a wounded man on a pallet between them. Stooping in an attempt to use them as a shield to protect her from the aide's quick eye, Melisende gathered her skirts in one hand and hurried alongside. As soon as they were in the yard, she slipped to one side, hiding within the shadows of the recessed doorway. The scene before her nearly stilled her heart.

Bodies lay everywhere, clogging the small yard. Several lay at odd angles, stacked against the far wall, flies buzzing their exposed flesh. A few men huddled near the gate, leaned together for physical support, their bodies sporting various bandages, their clothing dirty and torn.

Another group, men on pallets on the churned ground, waited quietly, some accepting drinks from orderlies who moved among them. A few spoke softly among themselves as they waited their turn for evacuation.

Her gaze slid to the last group, the men utterly silent save for an occasional weak cry. Motionless, they lay on the ground, bandages stained red, black, and an ominous yellow-green. No orderlies moved among them, and none came to their aid.

"They will be dead soon," a voice murmured in her ear.

Startled, she jerked away, facing the man standing beside her. It was Edward, the former guard at the back door. She uttered a small sigh of relief.

"What will happen to them?" she asked.

Edward jerked his bristled chin to the bodies stacked near the gate. "Many were given a draught of opium and now await their turn at the gate, though it is doubtful we will have time to bury them before your precious Bertran takes over the village. They will become his problem soon."

Melisende shivered despite the rapidly warming day. "It will be very hot soon. Will they not put up an awning to protect them from the sun?"

Edward shrugged. "The heat will likely hasten their deaths. Poor beggars."

A sudden warm breeze blew through the yard from the direction of the gate, bringing with it the sickening odor of corruption. Flies swept upward in a dark cloud above the bodies, only to resume their explorations a moment later. Melisende covered her nose and mouth with a hand and turned away.

Edward's cackle reached her ears. "So you no longer fancy yourself a healer, then?"

"I never did." Her muffled reply hid her animosity to Edward's callous disregard for the mortally injured men.

He edged closer, his whisky-laden breath tainted with the odor of onions and rotted teeth. "I saw you tending those poor wounded soldiers. Tenderly wiping their faces and spooning broth into their mouths."

Melisende's eyes flashed. "I also cleaned their English shit off the floor. Both jobs were simply compassionate gestures toward another human being," she snarled. "The fact there was a knife more or less at my throat to do so weighed heavily on my actions."

"The fact that many were young helped, aye?"

"And English," she spat. "I cannot tell you how glad I am to see you leave."

Edward favored her with a curious look and moved a half-step away. "I see you have plans to leave as well. Hoping to reunite with your lover?"

Melisende gripped her rolled cloak tighter. "*Oui*. No one will miss me in this confusion and I must see him." She forced a wide-eyed look of worry past her scowl.

"You will never get past the gate, confusion or not. And disgruntled soldiers in the street would be happy to take you as part of their loot." Edward cocked his head. "I can help you."

"Why would you help me? I have no whisky to trade for your services."

Edward laughed. "Now that is a downright pity. But I need through that gate as well, and together we can make that happen."

She eyed him warily and he shrugged. "I am too old to be of much use in battle, but they will force me to toil in other ways until I drop dead. Not much chance of a pension in enemy land. I wish to live simply back in England—or in France if I cannot get home." He straightened, giving her a hard look. "Aye or nay? We have no time before someone spots us and again puts us to work."

Melisende stared across the packed yard to the gate, mentally weighing her chances with Edward against returning through the house and shop to the front door. She turned to the grizzled man beside her. "How will we accomplish this?"

Edward grinned his gap-toothed leer. "Do exactly as I tell you."

CHAPTER 11

Melisende unrolled her cloak and pulled it over her shoulders, carefully hiding the leather satchel beneath it at the small of her back. Instantly, the heat of the day settled over her.

"Pull yer hood up, too. We don't want one of these soldiers seeing yer pretty face and getting ideas, now, do we?"

She glared at Edward, but did as he requested, hating the too-warm confines of the garment. Taking her firmly by the upper arm, he leaned close.

"Stay next to me, but hang back a bit. Don't appear too eager." His whisper carried the hint of a conspiracy and mild warning.

Before she could decide this was a bad idea, he straightened and jerked her arm, giving her a scowl. "Step lively, girl. We are late."

Heads turned as they made their way across the yard, but no one moved to stop them. As they approached the gate, a wagon, its wooden bed splotched with great dark stains, pulled to a halt. A tall, thin man, his uniform a dizzying array of colors and randomly attached silver and gold braid, hopped down from his lofty perch.

"Load 'em up, men! I haven't got all day." By pairs, soldiers grabbed the deceased men and heaved them into the wagon, uncaring of the solid thump of the bodies. The wagon driver halted one, snipping the trim from the dead man's uniform with a small knife before allowing him to join the others. He shoved the stained bit into his pocket and turned to Edward and Melisende as they edged to one side of the gate.

He grinned broadly. "What do we have here? Most of my guests do not walk to the wagon themselves."

Edward halted, jerking Melisende to his side. "Step aside, Marcel. She is not for the likes of you."

Marcel stepped closer, his head tilted to the side as he tried to peer beneath Melisende's hood. Without warning, Edward backhanded her, his fist striking her nose and upper lip. She gasped, one hand flying to her face at the pain. She tasted the coppery tang of blood and warm liquid filled one side of her nose. She wanted to scream at him, punish him for his assault, but the casualness of it stunned her.

"Save yerself the trouble. I'm taking her to De Ros—one last bit of fluff before he turns this dump over to the French."

Undeterred, Marcel raised the edge of her hood with grimy fingers. Melisende blinked her eyes, fighting back furious tears. She wiped the back of her hand across her face, smearing blood and mucus. Marcel grimaced and stepped back.

"I hope she cleans up better than she looks now—for your sake. De Ros likes his whores to not look as though they've been well-used *before* he gets them."

"Let us pass," Edward grumbled. "We're late as it is."

"*Mademoiselle.*" Marcel gave Melisende a sweeping bow, his dark red hair shining with oil in the hot sun.

Edward grabbed her arm and half-shoved, half-dragged her through the gate and into the alley. As soon as they reached the shelter of the darkened path, Melisende wrenched free of his grasp, twisting his thin arm between rigid fingers.

"Do not ever touch me again!" she seethed, flinging his arm away. Using the edge of her cloak, she wiped her face, grimacing at the pain in her nose. "I will not tolerate such behavior—I do not care what the provocation is. Do I make myself clear?"

Edward turned hard, unrepentant eyes on her. "I had to get you past that licentious bastard somehow. He has a lot of power among the soldiers, and not a one of them in the yard would have stopped him had he taken a fancy to you."

With a snarl, Melisende ripped the small dagger from the pocket of her cloak. Edward's eyes widened as the tip parted the grimy hem of his jacket. "Do not handle me again. I will play along—but only to a point." She pressed the blade against his soft belly. "Is my meaning understood?"

Edward raised his hands in surrender, a half-grin pulling at his mouth. "You are a feisty one, that's for sure. Too bad you aren't really going to De Ros. I hear he likes 'em lively."

Melisende shot him a disgusted look. "Get me out of here." She jammed the dagger back into her pocket and motioned him on with a jerk of her head.

He eased away from her and stuck his head around the corner of the building. After a moment, he turned back to her with a mocking bow. "All is clear—please remember the town is evacuating."

They stepped into an uproar of carts and horses, citizenry and soldiers. Cries rang out as people were jostled, horses squealed as people darted into their path. Bellowed commands and yelps of surprise or pain created more confusion. Dust billowed from beneath the hurrying feet of both man and beast. Melisende pulled a corner of her cloak over her mouth and nose to ward off the dirt and hide her face. There were few women on the street.

Around them, men carried what they could. The lucky few heaped belongings—owned and stolen alike—in small carts or wagons. A woman shrieked from an upper story window, and Melisende's head jerked sharply at the sound. An angry shout followed by muffled sobbing drifted downward.

"And De Ros said it would be an orderly surrender," Edward muttered.

"He cannot keep the mercenaries under control, and they know they will not get payment from Bertran for their troubles." Melisende eyed the rapacious lot angrily.

They hurried past the mob, taking care to move along the edge of the street, next to the buildings and away from the dangerous melee mid-street. Ahead, a group of rough-looking soldiers wove through the crowd, threading purposefully toward them. Weapons bristled from belts and harnesses as they shoved people out of their way.

"So they take what they can before Bertran's army marches through the gates," Edward noted, continuing their previous conversation.

"Have you chosen your loot yet?" Melisende mocked him.

He gripped Melisende's arm and shoved her sideways into a dark alley. Her head snapped back as he slammed her against the rock wall. Her breath left her in a *whoosh*, and her vision blurred. She blinked her eyes to clear them, and Edward's scarred face loomed before her. He leered.

"Aye, I have. You."

An explosion of pain ripped through her head and her world went black.

Kinnon leapt to his feet, but his wounded leg betrayed him. He snarled a curse and reached for his staff. Hobbling to the door, he held the dog at bay with the sturdy stick as he worked the latch. The instant a crack appeared, Jean-Batiste shoved his head through and was gone.

"Shite! Where is he?" Kinnon shouted, overcome with fear for Lucienne. He snatched his dagger from the table and jerked the door fully open. Glancing about yielded nothing—the dog was long gone. He fought to listen through the pounding in his chest, the roaring in his ears.

There! A shriek and a snarl drifted to him on the breeze. A masculine shout. Kinnon's head swiveled toward the sound. Certain he was headed in the right direction, he jolted unevenly across the ground.

He sweated, cursing his healing body. Pain stabbed upward through his side and his breath came in short gasps. He pressed on, ignoring the knife-like tugs in his leg. Cornering the ramshackle barn several yards behind the house, Jean-Baptiste's growls grew louder. A woman's voice sobbed and pleaded. Angry male shouts roared. Kinnon doubled his efforts.

He shoved aside a heavy limb, its leaves snapping with the force, slender branches raking his face as he pushed past. In a small clearing ahead, Lucienne stood splayed against a tree trunk, held there by a large knife pinning the shoulder of what remained of her dress to the tree. A few feet away, a man and Jean-Baptiste circled each other, a long dagger extending from the man's hand. Its blade winked in the mottled light and Lucienne cried out again.

"Do not hurt him! Please!" She reached for the knife at her shoulder and tugged at it, but the blade bit deeply in the wood and did not budge. She stomped her foot and sobbed her frustration, her fists clenched.

Kinnon jerked his attention back to the combatants as the man recoiled from a slashing attack. A red line opened on Jean-Baptiste's shoulder, but he neither whined nor flinched. His amber eyes remained locked on the man, his lips curled back from his impressive teeth.

It would only be a matter of time before the dog's wound proved deadly. A combination of blood loss and a slower response due to the injury would give the man the upper hand. Kinnon grabbed the point of his dagger between his fingertips and threw it with all the strength he could muster. The blade whistled through the air, startling the man. He paused, head up as he sought the source of the sound—exactly as Kinnon hoped he would. The slim, honed blade pierced the front of the man's neck, its tip protruding from the back. With a look of pained surprise, the man clutched the handle already drenched with heavy, pulsating blood. His legs crumpled and he crashed to the ground.

Jean-Baptiste raced to his adversary's side, sniffing him suspiciously as low-throated growls rumbled from his chest. Keeping an eye on the dead man, the dog turned on his haunches, lifted a hind leg, and let loose a healthy yellow stream.

Good for you, Jean-Baptiste! Choking on a slightly hysterical laugh, Kinnon lurched his way across the clearing to Lucienne. He reached for the handle of the knife pining her to the tree, partly straddling her to get close enough to leverage it from the trunk. With a grunt of accomplishment, he pried the blade free. He glanced down at Lucienne's tear-stained face.

Her eyes loomed impossibly large and round in her pale face. Tears matted her long lashes and sparkled in her eyes. Her soft pink lips parted.

"Thank you, Kinnon," she whispered. Her breath hitched in her chest and Kinnon's gaze drifted lower. The shoulder of her gown was torn and a trickle of blood trailed across her collar bone.

"Are ye hurt?" He felt the question inadequate, but could think of nothing better to say.

She touched her shoulder gently with her fingertips, wincing slightly. "'Tis a scratch. Thanks to you and Jean-Baptiste, I am otherwise unharmed."

Kinnon studied her face and saw bruise marks on either side of her mouth. Could the bastard have grabbed her face, forcing a kiss? Her hair was a snarled mess and he envisioned the man's fist trapped within the golden curls. The bodice of her dress was ripped, exposing the fullness of her creamy breasts. A long scratch curved downward across her chest. His wrath returned, rasping his voice. "It looks as though he handled ye rough, lass."

Lucienne stiffened. "Are you angry with me?"

Kinnon drew back, shocked. "Nae! 'Twas not yer fault. He had no right to touch ye. I am angry I couldnae prevent it." He shook his head forcefully as self-disgust roiled through him. "I couldnae stop him. I was no use to ye. Damn him and the others of his ilk!"

Lucienne's hands cupped his face, stilling his movements. She rained soft kisses across his cheek. "*Non*! You did not know he was here! You saved me."

The knowledge of what he'd barely been able to stop brought a curse to his lips. What if there had been more than one man? He could not have fought them off. What if his blade had missed? What if this had happened two days ago? Three? When he was still confined to his bed, unable to come to her aid? What if the man had dragged Lucienne further away where Jean-Baptiste's keen ears would not hear them? His stomach lurched.

His hands fisted tight as rage at his inadequacies roared through him. "I should have been here and prevented this—not cosseting my damn leg!"

"But, don't you see? You did stop him. You did not let your leg hinder you." Lucienne gently kissed the side of his neck beneath his ear.

The soft touch of her lips changed Kinnon's awareness. He breathed in the odor of her skin, warm beneath the tumble of her hair. He became aware of the crush of her breasts against his chest, the answering hardness in his groin. Slowly, he loosened his grip.

Lucienne snuggled closer. "Please do not let me go." She firmed her stance against him.

"'Tis not proper, lass," he answered, gently setting her from him.

"I *want* you to hold me," she replied with a pout, hands fisted at her sides.

"'Tis not right." Kinnon took a half-step back. Lucienne's face crumpled and fresh tears lit her eyes.

"Take me to the house," she choked. "Take me away from here."

She threaded her fingers through his as they crossed the clearing past the dead man and Kinnon did not have the heart to rebuke her. Jean-Baptiste ran ahead of them, a silent streak of muscled protection.

They reached the house and Kinnon shut the door behind them, locking away the horror. Lucienne came to an abrupt halt and he pulled up short behind her.

"You fixed supper?" She whirled to face him, a smile on her face. "You are so wonderful, Kinnon." Her fingers trailed down his sleeve. "Why can you not see how I feel about you?"

He struggled to ignore her half-exposed breasts, but his blood thickened, addling his thoughts. "I am a Scotsman—"

"Do Scotsman make love differently from Frenchmen?" Her voice, low and hypnotic, shortened his breath.

"Nae. 'Tis not the point." He ran his fingers through his hair.

"What is the point?" She glided closer, pressing against him, her breasts welling further out of their tattered, inadequate confines.

"Ye are but a lass, and not my wife. There can be nothing more than friendship between us."

Her eyes slanted, catlike, angry. "Is it Melisende? You like her better than me, *ai-je raison?*"

"Ye are too young to be worried about such things, Luci. I like ye and yer sister too much to cause a rift between ye."

Her face lit with a smile, throwing Kinnon into a spin with her rapid and unpredictable mood changes. "You called me *Luci.* I like that! No one has ever called me that before." She took his arm, pulling herself close as she peered up at him. "It will be your special name for me. Aren't I special, Kinnon?"

St. Andrew help me! Kinnon took a steadying breath. "Aye, Luci, ye are a verra special girl." He glanced at the dog, panting on his rug by the hearth. "Ye should take care of that wound on Jean-Baptiste's shoulder."

With a cry of distress for the dog, Lucienne broke away and began gathering items necessary to treat the gash. Feeling a bit unsteady, Kinnon sank onto a nearby chair.

CHAPTER TWELVE

Morning sunlight gleamed through the tangled web of golden hair laying across his face. Kinnon's nose wrinkled at the feather-light sensation as the gilded strands brushed his face with every breath he took. He shook himself awake, gently sweeping the locks aside as he took stock of his surroundings.

A slender arm splayed across his chest and one leg draped over his. Lucienne's head lay tucked beneath his arm, face downward, her entire body completely relaxed. He slowly slid from the bed, gently tugging her night rail down over her exposed calves. She had woken him during the night, crying incoherently about the monster coming after her. After a short check of the house and a glance at Jean-Baptiste who merely yawned at Kinnon's midnight ramblings, he had attempted to soothe the overwrought girl. But nothing would help except he allow her to curl up next to him on the narrow bed where she fell instantly into a deep, dreamless sleep.

He grimaced as his leg attempted to bear his weight. *Nothing like a lass draped across yer leg all night to stiffen it.* He stepped jerkily across the room and prodded the banked fire to life, wondering how he could leave Lucienne to see to his unit, and just how soon Melisende would be home.

* * *

Melisende opened puffy eyes to the pale streak of dawn's light outlining the door to the small room. She slowly sat upright, her stiff limbs protesting the hours spent on the hard floor. *Treacherous English bâtard!* She rubbed her arms, wincing as her fingers encountered the bruising on her left arm. Certain there was also a knot, or at the very least a substantial bruise, on the back of her head, she gently probed the area. *Aïe!*

She glanced at her clothing, but other than being rumpled and dusty, she found nothing amiss. Her satchel's strap still clung to her neck, and she felt its reassuring presence at her back. She patted the cloak's pocket and felt nothing. *Bâtard! He stole my money and dagger.* She rose to her feet, fingertips touching the wall for balance.

A noise at the door alerted her and she swung about to meet the intruder, her head suddenly clear. The latch slipped free and the door creaked open. Edward stalked inside and slung a bag from his shoulder to the floor. His eyes lit as he registered her standing form.

"Finished with yer nap, eh?" He propped his fists on his hips and grinned at her. "I was beginning to worry you were a delicate thing despite the spunk you showed earlier." He prodded the bag with the toe of his boot. "There is food in there. Fix us a bite to eat."

Melisende eyed him warily, but he did not approach her. Instead, he clomped to the narrow window and hefted the bar from the shutters. Letting it fall to the floor with a thump, he pulled the heavy boards apart, letting in the early morning light. "A nice day in the making, though `twill be quite hot again soon. Yer Constable Bertran should arrive for the formal surrender tomorrow." He gave her a lecherous leer. "We will celebrate from here."

Like hell! Keeping her features carefully neutral, Melisende approached the bag. She unknotted the drawstring at the top and peered inside. A loaf of bread, a chunk of cheese and a couple of rather withered apples nestled against a flask. Edward pulled a bench away from the wall and sat, leaning his back against the stone, watching her.

She glanced over her shoulder, not making eye contact. "I will bring your breakfast to you, but I think I will get comfortable, first." She fingered a pleat of her skirt, drawing his attention to her clothing.

Edward's boots scraped the floor as he sat upright, clearly interested. "I suppose you have done this for yer *beau* before?"

She lifted her shoulders in a negligent shrug. "It is different with each man, *monsieur.*" Turning her back on him, she grabbed her satchel strap amid a handful of the edge of her cloak and lifted both items over her head. Keeping the satchel covered with folds of fabric, she set it on the low table before the hearth.

"Don't be formal with me," Edward said. "I don't mean to keep you. Just a little play before I leave town. Yer *beau* won't mind a little wear and tear."

Melisende's eyes narrowed and she allowed herself a moment to clear her thoughts. *A bit of acting can go a long way, and I must distract him.* She loosened the tie at the neck of her gown and pulled the neckline wide at the shoulders. Lifting her hair with her hands, she finger-combed the tangled tresses as Edward's grunt of encouragement reached her ears.

Satisfied she had his attention where she wanted it, she resumed her task.

She turned to the sack on the floor and bent over it, making sure her gown gaped open enough to reveal the tops of her breasts to Edward's eager eyes. She played with the contents of the bag for a moment, finally pulling the flask from its depths. "Would you care for a drink whilst you wait?" Giving him her most innocent look, she held up the wooden vessel.

Edward licked his lips. "Aye. Bring it to me."

Melisende smiled and turned to the table. Her back to her captor, she worked swiftly and silently, removing three packets from the satchel. She picked a chipped mug from an array of worn dishes on the table and poured a measure of the wine into it. Quickly adding the powders to the liquid, she swirled it with her finger before turning back to Edward.

With a slow swish of her hips, she crossed the room and seated herself next to him. Predictably, his nose dropped to the level of her bosom. She rolled her shoulders forward, forcing her breasts to the top of her gown's neckline, displaying the exposed flesh. Edward swallowed and beads of moisture broke out on his forehead.

He raised a hand to her breast and she countered by meeting it with the mug. He accepted it absently in his outstretched hand and took a long draught. With an exaggerated wiggle, she nestled her hip against Edward's. He jumped. She smiled playfully and he took another pull at his drink. *Homme stupide. To think I would accept him after the way he treated me? Bah!*

"Finish this and I will fetch another," she murmured, fighting back the urge to slap the self-satisfied look from his face. Instead, she gently stroked a strand of greasy gray hair from the side of his face, then drew her fingertips down the length of the scar on his cheek.

Edward jerked his chin toward her bodice. "Let's have a bit more look, eh?"

Melisende hid her grimace and pulled the neckline further off her shoulders, baring a bit more skin. She slanted a look at him. "More after breakfast?"

Edward's eyes lit and his darkened teeth showed beneath an eager grin. He tossed the rest of the wine back in a single gulp and held it out to her. She reached for it and he grabbed her wrist.

"I want to see what you've been so eager to share with yer *beau*."

With a twisting movement, she broke his grip, unable to keep up the pretense. "I warned you about touching me," she growled. She shoved away, rising to her feet in a fluid movement.

Edward sneered. "I may be an old man, but I am still stronger than you and you have nowhere to go."

"I believe you are wrong on both accounts, *monsieur*." She took a step backward.

Edward lurched forward, his movements awkward. "What do you mean?" His eyes grew wide, the centers of his eyes almost obscuring the colored rims. "What did you give me?"

"To clear up our misunderstanding earlier, I *am* a healer, *monsieur*, and quite knowledgeable about herbs and such. I added a mixture of hensbane, opium and hemlock to your wine a few moments ago. I believe your *cirurgian* gives this to his patients before he performs very painful, unpleasant procedures."

Edward clutched his throat, trying to force himself to gag. Melisende's lips tightened in a small, satisfied smile.

"You will fall asleep and I will be on my way. Sometime tomorrow you will wake. With luck, your food and the rest of the wine will still be here and you can refresh yourself and make the most of whatever situation you find yourself in. I will not give you another thought. *Adieu, monsieur.*"

She pulled her gown back into place and knotted the neck closed. Crossing to the table, she retrieved her cloak and satchel, settling both over her shoulders. A moan and a thump rattled behind her as Edward slid to the floor. Returning to his side, she searched him, finding her dagger and several coins in an inner pocket of his coat. Pocketing the items, she strode to the door and escaped into an eerie stillness very different to the melee of the previous day. Her concern shot upward as the hairs on the back of her neck prickled.

The street was empty. Debris littered the ground. A rooster crowed nearby, snatching her attention. A baby's cry slipped past on a faint breeze. *So this is what the surrender of a town is like. I wonder what is left.*

* * *

Kinnon glanced at the bed and found Lucienne eying him sleepily through half-closed eyes. "Go back to sleep, lass. I will see to the animals."

She stretched contentedly, then hopped from the bed. She sashayed to her room where she dressed, returning to Kinnon for help with her laces. He quickly obliged her, keeping his actions smooth and brotherly. Relieved to avoid a repeat of the previous evening, he stepped away from her and grabbed his walking staff.

Kinnon hobbled to the barn, grinning at Lucienne's antics as she set about milking the three nanny goats. By the time she finished, Kinnon was willing to give it a try, and the cows' impatient low bellows hurried them into the large stall.

The gaunt beasts turned their heads in unison as Kinnon and Lucienne entered, their liquid eyes gentle though they stamped their rear feet against the swell of their full udders.

"You can milk Bibi, and I will take Jolie," Lucienne informed him, plopping herself down on a small stool next to the rangy cow.

Kinnon eyed Bibi dubiously. "She isnae verra big." He glanced at his hands, opening and closing them as he compared them to the size of the dainty cow's teats. "I dinnae wish to hurt her."

"Handle them as you would a woman's breasts," Lucienne replied, her forehead resting against Jolie's flank as she rhythmically squirted the cow's milk into the wooden pail.

Kinnon's face heated. *Impertinent lass.* Upending a bucket next to Bibi, he sat on the makeshift stool, knees sprawled apart as he tucked himself close to the cow. He stroked her flank. "Ye and I will get on fine, lass. I am a quick learner."

Bibi stomped a rear hoof and went back to chewing her cud.

Kinnon splayed his palm against her udder. His eyebrows quirked upward in surprise. *A bit hairy, but soft and warm.* He settled himself to the task, mimicking Lucienne's gentle squeeze from the udder downward, and was rewarded to see a stream of milk squirt into the bucket.

For several long moments, the silence was broken only by the steady swish-swish of milk as he and Lucienne filled their buckets. By the time Bibi's udder was depleted, Kinnon's hands cramped and his back ached from bending. But he held his bucket proudly for Lucienne to see.

"My first time to milk a cow!" he announced. Bibi stretched her neck and bellowed. Her tail swung through the air, catching Kinnon on the cheek. "Bah!" He wiped his face, scowling at the brownish muck on the back of his hand. "Auld besom! Ye can wait until tonight for yer next milking."

Lucienne laughed. "Oh, Kinnon! They only get milked twice a day." She scampered to his side, weaving around the cows' bony rumps. She stroked the side of his face with her fingertips. "There. No harm done. We can scrub it better once we are back inside."

Just then, Jean-Baptiste came bounding into the stable, barking his head off. Lucienne turned to him in surprise. "What is it?"

The dog leapt up, his paws on her shoulders, nearly knocking her to the ground. She staggered back a step against Bibi's broad side. Kinnon grabbed at her arm, waving Jean-Baptiste away. "Ye beast! Have a care for the lass!"

"And do not knock over the buckets, *s'il vous plaît.*"

Both Lucienne and Kinnon looked up in surprise at the new voice.

"Melisende!"

* * *

Kinnon stared at Melisende, calmed by her serene beauty, though she bore the marks of long travel. He thought the wisps of hair springing from her braid charming, the smudge of dirt on her cheekbone adorable—and stopped himself from wiping it away before the gesture was more than a thought. He wanted to settle her slightly askew cloak more comfortably about her shoulders, but managed to keep his hands at his sides.

Shocked by his impulsive response to her, he stepped away, fumbling for his walking stick. Her gaze followed his movement.

"Are you well, *monsieur?*" she asked, her voice low and rich, a sweet slide against his taut nerves.

"A bit of a wound, but Lucienne has taken verra good care of me."

Lucienne ran to her sister, hugging her and skipping about in turn. "Oh, Melisende! I used the herbs and I even stitched his leg! My sewing looked very nice and even. I did as I have seen you do, and it worked!"

Something within Kinnon lurched. *I was her first patient?* He released a whoosh of breath and the sisters glanced at him. He cleared his throat.

"'Tis good to see ye home, Melisende. What can ye tell me of the battle?"

"The battle is over. De Ros is to surrender the city tomorrow if reinforcements do not arrive." She moved to his side. "I am sorry to say your commander has taken ill. Rumors are he will not live."

Bertran dying? Kinnon shook his head. *He is the Constable of France. He has fought in a hundred battles, survived capture three times over. It isnae possible.* Memories of the man, hale and strong flashed through his mind. And then, only days ago, the unsettling feeling the man was hiding an illness.

"I must go," he said abruptly. "I must see for myself."

Melisende nodded. "I thank you for being here for my sister, no matter the circumstances. Had I known you were here, I would not have worried so much."

His gaze slid to Lucienne. "She saved my life. I am forever indebted."

Melisende looked from him to Lucienne's smile. "It seems you have both helped each other. I am grateful." She peered at him again. "Will you remain with your troops?"

"Ye remember?"

"*Oui.* I remember." Her eyes searched his, found his soul. "You had doubts."

Kinnon nodded. "I still do. I had planned to take my leave of Bertran and his army before this last battle." He scrubbed his face. "I cannae believe . . ." His voice failed, unable to speak the words aloud.

Melisende touched his arm lightly. "Go. Finish what you must. You will be welcome if you wish to finish convalescing here." Turning, she disappeared through the door.

Lucienne darted to Kinnon's side and wrapped her arms about his waist. "Do not go, Kinnon! I will miss you."

"And I will miss you, lass. Ye saved my life, ye know." He attempted to step away, but she clung to him. "Let me go, Luci. I have a duty to complete."

Lucienne snuggled closer, humming lightly under her breath. It was clear she paid little attention to his words.

Frustrated, Kinnon grasped her upper arms and pushed her gently back from him. "Are ye listening to me, Luci?"

Twinkling lavender eyes met his. "I like it when you call me Luci." She sighed. "*Oui,* I am listening. You care more for your duty than you do me."

"Nae. I will return—for a short time. I do not know what my commander will ask of me."

Lucienne dropped her gaze and gave a tiny nod. "You will come back?"

"Aye, lass. I will be back."

She glanced back at him, her features lit with pleasure. "Will you bring me sweets?"

CHAPTER THIRTEEN

The air was hot, dense. Kinnon wiped the back of his hand across his brow, cursing the mid-July weather. *'Tis nothing like Scotland*, he groused. *'Tis time I was home.*

"Shite!" He scowled at a bird that took wing at the sound of his voice, feathers flashing blue in the sun, then continued in silence, rebuking himself for the noise when he had no other way to protect himself. Armed with only a dagger, he would be easy prey to any who came across him.

He passed the camp's first sentry without challenge, but was halted by the next and questioned. The sight of his walking staff and stiff, hobbling gait—along with his name, verified by an aide—won him entry into the camp, and he made his way through the sea of tents to Bertran's pavilion where he was obliged to cool his heels on a tree stump while a guard conferred with someone inside.

All around him the camp spoke of a ferocious battle past. Few men did not bear some wound, great or small, clothing stained or torn. While not disheartened, the mood was serious, lacking the normal jovial comments of men taking their ease around the numerous campfires. Instead, the creak of leather and soft chime of metal reached his ears as men rode past. A sharp cry interjected a jarring note. Men hurried about the commander's tent, hushed and somber.

Kinnon sat on his make-shift seat as noblemen, knights and soldiers paraded past. Some were allowed entry to Bertran's tent, others milled about outside, talking quietly amongst themselves. He finally rose and stumped over to a small group of soldiers. They looked at him with worried eyes.

"What can ye tell me of Bertran?" Kinnon asked. The men shifted their feet, their gazes bouncing from one to the other until one man finally stepped forward.

"He is fatigued, *monsieur*, and the heat has aggravated his fever."

Kinnon's heart skipped a beat. "He has a competent *cirurgian*, aye?"

"More than one. And they all despair of his life."

Though Melisende had warned him, the words still struck like a hammer to his chest. He nodded to the men drifting in and out of the tent. "Who are these lads?"

"They are nobles and knights come to visit—" his voice dropped to a whisper, "—one last time."

"Many men wish to speak to him, but the *cirurgians* only allow a few at a time. They cannot deny them, but they try not to tire our Bertran more," another added.

Our Bertran. Those two words spoke volumes to Kinnon. *He will always be Our Bertran to the people. No matter their rank, he is simply Bertran.*

Kinnon reeled from the discouraging news, his heart connected to this great man who had treated him so well. Though Kinnon knew his commander had risen from less-than-auspicious beginnings and the nobles often despised him for it, today they vied for position at his side, verifying the soldier's disheartening words.

He glanced about the camp again, seeing its ugliness. Tattered women ghosted from tent to cook fire, scarcely heeded by the men they serviced. A glittering sword rested next to a disheveled soldier as he squatted in the dirt—unlikely the sword's true owner. Kinnon knew more riches lay hidden from sight, all taken as rightful spoils of war.

He wondered about the villagers. What injuries and thefts had they endured at the hands of the English? Would they fare better at the hands of the French? He remembered Melisende's memory of the shop keepers buying 'protection' from the very men who had once sworn to defend them—and what happened to those who refused such bullying tactics.

How do men fail so easily in their duty? Why do they find a comfortable hook to hang their misdeeds on instead of refusing to go along with the evil deeds? What religion or government needs to be so insular as to drive out all who disagree? Can they not learn from those they serve?

Bertran had used harsh tactics from time to time to force a quick victory—*better these few than an entire town.* Kinnon shuddered. Perhaps—but surely not to those few. And yet, those remaining had always capitulated, saving many. He shook his head, his thoughts too deep, piling on his grief for his commander. *He will be remembered as a great man—and he was. He has made a lasting impression on me, and for this past year, I would have laid down my life for his.*

An aide Kinnon recognized appeared in the tent's doorway, peering about the groups of men huddling near. His eyes met Kinnon's and he gestured at him. "Come. He wishes to speak to you."

Kinnon approached the tent with dread, his limbs drugged with apprehension. His throat was dry and he swallowed, working his mouth to gain moisture. He ducked his head beneath the tent's overhang and blinked his eyes against the semi-darkness.

Bertran lay upon his camp bed, one man hovering near his head, others standing about, glancing at Kinnon as he entered. Bertran waved the man next to him away as the aide urged Kinnon to approach. Shooting Kinnon a warning glare from beneath his brow, the man left Bertran's side.

"Come closer, Scotsman. I do not have much time." The once-clear, commanding voice Kinnon would have recognized anywhere was gone, replaced by the death-rattle rasp of a man clearly only a short time from the grave.

Kinnon stepped to the edge of the bed. "Ye willnae discount all the prayers of yer knights, now, will ye? They have to account for something."

Bertran's lips etched a tired smile. "Forty years of combat is apparently enough for this body. I am too weak to recover, despite their prayers."

Kinnon stared at the man who had become almost a father-figure to him in the past months. His eyes searched the familiar face, now gray and lined with fatigue. His features, considered ugly by most who knew him, now added sunken eyes and new wrinkles—unflattering in the candle-lit tent. To Kinnon, all that mattered was a great man was doomed to die—and soon.

"I was told you were dead," Bertran murmured.

"They were wrong," Kinnon replied simply, loathe to bring Herve into the conversation.

Bertran was silent for a moment. "I have made most of my arrangements. De Ros will, according to our terms, surrender the town tomorrow. As for me, it is arranged for my heart to be conveyed to the church of the Dominicans near my home." He eyed Kinnon. "Did you know Thiephaine de Raguenel is buried there?" He sighed a thin wisp of breath and closed his eyes. "She was the wife of my youth, and though I spent little time with her, with her is where my heart longs to be."

Silence lengthened between them, and Kinnon, rocked by his commander's acceptance of death, stood close, unable to move.

A hand touched his arm as a voice murmured in his ear. "The priest is here for the last sacraments, *monsieur*. Please step away."

Kinnon lurched about on his wounded leg and saw the tent filled with men of all ranks. Their figures weaved and blurred and he wiped his eyes, surprised to find them wet with tears.

Bertran roused and for the next several moments, all was silent except for the low murmur of the priest's words. After making his will, Bertran called for his sword. He unsheathed it, considering its glittering length as he raised it before the gathered crowd, his face strained at the weight. "I have always had pure intentions in my duty with this sword. But at times, I wonder if I have failed in any way." For long moments he perused the blade, then kissed the weapon and presented it with trembling hands to the *Marechal* de Sancerre.

"Return it to the king. Tell him I was ever his faithful servant, and if any faults were committed, I regret them deeply."

He embraced the *marechal* who wept unabashedly. One by one, each man in the room approached Bertran. He consoled them, reminding them to respect the Church, spare the ecclesiastics, and protect the poor, women and children.

Kinnon's eyes wandered the room, wondering which, indeed if not all, were guilty of disobeying Bertran's last words. *Though they arenae his last words—for I have heard him say so time and again. Yet among us are the thieves, the blasphemers, and those who have abused women and children to get what they want.*

His gaze returned to Bertran who now lay in silence, eyes on the crucifix in his hands. Time passed, but none moved away from the tent. Shadows drifted across the canvas, and at last Bertran heaved a great sigh, and his hands relaxed their hold on this life.

* * *

Kinnon sat beside the early morning fire, deep in thought. The camp had plunged into grief at the death of Bertran du Guesclin, and the silence was unbroken except for the crackle of the flames as they woke to new life.

He recited the names of his commander which he'd heard among the men, recalling their pride in serving Bertran. *The Eagle of Brittany, The Black Dog of Brocéliande, a Breton knight and French military genius. He won many a battle against much larger armies, and was ransomed by the king thrice—each time for a staggering amount. But he never quailed, never questioned, always persevered. Where would we be were it not for him? Where will we be next year? Next month? Tomorrow?*

A wave of voices rushed through the camp. Men scrambled for their weapons, and the guard on Bertran's tent snapped to attention. Kinnon followed the stares and caught the rising excitement. Within moments, a riding party, bedecked in splendid finery, rode into camp.

A man next to Kinnon nudged him sharply in the side. "'Tis the English commandant!"

"Why is he here?" Kinnon asked.

"The *marechal* went to the castle gate two days ago and demanded the commander surrender and evacuate the town as agreed."

Kinnon's eyes widened as he urged him on. "Though he knew Bertran was dying?"

The man bent closer, clearly enjoying himself. "Aye. De Ros replied that though his agreement was with Bertran, he would keep his word even after his death." He nudged Kinnon again. "But he would surrender to no one but the constable."

Men rode past, approaching the tent where Bertran's body lay. The sides of the tent were rolled back, and Kinnon could see quite clearly as De Ros and his knights dismounted and proceeded to Bertran's bedside. De Ros knelt and placed the keys of the castle at Bertran's feet. After several long moments of reverent silence, the stately procession remounted and rode away.

* * *

Kinnon stared at Herve in disbelief. Bertran's death and the attending ceremonies had left them all in shock, but Herve clearly sought to turn the events to his advantage.

Of all the dishonest, conniving, back-handed . . . Just because ye have wormed yer way into the marechal's good graces—`tis clear the man's head is muddled with grief.

He spat in the dirt. *No-good arse-kisser. I shouldnae have to answer to ye.*

But he did. Like Bertran, *Marechal* de Sancerre saw Herve's skill with languages as a blessing amid a group of men of different origins. Unlike Bertran, Kinnon feared the *marechal* was blind to Herve's faults.

Kinnon recalled the look of shock on Herve's face when they met inside the *marechal's* tent. *Aye, I remember yer kindness when ye left me for dead, ye wee bastard.* He bristled to realize he *would* be dead were it not for Lucienne's care . . . *Damn, Herve!*

"I will join the procession as far as Paris, but there my duty ends. I will help see Bertran is protected for the sake of his kindness to me, but I no longer belong to this army."

Herve's nose twitched as though facing a foul odor. "You are subject to the regulations of this army until your duty is done. And that means you answer to me."

"I answer to no man who leaves his comrades for dead on the field," Kinnon snarled. He pivoted on his walking staff and took a step to the door of the tent before spinning back around. "And I want my glaive back."

"You will rebuild your weapons cache at your own expense," Herve replied. He quickly dropped his gaze, shuffling papers on his camp desk.

"Ye took mine, and I want it back." Kinnon closed the distance between them.

"Any weapon taken from the field of battle is the property of the one who possesses it. If you cannot maintain your own weapons, mayhap its loss will improve your vigilance." Herve lifted his chin to stare down his thin nose, but his chin quivered.

"I want mine returned to me," Kinnon reiterated, his voice softly threatening.

Herve's Adam's apple bobbed up and down. "I will call the guards." His bluff rang hollow as his voice tightened into the next octave.

"Dinnae bother. Ye likely sold it. `Twas meant for a man's hand, after all." With a disgusted blow of breath, Kinnon stalked to the doorway, cursing his wounded leg at the hitch in his gait.

"And do not leave this camp!" Herve called after him. "I forbid it!"

Tight-arsed, know-it-all Frenchie needs to find another Scotsman to do his bidding. I have things to attend to before I help escort Bertran's body home. His nose twitched instinctively at the potentially noisome duty. *`Tis an honor to be a part of his escort, but a curse if the body isnae embalmed correctly. I hope the cirurgian is good at his job.*

He hobbled down the worn path between the tents, scarcely heeding the activities around him. A horse idled in its harness beneath a tree, and Kinnon approached the lad sprawled in the wagon seat. "I will bring this back soon."

He tossed his staff in the back of the wagon and swung himself into the seat with a grimace. The lad jerked to attention, his mouth open in protest. Kinnon waved him down. "Dinnae gawk at me, lad. I have an important errand to attend to."

The lad dropped to the ground, his hand on the horse's rump. "But, sir, no one is to leave the camp. `Tis *le capitaine* Herve's order!"

Kinnon shook out the reins and the horse pulled away. "Herve can take his orders and . . ." His voice disappeared beneath the clop of the horse's hooves.

CHAPTER FOURTEEN

Jean-Baptiste bounded from the yard, barking as he ran. For once, it didn't alarm Kinnon—for some reason the dog sounded more welcoming than aggressive. A tall, slender form followed in the dog's wake, her dark hair pulled back in its customary thick braid. A smile lit Melisende's face and Kinnon hesitated on the wagon seat, drinking in her silent greeting.

"Kinnon!" A burst of excited sunshine broke past Melisende, arms waving madly in greeting. Lucienne's golden curls bounced across her shoulders as she bolted toward the wagon.

Kinnon eased from the driver's seat, dodging Jean-Baptiste's exuberant reception as he danced around Kinnon's feet, leaping and barking. The poor horse shied at the commotion and Kinnon shoved the dog away. "Be gone, ye mangy beast! Ye willnae frighten off my horse."

Jean-Baptiste took the scolding well, calming long enough to sniff the air around Kinnon and his horse. With a satisfied *woof*, he bounded away.

Kinnon reached for his walking staff, turning back just in time to catch Lucienne as she flung herself into his arms. He staggered back against the wagon. "Easy, lass! Ye nearly knocked me off my feet."

She buried her face in his neck, arms wrapped tight about him. "You came back," she whispered forcefully. "Melisende said we must be patient, but you came back."

"Aye. I told ye I would." He gently disentangled himself, motioning to his wounded leg. "Can we go somewhere and sit?"

"Come this way, monsieur," Melisende called, waving him to the back of the house where a pair of mended chairs overlooked the tumble-down barns. Tucked in the shadow of nearby trees, it was a comfortable, cozy spot.

Her fingers wound through his, Lucienne guided Kinnon to one of the chairs. He started to lower himself to the ground next to it, but she pulled him up with a cry of protest. "*Non!* Sit here!"

Feeling definitely unchivalrous, he settled in the chair. Melisende took the other, and Lucienne curled at Kinnon's feet, staring up at him, her face aglow with happiness.

"How are things at the encampment?" Melisende asked.

Kinnon winced. "I have had a hard time believing Bertran is dead. But I was able to speak to him before he passed."

Melisende nodded slowly. "I was afraid it was true. What of the village? Did De Ros surrender before Bertran died?"

"Ye may not believe it, but De Ros and his knights rode from the castle the day after Bertran died to lay the keys of the city at his feet."

Her eyebrows shot upward. "*Réalité*? That is a tribute to *le Constable*, indeed."

"Aye. Many men, nobles and commoners alike, sought Bertran's blessing. 'Twas a sight like none I have seen."

"What will happen now? Are you freed from service?"

Kinnon frowned. "Nae. I have been asked to join the entourage bearing Bertran's body back to Brittany. `Tis my understanding the group will be made up of different representatives of the men who fought with Bertran. And I am the only Scot they have at the moment."

Lucienne wrinkled her nose. "I would not like the job of carting a dead body across France!"

"He will be embalmed, Luci. And `tis only several days' march to Dinan—which is where I will leave the company," Kinnon reassured her.

Melisende shook her head. "`Twill be closer to a fortnight, mark my words. Every town and priest along the way will insist on blessing the body. `Twill not be a simple thing to escort the remains of such a great man."

"I hadnae thought of that," Kinnon admitted, absently rubbing the back of his neck. "I want to be sure the two of ye are taken care of whilst I am away."

Melisende's lips tilted upward. "Who is to look after us, monsieur? We have been on our own for some time now. I think we can manage."

Kinnon banked his irritation. "I dinnae mean to belittle yer efforts. But there will be more lawless men in the area for a bit as they make their way from the village. `Twill be more dangerous than ever, and I cannae be here to help ye." His fingers dropped to his wounded leg, massaging the perpetual ache there. "Not that I am any help to ye at the moment."

Neither woman replied to his comment and the silence lengthened. He shifted uncomfortably against the complaining throb in his leg. Melisende tapped Lucienne's shoulder. "Run inside and fetch the stool for Kinnon's leg. And gather mugs for drink. `Tis an unseemly hot day."

Lucienne's lower lip slipped out in a pout. She unfolded to stand before them, hands fisted on her hips. "I do not like being left out," she scolded. When neither Kinnon nor Melisende answered her, she whirled and stomped off into the house.

Melisende rose. "Would a short walk improve your leg?"

"Mayhap." Kinnon stood and together they strolled to the small rocky area they had visited a couple of weeks earlier. He eyed the surroundings, checking for snakes, before he lowered himself clumsily to the ground.

"I am sorry your wound pains you." Melisende's clear blue eyes met his.

"`Twill take time to completely heal. Yer sister saved my life. I had been left for dead." Too late he realized his face was pulled in a ferocious scowl at the memory, and he jerked his lips upward, attempting to grin.

Melisende was taken aback by the darkness that stole over Kinnon's features and the harshness that jerked his eyebrows together and narrowed his eyes. But his struggle to change his frown to a smile amused her and she gave a short laugh. "We have both had a trying week, *n'est-ce pas vrai?*"

Kinnon jerked a startled look in her direction. "Ye could say that." He drew a deep breath. "I am sorry ye were detained in town. Ye must have worried about yer sister."

"You could say that," she tossed back at him, arching an eyebrow. She wondered at his return when he clearly had much on his mind and a sad duty to fulfill. He owed them nothing more for their brief war-time friendship. Her skin warmed. *Could he . . ? Non. It is absurd. We have had one serious conversation and `tis likely he was lonely and had no other person to discuss his concerns with. He has not returned today because of me—has he?*

She forced a slight smile, hoping to encourage Kinnon. He stared into the distance.

"I must be away home."

His voice sounded forced, tight—faltering. His gaze dropped to his hands as they twisted with uncertainty.

Melisende's heart ached and she ventured a gentle touch on his wrist in sympathy. Warmth where their skin touched bloomed, sending tingles of awareness along her fingers and higher. His arm twitched and they locked gazes.

"I wish circumstances were different," he murmured.

"What do you mean, monsieur?"

He gave her a wry grin. "At least say my name."

Her face warmed and she curled her fingers, breaking contact with his arm. "Kinnon."

Kinnon smiled, and the gentleness of it took her breath away.

"I dinnae want this to be the last time I see ye." His eyes clouded, his smile faded.

"You wish to return home." Melisende forced her voice past the quaver that threatened.

"I am a laird's son. I should follow him—lead my clan."

His voice revealed a struggle with such a possibility.

"I do not understand. Do you not wish to be their leader?" she asked.

"I no longer know. Fighting the English should have made me stronger, harder." He dropped his gaze. "It has made me question much."

Unreasonable hope that he would stay in France surged in her, but she shoved it back. It was not right for her to wish him to give up his birthright. "You will make a great laird. What you have experienced—"

"What I have experienced," Kinnon flared, "is a mob of men raping and pillaging where they will, justifying it as payment for fighting for the people. Yet the people starve and are driven from their homes, families torn apart by death and things beyond their control." He sobered. "Bertran's last words were to respect the Church, and protect the poor, the women and children."

She tilted her head. "Is that not every soldier's duty?"

"Every soldier," he mocked, his voice bitter, "routinely blasphemes the Church, and would take the last crust of bread from any unable to fend for themselves." He lifted bleak eyes to hers. "And many have left children fatherless, their mothers reduced to selling themselves for a few coins that their families might not starve."

Melisende's heart twisted, but she knew he spoke the truth. "You could ensure great justice for your people."

Kinnon's face softened. "Ye surprise me, Melisende. Every time I speak to ye, ye lift my heart. Ye see me as so much better than I see myself."

It relieved her to see the anger lift and she smiled. "It is because you are a good man, Kinnon. If I see you differently than you see yourself, please keep in mind you may not be correct."

"I hope our paths cross again." He took her hands in his. "I *want* our paths to cross."

Melisende's heart tripped. In the distance, Lucienne's voice shrilled, forestalling whatever else Kinnon would have said.

He released her hands and stood. "I must get back to camp. There is a command that no one leave without permission."

"And I suppose you did not receive permission?" A touch of humor rose as Melisende considered him. *He is unlikely to ask first. I like that.* She sobered. *It will never be my choice to like him or not. Wish it or not, we will not likely meet again.*

"I was commanded to remain," he answered with a shrug. "But there was nothing I needed to do to prepare for the trip, and you and Luci are important to me."

Loud warning barking sounded from the house and Lucienne's lilting cry filtered into their sanctuary. "Meli? Kinnon? There are *militaires* demanding to see Kinnon. Oh!"

She stumbled against a rock and fell. Kinnon grabbed her before she landed on the pebbly ground. She wrapped her arms about his waist and leaned close. Something in Melisende's heart clutched tight, almost painful, as Lucienne looked up adoringly into Kinnon's eyes.

Irate shouts punctuated the air amid Jean-Baptiste's barks and growls. Horses squealed. Kinnon set Lucienne aside and grabbed his walking staff. She reached out to him, but Melisende pulled her back. "Do not get in the middle of this, Lucienne."

"But they want to take him away!" the girl wailed.

"Oh, no!" Melisende gathered her skirt and hurried after him, overtaking him easily as he reached the yard.

Three armored men sat their horses as they plunged about, clearly agitated by Jean-Baptiste. The dog bristled, snapping at any horse that tried to leave the tightly guarded group.

"Jean-Baptiste, hold!" Kinnon commanded. The dog twitched an ear in his direction but did not back down.

Melisende paused at Kinnon's side. "Jean-Baptiste! *Garant!*"

The dog settled, though clearly not satisfied with the order.

A man urged his horse forward, but it stopped at a fierce look from Jean-Baptiste. "Call off your dog or I will order it killed."

"He is worth the lot of ye, and likely yer addle-headed commander as well," Kinnon drawled as he leaned upon his staff.

"An arrow through his chest will not improve his worth," the man noted.

Kinnon's eyebrows lifted. "Agreed."

Melisende started forward, alarmed at the brutal warning. Kinnon placed a hand on her shoulder in restraint. She halted and called to Jean-Baptiste. The big dog stalked to her side and sat, hackles still up, eyes watchful. Melisende laced her fingers through his collar.

Kinnon motioned with one hand to the men. "Why are ye here, frightening these women?"

The man glanced down his nose at Melisende. "They are not our concern. We are to take you back to camp."

"I am about to leave. Ye may be about yer business," Kinnon replied agreeably.

The leader arched his brow. "Mayhap I did not finish my sentence. We are to take you back—in chains"

Melisende sucked in a breath of alarm and gripped Kinnon's sleeve. He patted her hand reassuringly.

"There is nae need," he told the man. "I said I was leaving."

"You disobeyed a direct order. Herve has ordered you imprisoned."

Kinnon snorted. "Herve would like nothing better than to do away with me. He has tried once—" He turned to Melisende. "Do not be alarmed. Herve doesnae like me, but he willnae cause lasting harm."

Melisende stared at him, frightened by the look on the soldiers' faces. "They mean to imprison you!"

"Not much I can do about it at this point. Too many of them to argue with." He gave her a grim smile. "Dinnae fash about me. Take care of Luci. It may be longer than I expected, but Herve will have more important things on his mind than one disobedient Scotsman." He reached into his sporran and drew out several gold coins, shoving them into her hand. "Here. Ye may need these." He gave her an impish grin. "They werenae stolen from widows or orphans. I will be back. We havenae finished our conversation."

With a last look past her at Lucienne who clung to Melisende's waist like a frightened child, Kinnon hobbled toward the waiting men. Two soldiers dismounted and pushed him roughly toward the wagon. Kinnon shrugged their hands away with obvious annoyance.

"They will hurt him!" Lucienne whimpered.

Melisende pulled her to her side. "Hush, *ma petite*. It is a misunderstanding. All will be well."

A shout rose amid the men as they laid hands on Kinnon. He struggled against them but one knocked his staff away and Kinnon fell against the wagon. Jean-Baptiste sprang to his feet, barking. Melisende slipped the coins into her pocket and tightened her grip on the dog's collar.

One of the men delivered a crippling blow to the back of Kinnon's head. He crumpled and fell to the ground. *Bâtard!* Melisende wrenched free of Lucienne's grip, grabbing her dagger from her skirt pocket. She released Jean-Baptiste as she darted forward and the great beast covered the ground to Kinnon's side with a mighty roar. A few yards away, Melisende loosed the dagger, her forward momentum giving deadly force to the blade's flight. It burrowed deep beneath the chin guard of the mounted man's helmet and he fell to the ground with a groan.

Jean-Baptiste stood over Kinnon's still body, snarling at the two men to keep them away. Melisende grabbed his collar and spoke to the soldiers. "You have abused an honorable man. Return to your camp and I will send him *after* I have seen to his wound."

"He will answer to Herve," the man looked past her, "—as will you, *mademoiselle*."

She shook her head. "Be that as it may, I will waste no more time with the likes of you. Be gone from here before I release Jean-Baptiste to do his work keeping vermin off our farm."

Suddenly the dog whirled, a snarl on his lips. He broke free from Melisende's grip and she released him with a pained cry. The captain loomed over her, eyes wild with fury, dark blood dripping from the wound in his neck. He grabbed her by the throat and squeezed hard, shaking her violently.

Jean-Baptiste lunged at the man, his teeth making no purchase on the heavy leather and linked mail. An arrow twanged and Jean-Baptiste fell away. Lucienne appeared in the darkening edges of Melisende's sight, screaming as she flung herself at the man. He swatted her away with the back of a gloved hand and Melisende choked on a sudden rush of air as he partially released her.

With an angry roar, he flung her to the ground. Her vision sparkled with tiny darts of light and she coughed, struggling for breath.

The man's voice rasped with anger. "*Charger lui dans le wagon!*"

Scuffling sounds ensued, then a thump and a groan. Melisende propped herself shakily on one arm in the dirt, heedless of the tiny pebbles and debris clinging to her sleeve, fighting to regain her senses enough to see to Kinnon. The snap of reins and the creak of wheels told her she was too late.

CHAPTER FIFTEEN

Rumbling sounds grated beneath his head and sunlight streamed hotly on his skin. One side of his face felt as though it was on fire, and each breath burned like red-hot knives through his chest. *Wee bastards dinnae hesitate to take their revenge.* He tried to lift his head but a stab of pain exploded in his skull, warning him against movement. The muscles in his back and shoulders took up answering clamors and he settled grimly to the floor of the wagon, struggling to keep his breathing shallow.

Worry for Melisende and Lucienne rose in his mind. *Herve willnae take kindly to hearing a wee lass took on his soldiers in my defense.* There had to be a way for him to warn Melisende to take her sister and run far away from Herve's brand of justice. He groaned as the wagon wheels lurched over a rock in the road and pain took up permanent residence all over his body. Kinnon closed his eyes and gave himself up to thoughts of home.

In his mind, the rumble became the rush of waves breaking on the shore beneath the walls of Scaurness Castle. Lightning tore at the sky beyond the great tower and Kinnon could almost smell the sharpness of the air before the storm. Somewhere in the castle, his little sister would be lighting candles. A fond smile touched his lips. At sixteen, she wasnae so little anymore. Was she still afraid of storms?

The clop of the horses' hooves and rattle of the wagon across cobblestone broke through his reflections. He groaned and tried to move but chains rattled and manacles gripped his wrists, holding them in place. A wave of dizziness swept over him, highlighting the pain in his head. No longer able to keep his memories at the front of his mind, he gave in to the darkness.

Jarring motions slammed his head into the floor of the wagon, bringing him rudely back to wakefulness. His eyes squinted against the glare of sunlight, vision in one narrowed to a mere slit. Garbled noises fouled his ears, but he ignored them for the burst of pain in his leg. He moved his hand, disgusted by the faint rattle of a chain against wood.

He lay there for seeming hours as the sky darkened. His stomach growled and his bladder ached. *Stupid bastards havenae care about me. They are likely waiting for me to piss myself.*

He cursed under his breath, then louder, hoping to gain someone's attention.

"Shite!"

The sounds around him did not change. No one approached to see what he needed. He tried distracting himself by isolating and identifying the different noises. The stamp of a hoof and jingle of harness was likely the team hitched to his wagon. The subdued talk seemed to indicate they had arrived back at camp. The sharp crackle of a fire heralded the scent of the evening meal.

His stomach growled again. His abdomen cramped. Pain shot through his leg.

"St. Andrew's balls!"

A shadow fell across the wagon. "Sit up," someone commanded.

Kinnon heard the rattle of a key and his manacles opened. He tried to sit, but ribs grated in his chest. He groaned, his hands seeking purchase on the rough edge of the wagon.

"Do not try to jump out."

Kinnon grimaced and turned his head toward the voice. "I dinnae think I'll be jumping just now."

An age-gnarled face met his bleary gaze. "I am to allow you to prepare for your appearance in the commander's tent." He gave Kinnon a once-over look. "I would suggest you not waste any time."

Kinnon started to move his legs but fell against the side of the wagon, gnashing his teeth as pain stabbed like shards of glass once again. Sweat popped on his brow and slid down his neck. Getting himself somewhat under control, he gripped his leg, trying to hold the pain at bay. He pulled one hand away and blinked at the thick, un-clotted blood glistening on his palm. "Do ye think we could waste a wee bit of time summoning a *cirurgian*?"

* * *

Lucienne collapsed to the ground beside Jean-Baptiste. His tail thumped feebly as she cradled his face in her palms. Melisende eyed the big dog's form critically. A long gouge creased his head from ear to poll, and a sheen of fresh blood matted his fur. A heavy-shafted arrow protruded from the ground less than a foot away.

"He is lucky, Lucienne. The arrow stunned him and will likely make him a bit wobbly for a day or so, but he should regain his strength quickly."

"He will not die?" Lucienne quavered.

"I do not think so. But he would likely benefit from the wound medicine we have at the house. Can you see to it?"

Hope bloomed in her sister's eyes. "*Oui*! I can make him well!" She placed her cheek on the dog's muzzle, crooning to him.

Melisende gently touched Lucienne's shoulder. "Let us see if he can rise and walk. I do not wish to have to drag him to the house on a litter."

Lucienne stood, and together they helped the dog to his chest. After several moments, he seemed to get his bearings and climbed clumsily to his feet. He swayed, feet splayed, as he balanced precariously.

"Come, Jean-Baptiste. You can do it," Lucienne said, tears in her eyes.

"Let him take his time," Melisende admonished. "Help him to the house and dress his wound. I will tend to the goats and cattle."

"I will collect the eggs when I am finished," Lucienne told her.

Melisende gave her a fond look. "That would be a great help."

Lucienne nodded absently, her attention already back on the great dog at her side. He picked up one front foot, jerking it upward far enough to throw himself off balance again. Lucienne sucked in a breath of alarm and put her hands on either side of his shoulders. He steadied. Step by cautious step, they made their way to the house.

Melisende stared after them. *What are we to do? I attacked a soldier.* She shook her head. *And meant to kill him. It will not go un-remarked, or un-punished.* She looked at the small house that had been their refuge for so long. And at the tumble-down barns and neatly weeded garden. A cow lowed nearby. Tears sprang to her eyes.

I cannot simply leave the animals to their fate. But the cows's udders would eventually dry up—as would the goats's—and the chickens's eggs would lay snug beneath the hens and eventually hatch. There was grass aplenty and seeds and bugs enough to keep them for the summer, at least. Or until someone else took over their care.

We must leave. And soon. I do not know when someone will be sent to arrest me, but I cannot let that happen.

She started toward the barn, as she did every day, then halted. *I have no time to milk the cows today. We must pack.* She turned to the house, her mind instantly focusing on the necessities. *Lucienne will fuss, but it cannot be helped. Where will we go?* She halted again, suddenly feeling unbearably tired. *Mayhap the butcher and his wife will know of a place. Once we get our bearings, mayhap we can find Father's family.*

She opened the door to the house and caught sight of Lucienne as she slathered the wound salve on Jean-Baptiste's head. Her sister looked up, startled.

"Why are you here? Is something wrong?"

Melisende carefully hid her fears as she reassured her sister. "I threw a knife at a soldier, Lucienne."

"You were only protecting Kinnon," Lucienne protested.

"They will not see it that way."

Lucienne's face paled noticeably and Melisende sank onto the chair beside her. "*Ma petite*, we must leave here—now."

Her sister pulled back, a look of dismay on her face. "For how long?"

"I do not know. At least until the army has secured the village and moved on—and people no longer care what became of us."

Lucienne frowned. "That could be a long time. Where will we go?"

"I thought to stop a night or two at the butcher's home. He and his wife are kind. After that, we may go on to *Puy en Valey*. Father's family may be there."

"Back to the town . . ." Lucienne's voice faded and her eyes widened, showing her strain.

Melisende tenderly tucked a curl behind her sister's ear. "Do not worry, *ma petite*. It is my hope we are back here before the end of the summer."

Lucienne slowly nodded her head, though it was clear she put up a brave front.

Melisende patted her shoulder, becoming brisk and assured. "Pack what is necessary. We must leave soon."

"Jean-Baptiste is going with us!" Lucienne declared, her eyes hot with challenge.

"He will have to go," Melisende agreed. "He tried to hurt the soldier, also." She stood. "Let him rest for now. Pack only what you must. We can send for the rest later." She ducked her head so Lucienne would not see the lie. It was unlikely they would return anytime soon. Her eyes took in the contents of the small house, lingering on the pottery, infused with the memory of her mother's careful hands. And the buckets, brimming with her grandfather's patience and skill.

She blinked against tears of regret and grabbed a sack, stuffing it with enough food to see them on their way. A thump and a muffled word Melisende wasn't sure she should approve of drifted from the bedroom where Lucienne filled her own bag. Against her better judgement, Melisende picked a metal cup their mother had favored from the cupboard. Her fingertip traced the delicate etching on the side—now nearly worn away by years of use. The bluish hue had been her mother's favorite color. She wrapped it in a scrap of linen and added it to her bag.

She met Lucienne in the doorway. "Have you all that you need?"

"*Oui*, but what about you?" Lucienne glanced at the nearly empty bag in her sister's hand.

"I will add some clothing. Take one more look around and then we will leave."

Lucienne's eyes grew wide and she swallowed hard with a nod. Tears glistened, but she did not give in to her fears.

CHAPTER SIXTEEN

Kinnon slumped back to the bed of the wagon, his breaths short and shallow. The other man watched him impassively, fading in and out of Kinnon's sight as dizziness roiled over him. Voices buzzed in his ears and someone grabbed him beneath his arms and dragged him from the wagon. The sky darkened and the flames of a fire grew brighter as the sunlight faded. Kinnon lay on the ground, staring hypnotically through swollen eyelids into the crackling blaze.

"The wound has reopened." A new voice, low but distinct.

Aye. Yer men took great delight in kicking the hell out of me. Kinnon groaned as the man prodded his leg, but could not summon the strength to resist.

"Shall we take him to your tent?" The watchman was back, questioning his next move.

"I do not have time to treat this man. Bishop de la Tour wishes to bless Bertran's body. I leave for the cathedral shortly."

The voices lowered, murmuring below Kinnon's level of hearing.

Then dinnae bother coming back. Ye can take my body to be embalmed with his. For some reason, this amused Kinnon, and he chuckled. The movement shook his body and he ground his teeth at the fresh pain.

"Let us be about it quickly, then. Grab that dagger and place it in the fire. Heat it and bring it to me."

The thought of something warm seemed agreeable to Kinnon as chills swept through him again. But then the realization of what the *cirurgian* meant struck him with an unlooked for burst of energy, and he rose on his elbows with a bellow. Strong hands clasped his shoulders and his ankles, stretching him flat on the ground. He bucked his hips in protest, but someone sat astride his middle, holding him in place.

Suddenly the air filled with the acrid stench of burning hair and hide. Kinnon gave a hoarse shout as the fire seared deeper and deeper into his flesh, until blackness rushed in and he knew nothing more.

* * *

Lucienne plopped down on the bed, a scowl on her face. "I do not like it here. I miss the farm." Her hand scratched Jean-Baptiste's head and his tail thumped the floor.

Melisende turned from hanging her cloak on a peg by the door. "I know you do not like the confines of town, but we need to distance ourselves from the army for a bit." She brushed a golden curl behind her sister's ear. "We will go to *Le Puy-en-Velay* soon. But you must be patient. The butcher has offered me work here until travel is safe, and we need the money."

Lucienne sighed and slid to her feet. "But Kinnon gave us money. And at home, we have our own food." She wrinkled her nose. "I did not like what we had for supper tonight."

"You are entirely too spoiled, *ma petite!*" Melisende chuckled. "Let us get ourselves in order and we will see if we can find Father's family. `Tis a bit of a walk from here, but we will

74

do fine. This is a good place to wait until no one seeks us. The extra money will be a blessing."

Jean-Baptiste licked her hand and she glanced at him fondly. "My brave one. 'Tis good to see you on your feet."

"He is very lucky and very brave." Lucienne knelt and pulled the dog to her chest. The enormous beast allowed the hug, a silly grin on his face as he panted gently. "He protected us from them."

"Unfortunately, that is not a defense with the soldiers. They were doing their job."

Lucienne shot her an enraged look. "They shoved Kinnon to the ground! And punched him! Jean-Baptiste should have eaten them all!"

"They should have not been so brutal," Melisende agreed. She nodded to the dog. "You will need to keep him with you at all times. And you will spend much of your time up here. I will take you and Jean-Baptiste out a few times a day. The town is still too dangerous for you to stroll about on your own."

Lucienne slouched to her feet, disgruntled and obviously displeased with the new rules. "I told you I liked home better."

* * *

The only sense of time was a faint patterning of light through the holes in the tiny barred window in the circular tower room. Narrow strips of sunlight made its daily trek from one side to the other. Buried behind the thick stone walls of *Châteauneuf*, the days were terribly short. And the nights agonizingly long.

For weeks Kinnon did not care if he lived or died—he thought the odds of death far greater than survival. Each breath he took grated along the inside of his chest like a rusty blade carving its way through to the surface. Food and drink was passed through the door to him, but he paid little attention. He shook with fevered chills, and moving from the thin blanket he huddled beneath on the thin mattress on the cold floor was more bother than the stale bread and stagnant water was worth.

His eyes drifted to the small bag tucked against him, the remnants of his possessions and his only proof that he hadn't yet descended into hell. His little talismans nestled inside, the dirk he'd kept with him long gone. It was a mystery why Herve had allowed him to keep these small items—though no surprise he'd lifted the weapon—but their presence was a tiny comfort in his isolation, though he was unable to take them out and face them—and admit his failure.

Occasionally voices could be heard, arguing as the strident tones drifted into his prison. At those times, a pot of what he assumed to be a warm broth—judging from the aroma—was his daily meal, but his stomach had long since given up its desire for food.

Day after day, Kinnon mentally paced the tiny cell. His body was slow to heal, but his mind burned with restlessness. He eased into a seated position, seeing little to capture his attention in the dank cell. Surprisingly few rats rustled in the noxious reeds strewn about the floor. He rose shakily and hobbled to the wooden box that held his meal. A hunk of bread and something resembling a soft cheese huddled next to a flask of ale.

Breaking the bread in half, he sought a soft center. Much of it crumbled in his hands and he let it fall to the ground. He drank some ale and carried the flask back to his small island in the midst of his incomprehensible world. A movement in the corner of the room caught his attention and he flung the flask at the shadow with a harsh cry. A high-pitched squeal followed by a soft swish of sound marked the rat's hasty departure.

A tremor ran through him, for he knew if the rat grew bold enough or hungry enough, it would defy him, even to gnawing on him in the dark. He sucked in a breath of revulsion that ended on a ragged cough, reminding him his broken ribs had not yet healed.

He sat on the thin mattress and wrapped the thread-bare blanket around his wasted frame. Leaning against the thick stone wall, he eventually dropped off to sleep.

* * *

He woke to something warm and solid draped across his legs. The weight wasn't much, but it confused Kinnon in his befuddled state. Before he could react, his eyes registered the fact that the furry little body was light-colored, though he couldn't tell exactly what hue in the semi-darkness. But at least it wasn't the dull gray of the rats that haunted the towers. Nevertheless, his body jerked with startled surprise, and the creature lifted its head and meowed.

Kinnon blinked. A cat? No, more like a kitten judging from the small size. Perhaps half-grown, the animal set an impressive set of teeth on display as it yawned mightily. A rustle sounded across the room, and the cat's big ears instantly honed in on the noise. Sleek muscles bunched, gathering its legs beneath it. The feline eyes stared intently into the dark recesses, Kinnon either forgotten or ignored as the cat readied to tackle its prey.

The tip of its tail flicked then went completely still. An instant later, Kinnon felt the force of the cat's leap as it sprang across the room. A squeal and quick rustle that ended abruptly told the tale.

"Good work!" Kinnon approved, waiting for the cat to return. When it did not, the disappointment was acute, painful. He leaned his head against the wall at his back and stared at the tiny window in the door. He was again alone.

His thoughts went wandering, landing on memories of his beloved sister.

Riona, ye would like Melisende. She reminds me of Ma. She is tough, yet kind. Strong in the best sense of the word. And my heart is always lighter when she is near.

Lucienne, ye ask? Kinnon smiled wryly into the darkness. *The lass is fey. Fey and wild. She needs a man who appreciates her passions, be they childish or sultry. A man who can keep her curiosity satisfied.*

Ach, lass, I shouldnae say such things in yer presence. But ye are older now, and mayhap even a wife by now. He grimaced as a tear slipped from the corner of one eye. *I would have liked to have intimidated yer groom. Just to set him straight on how to treat ye.*

He imagined her laughter and how she would have stormed off, accusations of boorish behavior floating over her shoulder. Receiving no reply to his one-sided conversation, he drifted off to sleep, a prayer for all three lass' safe-keeping on his lips.

* * *

Summertime in France was a mixture of warm days and breezy nights. Or, it had been when she and Lucienne had lived on the farm. Melisende patted her neck with a folded piece of embroidered linen and shifted her market basket in the crook of her arm. Around her, the tall buildings of *Le Puy en Velay* effectively cut off the breezes sliding off the mountains and the air in the market place was close beneath the colorful awnings. Casting a critical look at the cloudless sky above, she decided it was time to hurry home—the small sweet cakes Lucienne loved could wait for another day. She lingered long enough to pay for a *baguette*, then exited the baker's stall into the full force of the late-morning sun.

The aroma of warm bread tickled her stomach, and it gave a tiny growl of interest. Knowing it would be time to open the shop as soon as she got home, she broke off a crust and nibbled on it as she wound her way among the lingering shoppers, feeling quite young and even a bit naughty as she pilfered her breakfast from the basket.

'Tis something I would expect Lucienne to do. Her fond smile was quickly followed by a frown, memories of her impetuous sister's actions the past few weeks contrasting greatly with the child she'd always known. *I do not know how much longer I can keep her under control.* Dismay tugged at her. *Her interest in the men who come to the shop is growing daily. It is difficult to send her to market by herself, and almost as hard to leave her whilst I go.*

Melisende doubled her steps as she thought back to Lucienne's sleepy *dishabille* as she waved good-bye that morning. *She is beautiful. My golden petite soeur is now a beautiful woman. And neither of us knows what to do about it.*

She turned the corner to Rue Goldsmith—named for the three jewelers' shops that dotted the wide lane. It was a lovely, restful avenue, lined with trees and small benches designed for opulent, leisurely shopping. Ahead, a horse nodded at the end of his tether in front of her uncle's shop. An early customer? She picked up the hem of her gown and fairly flew up the lane.

A bell chimed cheerfully overhead as she opened the brightly painted door. Light spilled in behind her, casting aspersions on the couple in the room. Lucienne leaned over the display counter, intent on whatever the young man on the other side whispered in her ear. Her curls, nestled close to the pale locks of a young man Melisende had seen previously in the shop, gleamed a burnished gold in the glow of the candelabra on the end of the polished counter top.

Melisende swept inside, sliding her basket down the counter, forcing the pair apart. "Still looking for a bracelet for your fiancé, *Monsieur* Depaul?"

The young man flushed, his eyes flashing with anger a brief moment before they became lidded, arrogant, unconcerned. "*Mademoiselle* Lucienne is willing to show me things of great beauty." He cast a look of promise over his shoulder at Lucienne who discretely pulled her robe closed. "I am a paying customer, after all."

"Not in this shop," Melisende bit out, clipping her words to keep from shredding his ears with what she wished to say. It would not help to completely antagonize the nobility in *Le Puy.* Her uncle would be scandalized by Lucienne's behavior and the risk to the shop would likely overcome his already reluctant familial duty. It would not take much for him to put her and Lucienne out on the street.

Monsieur Depaul's eyebrows shot upward, disbelief slapped across his face. "I assure you, *mademoiselle*, my father will hear of your lack of hospitality."

"*Oui*, I will be sure to tell him of it after I ask that he keep his son's intentions honorable around impressionable young ladies."

The man's lips pursed in a sneer. "You should ask your very pretty little sister what her intentions are, *mademoiselle*. I think you would be surprised at how impressionable she truly is."

"Enough! I will deal with her, and you will leave immediately." Shaking with fury, Melisende whirled on Lucienne, her hands shooing her away. "Upstairs with you! I will speak with you shortly."

Two red spots staining her white cheeks, Lucienne stormed to the apartment overhead. Melisende waited until the young man strolled insolently from the shop, then bolted the door behind him.

She took the stairs in a rush, closing on Lucienne's unslippered heels.

Lucienne spun about, fists clenched, curls tumbling about her shoulders in abandon. "You embarrassed him!"

Melisende reeled back in shock. "I embarrassed *him*?" She waved a hand up and down at her sister's attire. "You should be ashamed to be seen outside of your room in such a state of undress. Whatever possessed you to allow him into the shop?"

Lucienne twisted a lock of her hair about one finger as her body swayed with indecision.

"The truth, *jeune mademoiselle*," Melisende warned.

Lucienne sighed loudly and rolled her eyes to stare at the ceiling. "I cannot believe you are upset because I let a customer into the shop. His family is very important and spends a great deal of money here. Ask *Oncle* Ramon."

Melisende fisted her hands on her hips, refusing to let Lucienne turn the tables on her. "*Oncle* Ramon is on his way back from Paris, as you well know. And he would toss us both out on the street without delay if he found you entertaining his important clients in such a state."

"I don't see what the fuss is about. Raul only wanted to see—"

Fury ripped through Melisende. "He is *Monsieur Depaul* to you, young lady. Do not forget you are an unmarried young woman and he is engaged—not to you."

Lucienne dropped her offended act and drew herself up, a sneer marring her beautiful young face. "You are jealous because none of the men ever look at you."

Melisende jerked her chin up in surprise. "What absurdity. I have spent the last two years raising you, making sure you have a roof over your head. I have not sought marriage."

"And who would want you when they see me?" Lucienne preened. "I know you lost your heart to Kinnon, though it did you little good." She slanted Melisende a superior look. "What do you think went on whilst he slept in our house—only me and him? He would be unable to look you in the eye if you knew everything that happened."

Melisende froze inside and it took her a moment to find her voice. "You act like an ungrateful child—willing to hurt anyone who denies you. I will not listen to you speak of him in such a manner." She schooled her heartbreak behind a mask of pity. "He was grateful to you for your healing arts which saved his life. You should read nothing more into his actions than that."

Lucienne's eyes narrowed, her lips thinned in an ugly grin. "Think what you want. He preferred me over you. And he was *very* grateful."

"As he is no longer in France, it is a moot point. You are confined to your room until you can learn better manners."

Lucienne flounced into her room and slammed the door. Melisende stared at the closed portal and refused to shed the tears of doubt.

The remainder of the day flowed over her in a blur as Melisende poured her energy into waiting on customers in her uncle's jewelry shop. She shoved the problem of Lucienne's wanton manner to the back of her mind, but she could not shake the deep sense of betrayal she felt to think the one man she'd allowed herself to care for could have had relations with her sister. Until now, she'd not given their time alone much thought, too glad to know Lucienne had saved his life to read anything else into those days. Would Lucienne lie about this?

Had he made love to Lucienne whilst they were alone? He seemed so genuinely pleased to see me . . .or was it my heart wishing it so? She forced a smile as she greeted another customer, explaining her uncle would be back in a few days' time, and she, his niece, would be happy to help.

I do not even know what happened to him. Why should it matter? He has certainly gone back to Scotland by now. An unwelcome thought struck her. *Or is dead.*

Agitated, she rubbed her palms on her skirt, wishing the hours would pass so she could latch the door and be alone with her thoughts.

Oui, madame, non, monsieur she mocked in her head as she went about her duties in her uncle's absence. *Your wife already has too many diamonds crowding her throat. Why buy her more? And your mistress can scarcely lift her hands for all the pretty baubles you have placed on her idle fingers. I am sure she would love another.*

At last the shop emptied. The sun hovered low in the sky, highlighting the dust motes dancing in the air. Melisende picked up a broom from the back and swept the floor clean. She scrubbed the counter top, removing the final traces of the day's customers. She pulled her stained apron over her head and hung it on a peg. The door chimed.

Pasting a regretful smile over her burst of annoyance, Melisende turned to the door. A man stood there, hair wild as though he'd been lately pulling at it, his cloak hanging askew on his shoulders.

"How may I help you, *monsieur*?" she asked politely.

"Where is your sister?" he demanded.

Melisende blinked in surprise. "She has been in her room all day—"

He gave her a quelling look. "I beg to differ, *mademoiselle*, and I have no time for niceties. She was seen with my son not two hours prior." He took two steps forward, looming over her with his size and anger. "She has bewitched him, I tell you! Never has he disobeyed me before." He shook his fist in her face, spittle flying from his lips. "I will not allow her to ruin his life like this. When I find them, I will have her brought up on charges of witchcraft!"

* * *

Melisende knew her uncle was not pleased to return home and find one of his nieces missing, though presumably wed—even if against the elder Depaul's wishes—to one of the lesser nobles of the town. Raul's father was most adamant his son was acting under a spell Lucienne had cast. What else could entice him away from the mousy heiress to a modest fortune and six years his senior he had been engaged to wed?

She busied herself in the shop, cooking, cleaning, and keeping the books while her uncle chatted with the upsurge of customers. Many came to gossip about the pair's elopement, but most stayed to purchase pretty baubles for themselves. It was the one benefit, he muttered once beneath the influence of too many glasses of wine. After that, all Melisende had to do to cheer her uncle up was to place the day's accounting sheet beneath his nose. He was soon busy enough to hire an apprentice, and within a month's time, their lives had settled into a slightly new pattern.

"Melisende," her uncle called from the doorway to his office. She set her dust cloth aside and followed him into the small room, a bit startled when he closed the door behind her. He stepped hesitantly to his desk and sank heavily into the chair.

"Depaul had a message sent here today."

Melisende's heart skipped a beat. "What did it say, *Oncle*?"

He cleared his throat and Melisende felt a wave of dizziness sweep over her.

"He received a missive earlier. His son and Lucienne have settled in Italy."

She let out her breath in a *whoosh* of relief. "She is well? They are happy?"

He scowled. "I do not know more than what his message said. Two scatter-brained young people starting a life in a strange country, away from family." He shrugged expressively. "Depaul has cut them off pending his son's return to his senses. He still believes he is bewitched." His look turned grim. "God help them both."

CHAPTER SEVENTEEN

Days drifted by with no discernable march of time. Kinnon had to assume his meal came at the same time each day, and marked the placement of sunlight on the floor to determine if he was right or not. But sometimes long periods of time passed without light, and he did not know if one day or two had passed when his meal arrived at last.

I lift my cup to ye, Jamie, lad. He raised the flask of ale to his childhood friend—still alive in his memory when all he had in the world was his recollections of sunlight and days long past. Now, he hid whatever mirth came his way, for at such times he felt he stood on the edge of a terrifying darkness. He knew of men, when faced with more than their fear could hold, who succumbed to bizarre behavior marked with frenzied laughter and deep withdrawal. The realization of how easily he could become like them, existing nowhere except in their shattered minds, horrified him, and it became harder and harder to keep despair at bay.

Do ye think me brave, Brody? Kinnon pushed his uneaten bread aside. *I watched ye take yer last breath, and ye had no fear in yer eyes.* He clenched his fists. *There is no one to watch me die.*

Footsteps as silent as a sigh trailed through the matted rushes. Kinnon's head jerked up, instantly alert. Carried aloft like a standard, the tip of the cat's tail twitched in recognition as he sauntered across the floor. A faintly rusty *meow* trilled from his throat. Kinnon's lips crept upward.

"What brings ye here on this fine day, wee laddie?"

The cat strolled straight to him and rubbed its head against Kinnon's leg, arching its back as it replied with a second *meow*.

Kinnon rubbed the small head and the cat leaned into the caress. "Have ye no rats to prey upon?"

The cat placed one small foot on Kinnon's leg, then another, until it perched precariously on his thigh. Kinnon carefully slipped a hand beneath the furry belly. "Even yer wee weight doesnae fare well on my leg, lad. But ye are welcome to sit in my lap."

With peculiar feline grace, the young cat curled in the fold of Kinnon's legs, purring contentedly. His nose twitched, following the scent of the discarded bread. Patiently, Kinnon retrieved the remnants of his meal and fed them to his furry friend.

* * *

After an indeterminable amount of time, the heavy wooden door to the cell creaked open. Kinnon struggled to his feet, staring at the skirted figure silhouetted in the portal. A pale yellow aura beamed from the man's hand and torchlight reflected off his tonsured head.

"I am Frère Jean. I understand you are in need of a champion."

Kinnon's knees buckled. *Saints be blessed! Someone has taken notice of me!* He sank weakly onto the thin mattress as a cough racked his body. Frère Jean pounded him enthusiastically on the back until Kinnon caught his breath and waved the man off.

The monk gave him a wry grin. "I hope I did not over-do it. Healing is not my gift, I am afraid."

"Nae. A right-smart pounding was what I needed to get my lungs back in working order," Kinnon rasped.

Frère Jean laughed. "I appreciate your concern for my feelings, but I can see I have pained you. I will be more circumspect in the future."

Kinnon eyed the man thoughtfully. "If ye arenae given to healing, what is yer gift?"

The monk smiled and placed his lantern on the floor. Welcome light flooded the small room, and Kinnon blinked his eyes against the unaccustomed brilliance. Frère Jean gathered his brown robes and lowered himself to the floor next to Kinnon. "My gift is that I am temporarily assigned to *Châteauneuf* and have no pressing duties at this time. And it has come to my ears that men are searching for a Scotsman feared dead." He stared intently at Kinnon. "Tell me everything."

Dizzy with unlooked-for hope, and encouraged by Frère Jean's news, Kinnon told his tale.

"I shouldnae have disobeyed a direct order—and I wouldnae had it been anyone other than Herve—but I was verra concerned for the lass' welfare. I was beaten for my troubles— though it took six Frenchies to do it," he added, his eyes narrowed angrily at the memory. "I think I remember someone saying I had committed treason, but that is a verra long stretching of the truth." He stared at the monk, scarcely able to keep the tremor from his voice. "Are ye here to free me?"

Frère Jean looked thoughtful. "I can speak for you on behalf of your lapse of judgement due to your concern for the two women. 'Tis a tenant of chivalry after all, is it not? But the fact remains of your disobedience." He shook his head and leaned forward, resting his forearms on is thighs. "I confess I did not like your commander Herve when he was here—pompous little prick, may God forgive me. But things were in quite a turmoil, and he left rather quickly on his pilgrimage to escort Bertran to his final rest."

He shifted a bit sideways and propped a knee on the edge of the thin mattress. "I do not know what will become of you, though I will try my best to get word of your existence. I understand the men searching for you were told you were dead." He eyed Kinnon's gaunt form. "Not far from the truth, I believe." He shook his head. "But for now mayhap I can ease your mind as to the fate of the women you sought to protect."

Kinnon caught his breath and his eyes prickled with sudden moisture. *Finally! An answer to my prayers!* He leaned forward, urging Frère Jean's next words.

"I remember the stir among the men who grumbled of a woman who sicced her dog on a couple of soldiers who were 'just doin' their duty'." His voice lost its educated tones and slipped into the patois of the French soldiers.

Kinnon grinned—and it felt good. Frère Jean shrugged. "I did ask what the duty was that harassed the good woman sufficiently to provoke her to such an action, and they muttered something about a dangerous prisoner." His gaze returned to Kinnon, eyes rounded with pity. "Prison does not improve the man, does it, *mon ami?*"

"It has failed to be the best place to recover from my wounds," Kinnon demurred. He raised one arm, appalled anew at how wasted he had become. Letting his arm drop back to the coverlet beside him, he pinned the monk with a stare. "What of the women?"

"To the soldiers' great disgust, they were not captured, nor do they remain at the farm."

Kinnon's eyes closed, the relief almost too much to bear. "They got away. I knew Melisende would recognize their danger."

"But it is good to hear it confirmed, *n'est-ce-pas?*"

"Aye," Kinnon agreed, his voice choked with emotion.

"*Mon ami,* I will do my best to get word to your family, but my actions may take weeks or months to reach the proper channels."

"It is enough to know you are trying."

"Give me your full name and how I may send word. I will see what can be done."

"I am Kinnon Macrory of Clan Macrory. My da is Laird Niall Macrory. I pray ye are successful."

* * *

Later that night, as Kinnon prepared for sleep, he reached for the talismans in his bag. The flat piece of metal grew warm in his hand as he fingered the emblem etched in its surface. He set it aside and reached for the wine plug, drawing it beneath his nose. The scent of wine was gone, but the memories remained.

The carved tail of the tiny wooden horse brushed the back of his hand as he set the trinkets back inside the bag, and he lifted the statue on his palm. The dark was too deep to see the wee horse he'd once carved for his sister, but he knew every curve by heart. She'd given it back to him the day he left for France, telling him to bring it back to her when he was finished traipsing about.

"I am finished, Ree. I pray ye are well and Da hasnae married ye off yet. I do not imagine I will live a long life with my injuries, but I want to live it breathing good Scottish air. Someday soon, I hope to give this back to ye with my own hand."

Carefully, he stowed his treasures in the bag and stretched out on the worn mattress. A purring sound reached his ears as the tower cat curled beside him.

* * *

Melisende glanced up as the bell on the shop door tinkled. A young man with a leather satchel slung over his shoulder met her gaze.

"Are ye Melisende, Ramon the goldsmith's niece?" he asked.

Something cold touched the back of her neck and she nodded. He stepped forward, a bound missive in his hand. She accepted it, slipping two coins in his palm for his trouble. Touching his forehead in thanks, he hurried out the door.

Her feet didn't seem to be working, and she stared at the envelope for several long moments. Her eyes felt dry, and her pulse raced. She lifted a slender, jeweled dagger from a display tray and slit the seal on the missive. The dagger clanged against the counter as she set it down, her fingers nerveless.

She took a deep breath and pulled a single sheet of vellum from the envelope and unfolded it. Lucienne's looping, childish scrawl filled the page.

Dearest Melisende,

I hope you are doing well, and shop keeping has not bored you too much. Raul and I enjoy Italy very much, though money is tight and it is tiresome moving from place to place. We have stayed in some of the most fabulous houses! The clothes are incredible and I change as many as four times most days. The men are completely chivalrous though the women are quite catty.

I thought you would like to know that you are now an aunt. I have no idea when this will reach you, but I believe the babe—a girl—was a bit premature. At least, that is what I told Raul. She is growing, though I rarely see her. There is always a nursery with an over-worked nursemaid to care for her wherever we stay. With her dark hair she looks just like you.

Give my love to Oncle Ramon. Ask him if he could speak with Monsieur Depaul about money. Living completely cut off from one's family is such a bother.

Your sister,

Lucienne

The page fluttered to the counter top and Melisende's eyes welled with tears. "Oh, Lucienne!" she whispered. "What are you doing with your life? What possible chance does your daughter have?"

She stared at Lucienne's careless letter as her heart broke for the little girl who needed her mother's love.

CHAPTER EIGHTEEN

Off the coast of Scotland, summer 1377

Walking from the passenger quarters to the forecastle had taxed his strength, but the view was worth it. Trees clogged the far coastline as the cog ship turned into the firth. Mists drifted from the outstretched limbs into the clouds, pregnant with the promise of rain. A cool breeze swept the water spray over the tall sides of the massive ship, spattering Kinnon with his first taste of home.

Home.

Soon they would approach a bend in the River Clyde. Soon Scaurness Castle would loom at the top of a cliff overlooking the firth. Soon he'd be home.

Across the water, a red-sailed birlinn hugged the far coastline. Sunlight broke through a cloud, arcing above the beach in a multi-hued rainbow. Seagulls shrieked overhead.

Home.

A man appeared at Kinnon's elbow, red hair tossed in the wind, the bridge of his nose turning scarlet in the sun. "Sir, we will be ashore soon. We should be able to obtain a few horses from the smithy in the village. Hamish will get them ready."

Kinnon turned to the warrior who had appeared at the door of his tower cell almost three months earlier. "Thank ye, Rory. I am forever in yer debt."

The man ducked his head. "The men and I have been looking for ye more than a year. We are pleased to bring ye home. Even if the rumors are true and there is another as laird at Scaurness, the clan will want ye to take yer rightful place."

Kinnon hid his grimace. *I dinnae wish to be laird. I have no qualities to instill leadership or faith in men. I have failed in so many ways.* But he could not tell Rory this. He could not bring himself to cast away the men's success. Thank God, their diligence had brought him home.

The cog dropped anchor not far from the rock-strewn beach, and the men rowed ashore. Kinnon stared about him, drinking in the sights as though he sipped the finest wine. *I dinnae know why Brody, Jamie and I thought we had to leave to prove ourselves. Only now do I see my heart has been here all along, waiting for my return.*

"Kinnon? We must hurry. Something is amiss at the castle."

Pulling himself together, Kinnon mounted the proffered horse and gathered his reins. Rory and Hamish flanked him, a younger man bearing a worn blue standard—the symbol of the Macrory clan for generations—to one side. Twenty more men either walked or rode in their wake.

Soft morning light spilled through the lowering clouds, bathing Scaurness Castle in pale gold. A spiral of black smoke twisted upward, and shouts and the ring of steel clashed behind the thick walls. Hamish and Rory looked to Kinnon.

"I think they are having a wee problem, lads," Kinnon commented, tightening his legs about his mount's girth. A warning cry rang from the wall followed by the blast of a horn. A gust of wind whipped the blue standard, snapping the cloth defiantly. Kinnon's horse plunged sideways at the noise, but he settled the beast with a practiced hand. "They have seen us."

The small group advanced to the castle gate as the sounds of battle within rose. Without warning, the noise died.

"A Macrory! A Macrory!" The clamor built again.

"Is there treason behind the walls?" Kinnon asked.

Rory shook his head. "Yer father was on his death bed when we left over a year ago. 'Tis possible the lairdship has fallen into contention."

Helpless, Kinnon stared at the parapet as men fought and died. Nothing short of a siege could hope to open the gates if the men in charge wished to keep them shut. Kinnon's twenty men had no hope of changing the course of the battle.

Despair, an all-too-familiar sensation, crashed over him. *I have failed again—and this time people whom I know and love are likely forfeit. Damn! Damn all greedy, overly-ambitious men straight to hell!* He fisted his hand, pulling the reins tight. His horse arched his neck against the strain, prancing in protest. *I am sorry, Ree.*

His only course of action was to appeal to the king. Yet it would take days of travel to arrive at Dundonald Castle, longer still to present his case and wait until a decision was reached. The prospect was dim, untenable, not worth wasting time over. The Macrorys needed help— now.

Kinnon waved the men forward. "We will do what we can."

Horses broke into a gallop and men's feet pounded the turf as they ran, a shout from their throats rising as from one. "A Macrory!"

To Kinnon's surprise, the portcullis began to rise.

The massive, iron-clad gates swung inward with a groan. Men, all marked with battle, bloodied and grimed, bristled silently, swords outward, as they faced Kinnon's group. The stag on the faded standard danced in the morning breeze, announcing their presence as they rode through the gate. A woman's shriek pierced the air.

"Kinnon!"

With a moan of relief, Kinnon slid from his horse and staggered into his sister's arms.

Her head came to his shoulder-certainly taller than she'd been nearly five years ago—and her dark red hair sprang from the tangles of a braid that hung to her waist. Her arms wrapped tight about his waist, she clung to him with a sob. Kinnon staggered against the force of her welcome, his arms circling her in a fierce embrace. After a moment, he released her.

"What have ye done to the keep, lass?" he asked, motioning to the chaos. Riona's answer was a choking laugh as she wiped the back of one hand across her face drawing a line of dirt in its wake.

"Where have ye been? We received word ye were missing . . .or worse." Her eyes brimmed with tears that reflected longing and fear. And relief. Just then, a small form plunged against her legs and she bent to gather the child in her arms, her hands caressing the red-gold hair.

Exhaustion washed over Kinnon. "I'd like to come inside, if ye dinnae mind."

"Aye. It seems we have much to discuss," a deep voice intoned.

Kinnon's gaze jerked to the man who had appeared next to Riona. Blood matted against the side of his face, and his eyes glinted dangerously. Ranald Scott? The man bore scant resemblance to Kinnon's childhood friend, the man—battle lust raging—replacing the youth, but the recognition was there. Without another word, Ranald plucked the child from Riona's arms and strode to the great hall, his booted feet eating the ground in angry strides.

Kinnon followed as Riona took to her heels, obviously torn between him and the child in Ranald's arms. He frowned. *Riona would have had to marry right after I left to have a child, what, 4 summers old? She would have only been 15. Surely Da wouldnae have asked that of her.*

He entered the hall as Ranald plumped the little girl in a chair and stalked away. Riona sat next to her and the child scrambled immediately into her lap. Kinnon took the chair to their left with a sigh, recognizing all the effects of battle-lust in Ranald. He patted Riona's knee.

"Dinnae fash, Ree. He needs time to gather himself. A splash of cauld water will help."

She shook her head. "He is verra angry with me."

"Tell me what has happened," he commanded. Reluctantly, she complied, and her story crushed him to a level he hadn't known existed. "*Merde.*" He forced his gaze to meet hers, devastated to see the haunted look in her expressive grey eyes. The eyes mirrored so perfectly in the wee lass in her lap.

His chest tightened unbearably to think of his sister trapped by the pirate MacEwen, forced into an unwanted liaison by the honorless brute. "I should have been here to protect ye."

"Dinnae fash, Kinnon. `Tis in the past, and Gilda is much loved."

Talk moved to his sire, and Kinnon was stirred yet again by the effect news of his supposed demise had had on the man he'd always seen as indestructible.

"The king sent Ranald to protect the clan after Da died," Riona said. "But now that ye are home, Kinnon, ye will be laird."

Kinnon shook his head. "Nae, lass. I'll not be laird."

She drew back in surprise. "Why?"

"I may never recover my health, and I have seen enough of killing. I have chosen to enter a monastery." There, he'd said it. After the slow passage of time in the tower prison, made tolerable only by the occasional visits of Frère Jean and the company of a wee orange cat, Kinnon had no desire to step into the role of laird of Scaurness Castle. There were too many people eager to take over the position, and he did not relish the life-long fight ahead to maintain order. He'd seen all the battle-horrors he could live with. He was no longer an eager-eyed lad. He needed—craved—peace.

A shout from the stairwell drew everyone's attention. "Laird! He isnae here! The MacEwen is gone!"

From Riona's story and the knowledge of clan politics, Kinnon knew the pirate MacEwen had long coveted Scaurness and the portion of the River Clyde the castle controlled. That he'd tried to win control of the castle and nearly succeeded was a fearful thing. At least it appeared he was gone, though for how long was anyone's guess.

Kinnon lingered in his chair as Riona stalked to her room at Ranald's command to change, the ripped neckline of her gown exposing her white shoulder. *They are in for a long and miserable life if they care no more for each other than this.*

Ranald paced the room, anger vibrating about him. A large man approached him, confidence in his step. Instantly, Kinnon recognized him as likely Ranald's captain, for his rapport was close, yet respectful, and Ranald listened intently to the man's words. They cast a glance in his direction and Kinnon knew they would soon wish to know his intentions.

Rest easy, Ranald. The lairdship is yers. Though I wish ye better days with my sister.

Suddenly Ranald wheeled and stormed up the stairs, the other man hard on his heels.

Apprehension prickled along the back of Kinnon's neck. He surveyed the room, but nothing in particular caught his eye. Around him people moved with the stunned slowness of people still in shock from the battle. Groups murmured together, a child cried softly. An older woman, whom he recognized as Tavia, the clan's wise woman and healer, wiped her hands on her stained apron and reached for a tray of supplies on the trestle table beside her. Next to him, the lass Gilda sat in the lap of a lad mayhap boasting nine or ten summers, but his face was bruised and swollen, making him look older.

My niece. Gilda stared at him with wide grey eyes, her red curls reminding him of Riona as a child. He smiled, eager to know this young lass.

Ranald and his man approached the dais where Kinnon sat. "Have ye seen a man carrying a woman in a shroud?"

A shroud? "Do ye mean a corpse?" he asked. "Nae. A *ghille* wouldnae bring one through the hall."

"It isnae a corpse, and the man is nae *ghille*," Ranald growled.

Kinnon gave him a puzzled look. "Then who is it?"

Ranald's face was bleak. "MacEwen and yer sister."

* * *

How could I be so useless? I couldnae protect Ree when she was attacked by MacEwen five years ago, and I can do nothing to help now. Kinnon slammed his fist into the stone wall, taking the pain that shot up his arm as scant punishment for his inability to act.

Damn my leg! Damn my ribs! It was unfair to blame his injuries, but he felt worse than inadequate to face the difficulties at the castle. Worthless. Unfit to be a man. He halted at the entry to the hall, his breaths coming hard and fast.

A small hand tugged his sleeve. "Do ye know my ma?" Grey eyes bored into his, and Kinnon could not look away.

"Aye. Yer ma is my sister," he replied.

Gilda tucked her hand in his. "Ranald will bring her back," she told him with the matter-of-factness of youth. "He can do anything." She led him back to her seat. Kinnon sat and Gilda climbed into his lap. She patted his plaide draped across his shoulder.

"I havenae seen ye before. Ye look like my grandda." Her face rounded solemnly. "He is an angel."

Kinnon's heart lurched. "Did ye know him?"

She nodded, red curls bouncing across her shoulders. "Aye. He was verra sad when the men told him his son was dead." She tilted her head at him. "Was that you?"

"Aye. 'Twas me," Kinnon choked. The lass settled against him.

"I'm glad ye arenae an angel."

Her simple words touched something inside of him. A warmth he had never felt before seeped through him, promising healing. "I am, too, lass." And for the first time, he meant it.

CHAPTER NINETEEN

Tension heightened. High-pitched voices resonated with apprehension, movements about the room appeared furtive and disjointed. Kinnon did his best to entertain his niece, and welcomed her tales of the kittens she and her friend, the lad who'd apparently helped her escape the pirates, had discovered in the run-down stables. From time to time, he stood and paced the room, anxious to learn what happened to his sister and the MacEwen. With calm perseverance, Gilda brought him back to her story, forestalling his return to the storerooms below.

He was uncertain how a day could last so long, but his prayers were answered just before nightfall as his sister and Ranald returned to the great hall, wet, disheveled, and with the glow of renewed promise on their faces.

The next sennight was spent in feasting and gaiety, even amid the hard work to repair damage to the castle and grounds, though the evening of the funerals for the brave, deceased Macrorys was somber enough. Kinnon found himself surrounded on every side by well-wishers, and plumped with more food than he'd eaten in the past three years. He escaped in much-needed rest, wherein he was assured he would wake on the morrow among friends, neither wet nor cold nor hungry, and without fear of sudden execution.

* * *

Kinnon shifted uneasily in his seat, still uncomfortable in company after many long months alone in his cell. People cast speculative looks his way, and the room was abuzz with questions. Ranald, Finlay, his captain, and Riona lingered at the high table after supper. It had been over a week since the MacEwens had been routed and the castle set to rights, and it was time to firm his plans.

He addressed Ranald's question first. "I have nae desire to be laird. Though `tis within my right to ask it, I believe `tis best left in yer hands."

Ranald's face was uncertain, his brow furrowed as he considered Kinnon's response. Riona turned worried eyes on her brother.

"But, Kinnon, `tis yer birthright," she said.

He gave her a tight smile. "I cannae tell ye how much it grieves me to have been absent when Da died. I know how much my presumed death hurt him." *Damn ye, Herve, now and forever for yer lies!* "Though I dinnae wish to speak much of it, my time as a soldier produced many doubts in my mind. For a time, I thought I could be a laird who could bring peace to the clan, but `tis not the reality of life here."

Ranald spoke up. "I dinnae think I understand. If ye are so determined to have peace, why would ye not wish to give it to yer people as their laird?"

Kinnon glanced about the room, so different from the shock of the battle with the MacEwens. "Did ye not notice the day I arrived, how ye were at war with yer own people? There will always be those who covet Scaurness and its pivotal role protecting the firth. Ye need a strong man as laird, not someone who has seen too many atrocities and has trouble sleeping at night."

Riona's pale hand covered his, and he felt a measure of comfort.

"What will ye do?" she asked softly.

"As I mentioned before, I will retire to a monastery and seek absolution. And mayhap healing."

"Where?" Riona's voice caught on a tremor and Kinnon winced.

"I have chosen Iona."

Ranald glanced sharply at him, clearly startled. "'Tis a desolate island with harsh storms. Ye'd live completely isolated. Are ye sure?"

"Why there?" Riona chimed in.

Kinnon felt his chest empty of all emotion. "Because it is said the sanctity of the soil can dissolve one's sins."

* * *

Kinnon sprawled in the chair, alone in his room. Riona had turned on him furiously at his mention of the soil of Iona. *If you are buried in it!* she challenged him. It was true many kings of Scotland had chosen the isle of Iona for burial in order to be sanctified, and Kinnon felt the pull of the holy island.

It took a bit to calm her down when anyone could see he stood closer to death than he did life. He understood Riona hated to lose her brother again so soon. She wished him to remain at Scaurness where she could nurse him. He cringed at the thought of being venerated as the long-lost son, and did not wish to be a hinge-point on any plan to replace Ranald as laird. Well and whole or feeble and infirm, as the auld laird's son, he could be used by anyone who wished to usurp the leadership at Scaurness. He had more respect for Ranald than to allow himself to be a distraction or a tool for those who wished to stir up trouble.

In the past several days, it had become clear Ranald and Riona were on their way to a reconciliation of whatever had caused their earlier rift. Kinnon knew, from the little Riona had confided, that her protectiveness of Gilda had led her to believe Ranald could not love the child as his own. Kinnon had yet to see evidence Ranald was anything but besotted with his adopted daughter—and quite possibly his wife—and Riona admitted he was a considerate and caring father.

'Tis good to know they will likely soon present me with another niece or nephew. He sobered. *One I will likely never meet.* It was the only unresolved problem with his plan, and after spending the sennight in Gilda's presence, one that tore at his heart.

"Are you going to be an angel?" A tiny voice at the door to his room jerked him out of his musings. He pulled himself up in his deep chair, hiding a cough as he turned to his niece.

"Not any time soon, lassie. I believe I have some time left on this earth."

Gilda crossed the room and climbed into the seat next to his. It was late and she wore a night shift that would soon need replacing if the sight of her ankles was anything to judge by.

"How many summers have ye?" he asked, eager to redirect her questions.

She curled her feet beneath her and leaned against the chair's high back. "I have almost five summers, and ye look tired."

Kinnon grinned. "If that is a polite way to say I look old, I thank ye."

She cocked her head at him. "Nae, not old, but verra tired. And ye breathe strangely,

90

too."

He nodded soberly. "'Tis one of the reasons I will go to Iona. Mayhap they can heal me."

"Tavia is a good healer," Gilda offered. "Ye could stay here."

"Nae, lass. I need more healing than she can provide."

Gilda's lower lip quivered. "I dinnae want ye to go."

"Ye hardly know me, lass."

She nodded vigorously. "Aye. But ye are my uncle."

He ruffled her red curls. "Aye. I am. I willnae leave for a few more days, and after that, mayhap I can visit from time to time. Would ye like that?"

A smile split her impish face, instantly replaced by an outlandishly large yawn.

"Should ye not be in bed, lass?" Kinnon regarded her skeptically.

"Aye. Ma willnae like me running up and down the halls." She cast him a narrow, pleading look. "Ye willnae tell her?"

"Not if ye hurry off. I will walk ye to yer room."

She shrugged carelessly. "Och, I willnae get into trouble. I know all the good hiding spots—should someone see me."

Kinnon smothered a laugh. "I am sure ye do. But, as yer uncle, 'tis my job to see ye safe abed."

Gilda hopped off the chair and took his hand, hauling him to his feet, her wee body angled far backward as she pulled. She leaned heavily against him as they ambled the length of the hall to her room, the torchlight no match for her brilliant red-gold hair that bounced across her shoulders with each step.

"Here ye go," Kinnon said, holding the door to her room open for her.

She faced him with a winsome look. "Tell me a story?"

Kinnon hesitated, racking his brain for a tale fit for his young niece's ears. Then, with a nod, he followed her inside. Eyes bright, Gilda settled herself in her narrow bed and Kinnon took a seat in the comfortable chair beside her. He held his fist to his forehead.

"Beira, the queen of winter, had only one eye, but it was as keen as an eagle's."

Gilda giggled and squirmed beneath the covers.

Encouraged, Kinnon continued. "One day she took for a servant the beautiful young princess, Bride. Nothing Bride did ever seemed to please the grumpy old queen, who was jealous of Bride's youth and beauty, and Bride was often in tears.

"One day, Angus, the youthful king of summer, dreamed of a beautiful young princess who was crying, and he resolved to find and marry her. But 'twas the depth of winter and the weather was uncertain and often foul. Borrowing three fine days from summer, he flew over the ocean from the Green Isle of the West and found Bride at the foot of a mountain with snowdrop flowers in her hands. She was as beautiful as his dream and he begged her to marry him. She shed tears of joy, and where they touched the ground, violets sprang up. Everywhere, the birds began to sing, and flowers raised their faces to the warm sun, welcoming spring.

"Without a word to Beira, her mistress, they were wed by the queen of the faeries. Beira was verra angry, and to this day, each year she sends winds and storms to keep spring away. But everywhere Bride dips her fingers in the water, the auld hag falls into a deep sleep and doesnae wake until after the harvest."

Gilda looked at him from beneath heavy lids. "'Tis almost harvest, Uncle. Will ye return like Bride?"

He rose and placed a soft kiss on her forehead. "Aye, lass. I will return in the spring."

* * *

Kinnon stood beside the standing stones on the Isle of Mull, awaiting the boat that would carry him to his new life. The wind whistled through the stone, whipping his plaide about him, whispering in his ears.

Do ye deserve to be saved? Will the rest of yer life atone for the atrocities of war?

Kinnon scowled and huddled deeper into his plaide, pulling a corner of it over his head. It kept out most of the wind, but not the voices.

Why do ye think ye should be forgiven?

"Och, damn voices. Be gone!" He glanced about him, but the others near him were too concerned with keeping warm to pay attention to his words. One man peered at him briefly from the depths of his cowl, then turned away. The men of his guard, sent on Ranald's insistence, made no remark.

The boat from Iona slipped into its moorings, bouncing lightly on the waves. Silently, people climbed aboard, settling the craft deeper in the water. With quiet words of thanks to his men-at-arms, Kinnon bid them farewell. Within moments, the boat was loaded and the ship's captain urged it out into the bay.

The trip was no more than half an hour's time, but it was several minutes before the single peak on Iona appeared from the fog. It crept closer and closer, until the large stone boulder marking the port at *nam Mairtear*, Martyr's Bay, was clearly visible. The boat slid to the shore and the passengers disembarked as silently as they'd entered. Heads bowed, they disappeared like wraiths to wherever their paths led.

Kinnon glanced around. A monk stood nearby, his black robe and tonsured head marking him as a man of God as clearly as his patient demeanor. A smile crossed his face as he noticed Kinnon's gaze.

"*Failje a Eilean Idhe*, my friend." He swept his hood over his head against the cold and motioned for Kinnon to step forward. Picking up his small bag of belongings, Kinnon obeyed.

"I am Brother Padraig. We will get you inside the abbey and then talk, aye? `Tis a *dreicht* day and not one to stand about in longer than necessary."

Kinnon agreed wholeheartedly, indeed his left leg ached abominably in the cold dampness, and he sensed a round of coughing was imminent. Something warm to drink would not go amiss.

They filed up the Street of the Dead, past St. Oran's chapel and the *Reilig Odhrain*— burial site of Scottish kings—and approached the abbey. Brother Padraig opened the door, and Kinnon was relieved at the soothing warmth inside.

"Set yer belongings along the wall. We will take them to yer room in a bit," the monk instructed. "Then come warm yerself by the fire."

Kinnon started to place his bag on the floor, then hesitated. He felt his face heat. "I have a small request," he began.

"Only a small one?" the monk rejoined with a smile. "What is it?"

"My niece gave this to me as I left her three days ago. She said it was to be my friend and remind me of her."

Brother Padraig strolled to Kinnon's side, curiosity on his face. "What could the lass have given ye that has ye confused?"

"Not confused, just unsure of its welcome." Reaching inside the worn bag, Kinnon pulled forth a small bundle of orange fur. It stretched and looked about cautiously, its tiny mouth emitting a squeaky *meow*.

The monk drew back, startled, then laughed. "A wee ginger tabby! Though even the rats are God's creatures, I believe I speak for all of us if I say it would hurt no feelings here if the rats chose to live elsewhere—out of respect for our new friend."

Kinnon grinned. "I hoped ye would feel that way. My niece is a charming lass of four summers, and it would have broken her heart if I had turned her gift away. And once I was on my journey, it became difficult to give wee Angus over to another family to raise." He lifted his gaze to Brother Padraig. "I have had no family to speak of for the past three years, and only recently met my niece, Gilda. I am happy to dedicate this lad to the greater good of the abbey, but ask that we take good care of him."

Brother Padraig clapped Kinnon's shoulder. "Dinnae fash! He is a welcome addition to our family." He waved to a young man nearby. "Warm a bit of broth for our wee new brother. He can eat with us until he is old enough to hunt on his own."

Within a short time, Kinnon found himself seated next to the hearth, Angus contentedly full and asleep on his lap. Brother Padraig took his seat.

"Tell me, my friend, what brings ye to our fair isle? I have read yer missive, but wish to hear from yer lips what ye believe God has put upon yer heart."

With some trepidation, Kinnon began his story.

CHAPTER TWENTY

The days grew shorter, the winds more fierce, roiling the seas on the western coast of the island. And the voice in Kinnon's heart disturbed the peace he wished to find. He'd entered the daily life of the abbey, praying and working as he was able. He was content to help with cooking—a skill he'd learned as a lad when away from the hall for more than a day—adjusting to their fare of mostly vegetables with only a wee bit of longing for a bite of mutton or fish during the week as Sundays and special occasions were the only days meat was served at the abbey. Prison had taught him all sustenance was to be valued.

There was little work to do on the grounds. The gardens had been harvested and food preserved for the winter before Kinnon arrived. Though fair days often interrupted the winter tempests, and the more intrepid souls ventured out of doors, Kinnon found his health did not allow him the freedoms he was used to.

He spent much of his time in the scriptorium St. Columba had established many years ago, reading the ancient works collected carefully by the monks. Much had been lost in previous years during Viking raids, and the marvelous Book of Kells had been transported to Ireland for safekeeping. But in the scriptorium, Kinnon could for a time lose himself in thoughts of pious men long dead and ignore the unrest in his heart.

The long winter evening hours were set aside for respite and many of the brothers enjoyed the company in the main hall. Most were engaged in mending clothes and other minor chores or quiet reflection, though Brother Padraig rarely left Kinnon to his own thoughts. As his mentor, Brother Padraig often engaged Kinnon in deep conversations on a variety of subjects, many of which contributed to the restless feeling Kinnon harbored inside.

"I understand yer attraction to our simple way of life, Kinnon. Do ye believe it to be a true calling to a deeper commitment to the Lord here on Iona? Or is it a distraction for God's greater calling for yer life?" Brother Padraig leaned back comfortably in his chair in the main hall.

Kinnon struggled with the question as he stroked Angus' orange fur. "Am I pursuing God or hiding from Him?"

Brother Padraig nodded. "Well put, my friend. Do ye have an answer?"

Kinnon frowned. "God is hiding from me. How else to explain this feeling of incompleteness inside? Every day I join men who are completely at peace, listening to their murmured prayers as they go about their tasks." He strove to control his agitation. "They have such an ease about them, as though nothing else matters in the world."

Brother Padraig gave Kinnon a shrewd look. "As though the horrors ye have seen matter not?"

Kinnon lifted his hands. "They are untouched by them. They have not seen the hell we call war."

The monk offered a wry grin. "Kinnon, every man here has his story. 'Tis true a few were dedicated at a young age and know no other life. Others willingly chose this vocation because of a thirst for the scripture, a love of a holy and simple lifestyle—a desire to seek God in every aspect of life. Some sought refuge such as ye have. Their stories would curdle yer blood. Here, on Iona, we are no stranger to war. Our island has seen much bloodshed from Viking raids. Martyr's Bay was not named simply to honor the saints. Real blood stained the water. Real men died here. The cemetery holds the bones of many men who died before their time."

Brother Padraig leaned forward. "God does not hide from men. Man sometimes takes his eyes off Him. Renew your focus on what matters most. Look at the small things, Kinnon. For in them, ye will see the work of God's hands. And from there, 'tis a short journey to find His heart."

* * *

Angus, no longer a wee kitten, slept curled upon the window sill, soaking in the watery late winter sun.

Kinnon paced the scriptorium, his sanctuary against the steady rain outside. Thick rock walls protected the ancient manuscripts, but naught protected his soul. "I cannae rid my mind of the life that called me to prove myself as a man by contradicting everything the chivalric code required."

"Was it always thus?" Brother Padraig asked.

Kinnon called Bertran to mind. "Nae. My commander's last words were to protect the poor, women and children, respect the Church and spare the ecclesiastics."

Brother Padraig chuckled. "Mayhap there was a reason he asked ye respect the Church *and* spare the ecclesiastics in the same breath."

Kinnon felt the ghost of a smile on his face. "Aye. 'Twas sometimes difficult to tell whose side the priests were on."

"My friend, at some point in everyone's life, ye discover ye are human. A priest may make a poor decision as he stares at death, just as any man."

Kinnon shook his head in disagreement. "Our precepts were generosity, fidelity, liberality and courtesy. And yet I saw looting, murder of innocents, rape, blasphemy."

"Which bothered ye most?"

Kinnon sobered. "That they were innocents. How could men sworn to protect . . ." Kinnon turned away, unwilling to voice the scenes in his head.

"Murder, rape and blaspheme?" the monk supplied. "Consider this. Ye have a bit of a command of the French tongue, aye?"

Kinnon nodded.

"What does the word *chevalier* mean?"

"A military follower—one who owns a warhorse," Kinnon answered.

"Nothing else?"

"I dinnae understand. A *chevalier* is a heavily armed horseman."

"*Chevalier* is the root of the word *chivalry*. There is a verra big step from one to the other."

Kinnon turned to Brother Padraig, eyes narrowed. "What are ye hinting at?"

"Mayhap ye wish all soldiers to live up to the noble standard of yer code, when many are nothing more than men given a job others either cannot or dinnae wish to do."

Kinnon's brow furrowed. "What of the murder and thievery and rape?"

"They will pay for their sins. But their sins arenae yers."

Kinnon was silent. Finally, Brother Padraig rose to his feet.

"Think on things that are lovely. Even in the midst of great turmoil, find beauty and it will give ye rest."

Angus yawned and shifted his perch as the monk exited the room.

Things of beauty? In the midst of bloodshed and injustice? His gaze traveled over the shelves of manuscripts and the tomes piled upon the scattered tables. *Peace, yes. But beauty? Is beauty contained within these walls?*

A small voice entered his mind. *What need do I have of a man who will insist I cook his meals, clean his house and dance to his tune? Lucienne and I make it fine on our own.*

Memories he'd tried to hold at bay rushed over him. In his years of dark despair in the tower prison, the memory of gentle spring sun on his skin had warmed him. Remembrances of a few hours of time-out-of-time had invaded his dreams of war and bloodshed. Reminiscences of a laughing face and clear blue eyes had replaced his distress with comfort.

He'd gladly left France after he'd won his freedom, with only a bittersweet thought to the two young women who'd saved his life—and his sanity. Faced with ill-health and the overwhelming desire to put France far behind him and return home as swiftly as possible, he'd not pursued further information of Melisende and her sister beyond the reassurance they'd not been captured by Herve's soldiers.

In the midst of the war, he'd found peace, strength, and—Lord help him—beauty. And to his eternal regret, it was lost to him now forever.

* * *

Seagulls shrieked as they circled overhead. The promise of spring was in the warm breezes and the green grasses. Young boys hurried after their wooly charges as the sheep eagerly sought the new fodder, tiny lambs tottering behind their dams on shaky new legs across the rocky landscape.

Brother Padraig clasped Kinnon's shoulder. "My friend, ye are doing the right thing. Some serve in the world by preaching the Gospel, and a few give themselves over to God in solitude and silence with constant prayer and penance." He smiled. "Yet others are called to married love, mayhap bringing new life into the world. I pray ye find whom ye seek, but there are always places to tend the poor and needy in this world. Ye need not take vows to help God."

Kinnon gripped the monk's upper arm, conveying his thanks in the strengthening grip, the earnestness of his gaze. "I have no words powerful enough to thank ye, brother. Ye have given me much to contemplate, and have healed more than my poor body."

"Rest is a balm for the soul and healing for the body," Brother Padraig quipped. "I will take good care of wee Angus. 'Tis a good thing ye decided to leave him here. After these past months without battling the rats for the last of the winter stores, I fear we would have had an uprising amongst the monks had ye insisted he go with ye." He grinned. "Take care, my friend. If possible, I would hear word of yer travels."

Kinnon stared deep into the monk's kind eyes, hesitant to bring himself to the moment of parting. But the gentle thumping of the waves against the boat's waiting hull reminded him the time to tarry was over.

Ranald's men-at-arms met him as the boat docked on Mull, a horse saddled and waiting for him. Kinnon greeted them warmly, wondering at the sense of freedom stealing over him. It had begun as a flash of clarity the moment he'd resolved to search for Melisende. At first he wasn't sure if he simply needed to be certain she and her sister had survived and were doing well, or if he truly longed to be with Melisende again. But the thought that she could have married in the years they'd been apart struck his chest with a peculiar agony that was a curious mix of anticipation and fear. The thought of another man holding her, loving her, being the center of her life, sent strong jolts of alarm through him.

It was then he realized he had to find her—for himself, not so he could worry less, but so he could care more.

CHAPTER TWENTY-ONE

Melisende sighed as her fingertips hovered over the last fruits in the seller's cart. Even with extra money from the surge of business following Lucienne's elopement with Lord Depaul's son almost three years earlier, it was almost impossible to purchase decent foodstuffs this late in the winter. Spring was evident in the tiny flowers that poked their heads through the ground, and the warm breezes and rains all but washed away the winter snow. The ground was still too cold and hard to consider planting gardens, and the crops harvested months earlier were nearing the end of their appeal.

Resigned, she placed six withered apples in her basket, after checking them carefully for worm holes, and paid the exorbitant sum asked. They would add a bit of sweetness to the dried bit of beef she planned to stew for dinner tonight. Along with the herbs she carefully tended on the window ledge in the kitchen, it should be a tasty meal.

Even on the farm, we would have only what survived the winter. And we would have already put seeds in pots to have the young plants ready to set out once the weather warmed. She sighed. As much as she longed to return to the farm, and as much as she considered it home, she did not want to face living there alone.

Mayhap Kinnon was right. Mayhap a family is needed there. She gave herself a mental shake. *What am I saying? I am twenty-and-three, hardly a young woman any more. Who would look to me as a wife and mother?*

Her steps slowed. *Lucienne's little girl is nearly two, and I will likely never see her—or any other children Lucienne may have.* It was a jarring thought and she worried over her niece daily. Since the letter telling her of the child's birth, she had received only one other from Lucienne, also asking for money. There had been no response to queries about the little girl—not even her name, and Melisende certainly did not ask what she'd meant by telling Raul the baby had been premature. It broke Melisende's heart to dwell on the choices her sister made in her life.

She turned her thoughts to the child. *When did she first walk? Talk? Does she like the outdoors? What is her favorite food? Is she precocious?* Melisende sighed, her chest tight. *I will never know.*

People rushed around her, laughing and calling to each other on this fine morning. It was easy to feel confident with the long winter behind you and spring sun on your face, but Melisende suddenly felt alone even in the midst of the busy market.

Someone bumped her shoulder—hard. Her basket slipped from her grasp and she cried out as she lunged for the apples that threatened to disappear beneath the bustling feet. A set of boots, scarred and muddy, planted themselves in front of her. She grabbed the last apple and rose, dusting the wrinkled skin on her skirt. The man who owned the boots did not move away, forcing Melisende to take a step back.

"I beg your pardon, *monsieur*," she said with some asperity. *Arrogant ass.*

He leered at her. "Well, bless me if it isn't the Scotsman's tart."

Melisende's eyebrows shot up and she gripped her basket to keep from smashing a fist in the man's stubbly face. A streak of alarm shot through her as she envisioned her dagger in the pocket of her cloak—which she'd left at the shop this fine morning. She'd felt safe in *Puy-en-Velay*—apparently too safe.

"I am certain I do not know what you mean," she replied crisply. "And I will thank you to keep your slanderous words to yourself. I do not know you."

He nudged the smaller man next to him. "Isn't there still a notice up for her arrest?"

Her blood ran cold. Her gaze flew over the crowd of people hurrying past, not a one of whom would hesitate to turn her in if there was a reward involved. "You are mistaken," she told the man firmly, gathering her skirt to walk around him. With a deliberate side-step, he countered her move.

"You will come with us, mademoiselle." His voice was no longer arrogant, and his face hardened.

Melisende drew herself up with assurance she was hard-pressed to feel. "I think not. My *oncle* is an important man. If you wish to have dealings with me, you must speak to him first. *Adieu*." With a curt nod, she attempted to force her way through the space between the two men. They closed ranks, blocking her path.

The first man held out his hand to her, palm up. "Come with us."

Melisende narrowed her eyes. "If you touch me, I will scream."

He grinned, calling her bluff. "We'll risk it."

Dropping her basket, she snatched up her skirts and darted to one side. The soldier grabbed her from behind, halting her flight. She whirled within his arms and stomped down hard on the top of his foot, bringing all her weight to bear, her sturdy boots adding to the force. He yelped and bent at the waist, grabbing at his lower leg. Stiffening her fingers, Melisende aimed for his face—now on level with her own—digging her nails into the skin at the top of his cheeks. Narrowly missing his eyes, she raked long gashes in his flesh before dodging his partner and dashing away.

"After her!" he roared.

A murmur of excitement rippled through the crowd. Someone shouted at her to stop, but she ignored him and ran faster. Weaving in and out of the stalls she'd patronized only moments before, she registered the shock on the merchant's faces as she sped past. There was no time to think, only to respond as footsteps and voices closed in.

* * *

Blackness enveloped her. Glancing about her furtively, she scratched softly at the back door of her *oncle's* shop. Beyond the bolted portal came a snuffle and a low growl.

A single word reached her ears. "Quiet."

The dog's growl turned to an anxious whine. He recognized her.

The moments it took for her uncle to unlatch the door seemed like hours and Melisende's heart began to race. She clenched her fists. "Hurry, hurry," she chanted softly.

With a sturdy *snick*, her *oncle* released the latch and opened the door. He stared at her. "I thought it was you." He glanced at Jean-Baptiste who wiggled his entire body in silent greeting. "Your dog dragged me downstairs in the middle of the night—after the day I have had," he finished dramatically.

Without answer, Melisende slipped past him into the shop's storeroom. He followed on her heels.

"You have no idea what it has been like! Soldiers in and out of the shop all day, questioning my customers. Questioning *me*." He rocked back on his heels as Melisende leveled a bland, disinterested gaze on him.

He rallied. "I told them that if you were smart, you would have already left town—followed your sister to Italy."

Melisende felt the weight of every single second of the hours she'd spent in hiding, smelling the questionable places she'd huddled in, listening for footsteps, deciphering even the slightest noise, assessing it for possible threat. Her stomach rumbled, she smelled like a sewer, and she felt a hundred years old. His day was of no importance to her. "Close the door, *Oncle*."

With a start, he rushed back to the door and threw the latch before hurrying to catch up with her as she climbed the stairs.

"Where are you going?" he demanded as she reached her room and began flinging her possessions into her bag.

She flashed him a look of impatience. "If I do not tell you, you will not have to lie when the soldiers return tomorrow."

"You cannot think I would tell them . . ." he blustered, red-faced.

Melisende slammed the flat of her hand on the bed and leaned forward menacingly. "What did they pay you, *Oncle*?" she snarled. "What did they promise if you helped them find me?"

"You are ungrateful!" he shot back, edging toward the door. "I took you and your shameless sister in when you had nowhere else to go. Lord Depaul still threatens me after all this time with an inquisition from the Bishop, still claims your sister is a witch."

Melisende released a breath of frustration. "Lucienne is not a witch, *Oncle*. Raul simply lost his head." She shoved a thin shift inside the bag. "Though faced with the alternative of marrying the heiress almost six years his elder—well, 'tis hard to blame him."

Jean-Baptiste whined, clearly upset by their voices.

Oncle Ramon whirled at the distraction. "And your enormous dog! You are both a menace and a burden. I will be glad to be rid of the both of you."

With a final step to the door, he dashed through and slammed it closed. The scrape of a heavy object across the wooden floor told her that exit was now blocked. With a shake of her head, she crossed the room and threw the bolt. Locking it would give her an added few minutes before anyone entered and discovered she was no longer there.

She flung her cloak about her and hefted the strap of her bag over her shoulder. A quick pat told her that her dagger was still in her cloak pocket. She turned to Jean-Baptiste.

"Come on. We will do it the hard way."

Opening the single narrow window, she eased out onto the ledge. Jean-Baptiste stuck his head through the casement and whined.

"Don't be a baby," she chided. "'Tis not so far." She pointed to a low shed only a few feet from the wall. "See? No problem." She paused, gathering herself as she judged the distance. "Of all times to wish I was a boy," she muttered, pulling her skirts to her knees.

She hunkered down, bracing a hand on the window sill. Jean-Baptiste whined again. Ignoring him, Melisende leapt across the short distance, landing on the shed's rooftop with a thud, catching herself on her hands and knees. She stood and motioned to the dog. "Come on, Jean-Baptiste. You can do it."

He leapt lightly through the window, landing on the ledge with a scramble of toenails. He looked down at her and slowly wagged his tail.

"Come on," she urged again. He glanced at the ground and for one fearful moment, she thought he would jump straight to the ground. Then his muscles bunched and he flew across the space to land next to her. She rubbed his ears in relief. "The next step is easy. The one after is not. Where are we going? Do we join Lucienne and her husband in Italy?" There was no answer, only faith in Jean-Baptiste's eyes.

Melisende knelt and grabbed the edge of the roof and slipped over the side. Jean-Baptiste was quickly at her side, following her into the night.

CHAPTER TWENTY-TWO

The French countryside was ablaze with flowers. Birds sang overhead and Kinnon's heart lifted. With him rode twenty men-at-arms, eager for adventure, or at least a journey to reunite their clansman with the woman who had saved his life. After visiting with Gilda as he'd promised, he'd announced his plan to Ranald and his astonished sister to find Melisende. Ranald had responded with the food, men and money to assist his journey. Riona had gifted him with her prayers and good wishes. He'd need all of it.

He guided his horse around the rocks and boulders, as familiar as a distant dream from the weeks he'd spent visiting the farm which housed the fierce Alaunt, Jean-Baptiste—and Melisende.

But today Jean-Baptiste did not leap from the barnyard, snarling his warning. All was silent at the little house. The ramshackle barn leaned perhaps a bit more precariously and a few chickens clucked and pecked their way across the dusty yard, cackling in indignation as Kinnon's horse strolled through their midst.

He saw Melisende everywhere in his mind. Eyeing him distrustfully from the far gate. Smiling as she placed a reassuring hand on the dog's head. Motioning for him to follow her to their private spot overlooking the valley. But she was no longer there.

Desertion was evident everywhere. The far gate hung askew, its top hinge worn through. No cows waited for milking; the absence of the goats apparent in the overgrown shrubbery. Kinnon glanced to the house and frowned at the broken crockery spilling from the open door. He swung down from his horse and handed the reins to the soldier beside him. Rory accepted them without a word.

Kinnon stepped over the crockery, eyes intent on the darkness beyond the door. He touched the ripped wood where the metal latch had hung. But the scar was old, its color nearly that of the ancient door. Alert, though more concerned with Melisende and Lucienne's fate than his own, he crossed the threshold into the house. The air was fresh, with no lingering odors of death or decay. *I wonder if it has been empty since they left nearly four years ago?* He crossed to the spare room and peeked inside. The narrow bed was overturned, the thin mattress slouched against the wooden frame. But there was no trace of the young girl who'd once called it home.

He walked back through the main room.

`Tis a large wound and you cannot care for it yourself.*

Dip me in pitch! Startled, he glanced about the room, but saw nothing but the second bed in the corner where Lucienne had tended him. The memory of her unyielding curiosity warmed his blood and he hurried from the temptation he'd felt to toss her over his knee for her brazen ways.

"Is aught amiss, sir?" Rory asked anxiously as Kinnon darted back into the sunshine.

Kinnon collected his reins and mounted. "Nae. There has been no one here in years. Let us ride to the village."

The men turned their horses's heads in unison and picked their way carefully back down the rocky trail. On reaching the main road, the pathway smoothed and they set their mounts to an easy canter. They reached *Châteauneuf-de-Randon* and slowed their pace as they rode down the main street. Nothing was familiar to Kinnon, but he'd been on the outside of the village during the siege, and his time inside had been restricted to the tower room at the *château,* itself.

He searched each building front. *There was a butcher she trusted* . . .At last he spied a shop displaying meats. He dismounted and handed the reins again to Rory, who tossed them to Hamish. Rory slid from his horse and followed Kinnon inside the building.

The light was dim after the brilliant sunshine outside. Kinnon gave his eyes a moment to adjust as he glanced about the moderate-sized room. A counter with a white cloth draped over it sat along the far side, with a door presumably leading to the back courtyard directly behind. A cloying smell filled the air—not quite rancid, but similar to what Kinnon associated with a battlefield. He wrinkled his nose.

A large man entered the room, wiping his hands on another white cloth, though this one bore several stains. He was jovial and eager to do business.

"How may I help you gentlemen today?" he asked, a broad smile on his face. "It is late in the day, and much of my product is sold, but I have a young stoat in the barn I could have dressed for you . . .?" He lifted his eyebrows in query. Apparently he'd seen Kinnon's soldiers waiting out front.

Kinnon shook his head. "Mayhap another time. Today I have a question for ye."

The man's face fell in disappointment, but he shrugged. "Answers are generally free."

Kinnon's lips quirked upward. "Mayhap my men would not be averse to something fresh for dinner." He raised a hand to halt the butcher as he hurried toward the rear door. "And they can help after ye have answered my question."

The butcher spread his hands wide. "But of course, *monsieur*. I am Piers the butcher. How may I help you?"

Kinnon stepped closer. "I was a soldier here when Constable Bertran took the town from De Ros."

"He was a very great man," the butcher intoned, his voice deepening with respect. "It is said his body was buried in the *Basilique royale de Saint-Denis*—with the kings of France."

Kinnon nodded. "I have heard that as well. But his heart lies with Thiephaine de Raguenel, the wife of his youth."

"*Oui, monsieur*, but how did you come by that knowledge? Is Bertran spoken about in Scotland?"

"To my knowledge, no—or at least very little. I was among his junior officers when he died."

Piers' eyes widened. "It is an honor to have you in my humble establishment."

Kinnon laughed. "Forgive me—I am Kinnon Macrory. And I was a brash young Highlander when I first met yer constable. I was once of some small service to him and I believe he appreciated the fact that as a Scotsman, I stood to gain little by advancing myself in his army."

"By needing little, you gained much," Piers noted.

"His friendship and respect was my everlasting gain, but I also received unasked-for enmity from other officers. Which brings me to my question."

Piers made an inviting gesture with his hand. "Of course."

"During the siege, I made the acquaintance of two young women who lived on a farm in the hills north of town. They sometimes supplied Bertran with fresh eggs and vegetables. I collected them for him."

Piers's look became guarded, but he said nothing. Kinnon continued. "I was injured during the battle and the younger—the eldest being away from home at the time—saved my life." He focused directly on the butcher who seemed to shrink. "I returned to my unit just before Bertran passed, then attempted to help the two women before I left town, as they were verra much alone. I had become quite fond of them and wished to see them safe."

The memory of the utter terror in Lucienne's voice drifted through his ears and he glimpsed again the uncertain fear in Melisende's expressive eyes the last time he saw her. He paused, placing a finger next to his nose to control himself.

"I am not sure I understand your question, *monsieur*," Piers mumbled as he took a step backward. "Mayhap now would be a good time—"

Kinnon interrupted him. "I spent three years in the tower prison at *Châteauneuf* for trying to help them, and six months after that regaining my health. I wish to find them."

Piers shrugged expressively, his hands spread wide. "What would I, a poor butcher, know of two young ladies? There were many refugees both during the English occupation and after."

"But, *mon ami*," Kinnon said softly. "Melisende mentioned *you*."

It was a calculated risk. Kinnon did not know if this was the correct shop, or if this was the same man who had sheltered Melisende in the past. He had just spent several minutes proving himself worthy of the butcher's trust by aligning himself with Bertrand. He watched Piers's eyes as they glanced about, weighing his options. A voice from the doorway called the butcher's bluff.

"Tell him, husband. Tell him what you know."

* * *

Kinnon, Rory and Hamish sat at the table with Piers and his wife, Cateline, while the rest of his men took their meal in the open air beneath the first of the evening stars. A dark-eyed maid served them, her belly lightly rounded with child.

"I remember your Melisende," she announced loftily. "'Twas before my Gautier and I wed." She placed a hand protectively over her belly as her gaze fell on Kinnon. "She did not mention you."

Cateline sent the maid a stern look. "That will be all, Mariette. You may begin clearing the kitchen."

Kinnon held the maid's gaze. "No offense, *madame*, but she dinnae mention ye, either."

With a huff, Mariette flounced from the room. Cateline turned to her guest. "Melisende was always gracious but spoke little of herself. We were, quite frankly, surprised to see her a day or two after Bertran died. She had been forced to stay with us the better part of a week during the siege, and left without a word to anyone."

"It seemed affronting at the time," Piers added. "But when she returned, she was able to tell us what happened."

Kinnon listened intently, bitterly disappointed to find the trail continued on from here, but enthralled to hear Melisende spoken of by people who had known her as well as anyone.

He winced to hear of the insolent old goat who'd tried to take advantage of her, and grinned broadly when she'd left him passed out on the floor of the run-down house and at the mercy of any who came across him.

Good lass! Ye are so verra brave.

"I thank ye for caring for Melisende and her sister. If there is anything ye need—if `tis in my power . . ."

Piers belched pleasurably. "Duly noted, *monsieur*, but we were happy to help Melisende."

Kinnon caught the look that passed between the butcher and his wife and the deliberate omission of Lucienne's name. *What trouble did ye stir up, Luci?*

Piers waved an arm about the room. "And we have what we need."

Kinnon rose to his feet and bowed over Cateline's hand. "Then, with your permission, *madame*, my men and I will retire for the night and be on our way to *Puy-en-Velay* at first light. Your hospitality overwhelms me."

Cateline beamed at him. "I hope you find her, *monsieur*. Melisende deserves to be happy."

* * *

The town of *Puy-en-Velay* clustered around the base of the cathedral, its alternating black and white façade a contrast to the tile-roofed buildings at its feet. Just to the north, the *fortress de Polignac* rose from the great black rock, hovering protectively over the town.

"Where shall we start?" Rory wondered, echoing Kinnon's thoughts.

"The butcher said Melisende was searching for her father's family. He had been a goldsmith, so we will try the market place."

Rory nodded. "Hamish will find us lodging and food for the noon meal."

Kinnon was too anxious to wait. "I will find something to eat in the market."

"Then I will join ye."

Kinnon's steadfast captain who had spent so much time searching for him a year ago, seemed reluctant to let him out of his sight. Kinnon appreciated his loyalty. "Mayhap a guard of three would care to follow me?"

Rory signaled two additional men and the group parted ways. Kinnon's path wound past the cathedral. A youth helpfully pointed out the *Place de Breuil* where the market was held. Kinnon and his men dismounted and strolled through the packed stalls, munching food from vendors and admiring the colorful extravagance that was *Le Puy's* market.

A merchant directed them to the Golden Street. "There was a terrible confusion last week at Ramon's shop," he added. "Soldiers tried to arrest his niece—a lovely young woman who was always kind to me and others here."

"Was she arrested?" Kinnon demanded, his heart pounding in his chest.

"*Non, monsieur*. I do not think so, because the soldiers have lingered about the shop since. Poor Ramon, After his other niece eloped with Lord Depaul's eldest son three years ago! His reputation was only just recovering before this happened." The merchant chuckled. "After a lifetime of being a bachelor, he is even less likely to marry now."

"Which niece eloped?" Kinnon's heart stuttered. Was it in Melisende's character to run away to marry? Nae. `Twas more likely Lucienne.

"`Twas the youngest. A bit fey, she was, though I've never seen a lovelier woman in my life. Too beautiful, if you ask me. But I was never comfortable around her. No one could deny her anything, and she knew it."

With a word of thanks, Kinnon led the way to the wide street the merchant indicated. Trees and scattered benches marked the elegant shops. A few well-bred horses loitered in the shade, servants keeping watch over their charges. Bells chimed cheerfully as a door opened part way down the street. A woman in rich clothing, escorted by an elegantly dressed older man, strode from the shop, her hand held up before her as she admired a ring on her finger that winked blindingly in the midday sun. She tucked her hands in the crook of the man's elbow and snugged his arm tight against her breasts, her well-pleased giggle drifting on the breeze.

"I believe this may be our shop," he noted. Rory handed the horses to the other two soldiers and he and Kinnon stepped across the street to the red-roofed shop.

The same bells tinkled as Kinnon opened the door. The interior of the shop sparkled with polished wood and stone surfaces that glittered in the abundant candle light. A man in a supple leather apron glanced up from the exquisite, multi-stoned necklace he was showing to a gentleman at a nearby table.

"I can be with you shortly, *monsieur,*" he called.

Kinnon acknowledged him with a wave of his hand, aware he once again had reached Melisende's trail too late. He peered about, imagining Melisende entering the room, a smile on her face as she greeted each customer. She would be intimate with the details of the room, leaving no cobweb or speck of dust to mar the perfection of the displays.

I had no gift for creating beautiful things, but I was quick with numbers and did his accounting. Her words drifted through his head. *Nae, lass, for ye outshone them all. Yer greatest beauty is in yer heart and it surfaces in yer smile and yer eyes.*

"How may I help you, *monsieur?*"

Kinnon dragged his attention from the past and stared at the goldsmith. Delicate tools peeked from various pockets in his apron, and his hands were surprisingly large to produce fine jewelry.

"Are ye Ramon the goldsmith?"

His eyes darted about the room, but other than Kinnon and Rory, it was empty. "*Oui.* Who wants to know?"

"I wish to speak to ye about yer niece."

The man scowled. "I was better off before those two showed up on my doorstep."

Kinnon tilted his head. "I thought caring for family was a cornerstone of Christian charity."

"They brought their own trouble. Though sales improve as people come to gawk and linger to purchase, the gossip is enough to drive a man to madness."

One side of Kinnon's lips quirked upward sardonically. "Pray to be delivered from such madness."

Ramon shrugged. "It brings customers," he repeated.

"What happened to the eldest—Melisende?" Kinnon asked softly.

The man looked at Kinnon in surprise. "You knew her?"

"Bertran's army compensated her poorly for her gardening and cheeses."

As Kinnon had intended, the mention of Bertran's name caught the goldsmith's attention.

"Bertran was a great man. `Tis right she helped him." His attitude seemed to mellow. "She was good, competent help whilst she was here. Never a number out of place in the books, nor a speck of dust to be seen." His eyes narrowed. "Not that I can say as much for that sister of hers."

"Lucienne had her own problems," Kinnon demurred.

Ramon raked a hand through his hair. "Even as a young child she was beautiful. Men wanted her." He cast Kinnon a sharp look. "You knew of this?"

"Aye," Kinnon replied placidly. "'Twas why they moved to the farm."

The goldsmith seemed satisfied with Kinnon's response. "About three years ago, Lucienne eloped with Lord Depaul's eldest son. He was betrothed to a wealthy merchant's daughter, and the lord threatened to bring Lucienne up on charges of witchcraft." He snorted. "As if the young man hadn't excellent reason besides a love spell to choose Lucienne over the sour-faced woman more than a few years his elder. Nevertheless, until word came that they had married and planned to take up residence in Italy, I was hard-pressed to keep out of the magistrate's clutches, Lord Depaul was that angry."

"Loss of the wealthy heiress was a problem?" Kinnon queried.

"He has sworn to bring his son home and arrange an annulment. Seems the heiress wants a title."

Kinnon nodded. "What about Melisende?"

Ramon's gaze grew furtive. "Her trouble was with the army—for aiding a man who had deserted his post."

Kinnon locked his gaze on the goldsmith's. "I was that man."

The man's eyes grew large, frightened, and he glanced about the room. As before, only Kinnon and Rory were in attendance, and Rory took a step toward the door, crossing his arms over his chest as his bulk obliterated that exit. Ramon gulped.

"I did not betray her to the soldiers," he whispered.

Kinnon's ears caught the nuance of the phrase. "But she thought ye did, aye?"

The man nodded. "They threatened me, and I did not wish to land in prison. Then they promised me part of the reward for her capture. I was tempted."

"I hope ye dinnae believe ye would receive coin for yer efforts."

Ramon hung his head. "I lied to them to save myself."

"And Melisende?" Kinnon's blood began to boil.

"*Oui*. It saved her, too."

* * *

Kinnon patted his horse's neck and checked his manger to be sure it had an adequate amount of grain in it. "Greedy bastard. Ye have nearly licked the wood slick." The horse snorted his disregard for his master's concern and went back to cleaning the corners of the small box.

Kinnon turned to Rory, one stall away as he tended his steed. "I dinnae know where to go from here," he confided.

"Mayhap a stroll to the cathedral will help clear yer head," Rory mentioned.

The red, white and black mosaics gleamed in the late evening sun. Pilgrims seeking to be blessed before their journey to Santiago de Compostela clogged the streets, many hoping to obtain their blessing that evening in preparation for an early morning departure. Rory and Kinnon approached the cathedral from the west. The *Rue de Tables* was narrow, the half-timbered buildings overhanging the street. Stalls jammed the way, filled with trinkets and items for sale, snatched up at the last moment by eager pilgrims. Men and women alike, adorned with the scallop shell—the symbol of St. John—on their clothing and walking staffs, wound past the tables, some chattering excitedly about the journey ahead, others silent with equal parts of hope and despair reflected in their eyes.

Kinnon glanced at the carved wooden doors of the cathedral, still open at this hour. Reliefs showing the nativity and the passion caught the shadows and the last of the golden light, revealing their precious stories of life and death, beckoning to all who believe.

Rory turned to the street stretched below. "'Tis a wicked thing they do to these poor pilgrims. Paying an exorbitant price for a vial of the tears of St. John willnae protect them any better than a good walking stick and a bit of common sense."

"If desperate enough, they will purchase anything to alleviate their burden," Kinnon replied quietly.

"Do ye think to travel to Italy, then?" Rory asked.

"My own pilgrimage is to find Melisende. Yers may end at any time, with no harsh words between us."

"Nae," Rory replied comfortably. "I meant no criticism. I wondered if I should learn a wee bit of Latin, 'tis all."

Kinnon returned Rory's affable grin with a duck of his head. "I am sorry I seem touchy about Melisende's plight. There are so many questions, and I have come so far to have so few of them answered. Did she travel to Italy to meet with Lucienne? Has she left on foot? Alone?"

He turned abruptly on the stair and stepped into the heavy foot traffic, scarcely able to stir except in the direction of those around him. He hid a curse beneath his breath, mindful of the cathedral and the carved doors now looking down on him with disapproval.

Rory clapped a hand on his shoulder. "Dinnae worry. We will find yer Melisende. It should be easy to find a wee lass and her dog."

The seller of rosaries at the table next to them glanced up, a startled look on his face. "Did you ask about a woman and a dog?"

Kinnon eyed him curiously. "An English-speaking trinket seller in France. Truly a sacred miracle."

The man flushed. "I was once an English merchant who spent a goodly amount of time in Edinburgh. Your speech caught my ear as much as your words."

"And do rosaries sell better here on the steps of the cathedral than on the streets of Edinburgh?"

A grin split the man's face. "Aye. But the price of information you seek is more dear."

"If 'tis worthy, ye shall have yer price," Kinnon conceded.

The man leaned forward eagerly. "I remember the lass because of her great dog. He was very calm, but showed his teeth if anyone approached his mistress." He canted his head in remembrance. "They were quite large teeth and deterred several advances. It is not good for a woman to travel alone."

"What else do ye remember?" Kinnon prodded impatiently.

"I remember she asked about the *Chemin de St. Jacques*—the pilgrim's road to Santiago."

"Do ye think she travels with the pilgrims?" Kinnon's voice was urgent as he pried the last bit of information from the table merchant.

He gave Kinnon a smug smile. "I know she does. I saw her leave *Le Puy* six days ago, just after Matins, with a small group of pilgrims. She could be at the *Domerie d'Aubrac* by now."

CHAPTER TWENTY-THREE

Jean-Baptiste settled close to her side. Melisende lowered a hand to his head, seeking the dog's comforting contact. Fog had rolled in during the night and she could scarcely see more than a few feet around her and his touch brought reassurance. Hidden by the heavy mist, the group of nearly thirty pilgrims had all but vanished, leaving only the two women closest to her within her view. Fine droplets of water clung to everything. Even the glow of the fire was dimmed as it struggled to life in the saturated morning air.

Already weary though the day had hardly begun, Melisende reached inside her bag for rags to wrap about her feet. The cloth was dry, but the insides of her boots were damp from the mist and she knew the end of the day would see her feet blistered and sore.

"I thought the boots needed airing out," she confided to the dog, explaining why she had not simply slept with them on. He thumped his tail on the ground at the sound of her voice and she eyed his feet. "You need a break, too, *mon ami*. Your foot has not had a chance to heal since you slipped on the sharp rocks on that last pass. The *Domerie d'Aubrac* may be a good place for a day or two of rest for you as well."

Jean-Baptiste accepted a bit of bread from her bag, then returned to licking his wounded paw.

The heavy mists dulled the sounds around her nearly as effectively as drawing a curtain. The pilgrims huddled together in near silence, hoping to avoid the attention of bandits in the area, praying for the sun to pierce the fog and show them the way down off this accursed plateau. Melisende slipped behind a copse of trees to complete her morning routine. As she made her way carefully back to camp, doing her best to avoid stumbling over stones hidden by the mists swirling around her ankles, a strange rumbling noise caught her attention.

Jean-Baptiste lifted his nose, testing the air. The hair on his back rose and a low growl slipped from his chest. Melisende froze, her gaze quickly seeking shelter. The fog changed from dull gray to palest gold as the sun fought its way over the mountain tops. The rumbling sound increased.

Anxious cries echoed around the camp. "Bandits!"

Melisende wound her fingers about Jean-Baptiste's collar. "Would they be so bold?" she wondered. "Or would they have slipped in quietly and robbed us during the night?"

The fog thinned, but her view was still limited. In the distance the chime of a church bell could be heard.

"Maria!" someone called out, and the tone of the little camp changed. Pilgrims ceased their frantic movements and some even hugged each other, chattering excitedly. Curious, Melisende stepped forward.

"They are coming for us!" a woman cried, and yet her posture was of thankfulness, not fear.

The fog burst into flames of color as men on horseback entered the camp, the bold red, eight-pointed cross on their white mantles burning brightly in the morning sun. They wheeled their mounts to a stop in a great show of horsemanship. One knight called to the pilgrims.

"We have come to escort you to *Aubrac*. It is our sworn duty." The spokesman nodded at the group. "Gather your belongings and come with us. There are bandits in the area."

The bell continued to ring its slow, steady strokes. Following the sound and the scuffed path—one of many that cut across the plateau—the knights herded the pilgrims down the hill. The vast tableland stretched before them, enormous rocks looming suddenly out of the heavy mists. The pilgrims spread out, avoiding the boulders, and Melisende could understand how they could easily be lost in the fog were it not for their protectors who pushed the stragglers back into the group.

The bell continued to ring, the tone growing louder as the pilgrims approached the village, and Melisende turned into the sound.

"It is the bell of the lost," a masculine voice murmured.

Melisende looked over her shoulder to see a knight walking his horse beside her.

"She is known to us as *Maria*," he added.

"I heard a woman call the name," Melisende replied, "but thought she appealed to *Notre Dame*."

"The bell is rung to assist those lost in the fog and snow, and perhaps warn away bandits as well."

"I suppose knights do a better job of deterring bandits than the ringing bell," she observed.

"The bell is well-known to herald knights in the area," he agreed. "It is engraved: *"Jubile pour Dieu, Chante pour les clercs, Chasse les démons, Rappelle les égarés"*. --Jubilee for God, sing for the clercs, hunt the demons, recall the lost.

"A large job for such a tool." Melisende smiled. "It is good the church supplies additional help."

"As you say, my lady." The knight jostled his horse's reins, slowing his walk further. "The monks will take care of you at the *domerie*, but should you have need, I, Jean-Luc, would be pleased to be at your service."

Melisende patted the large dog beside her. "This is Jean-Baptiste. He is all the protection I need."

"I mean you no disrespect, and you likely will enjoy the rest provided at the *domerie*. Should you wish to walk the town or visit the market, however, I would be honored to provide you escort."

They continued on for a few moments in silence. Jean-Luc nodded his head to her and urged his horse forward. Melisende stopped.

"Melisende," she called after him. "My name is Melisende."

Jean-Luc paused, glancing back over his shoulder. Applying his heels to his horse's side, he cantered slowly through the gates of the town.

* * *

Melisende entered the *domerie*, Jean-Baptiste at her side. The monk receiving the pilgrims gave her a startled look.

"We do not house dogs here, *mademoiselle*."

"He is my companion and protector," Melisende replied.

Another monk hurried over, and the two murmured together for several moments. "You

110

will be safe here without the dog. He may stay in one of the barns."

Melisende gave a respectful nod, weaving on her feet as exhaustion drained her muscles. "I will take him elsewhere."

She turned and stumbled through the door and into the afternoon sunlight. Tears and the sudden brightness blinded her unexpectedly, and she drew up short. People surged around her as she blinked to clear her vision.

"Is anything wrong, *mademoiselle*?"

She jerked, recognizing the voice, and pivoted to the young knight behind her. "I must find a place for Jean-Baptiste," she said, not mentioning she would not be parted from the dog and planned to sleep wherever she found him space. "The monk mentioned a barn."

"The barns are emptying but quite filthy after housing cattle and other beasts over the long winter. They are now being moved to their grazing in the highlands for the summer." He waved a hand around them. "Do you see the crowds, the sheep and cattle?"

For the first time Melisende was aware of the noise around her. Cattle bellowed, and sheep added their high-pitched bleats to the chatter of the two-footed crowds. "I thought this was a market day, but had not noticed the numbers."

"'Tis almost like a festival," he agreed. "There are extra vendors in the market, jongleurs to entertain the travelers. However, there are pickpockets and other evil-doers as well. Might I accompany you?"

Melisende remained undecided. He seemed to be in good standing with his regiment, and the eight-pointed cross on his cloak promised chivalry. She glanced at the dog next to her. "I am at a loss to find a place for Jean-Baptiste. He has been with me since he was a puppy and there was no place to leave him when I left on pilgrimage. Could you suggest a safe spot?"

"I am ever at your service, *mademoiselle*." Jean-Luc bowed to her and the dog. "However did he acquire such a name?"

* * *

He has changed more than one man's religion. The memory of her first meeting with Kinnon softened her, eased a bit of the tiredness from the days on the harsh trail. She managed a small smile for Jean-Luc as he laughed at her tales of Jean-Baptiste.

"What brings you on pilgrimage?" he asked.

Melisende frowned, the past few days blurring together. What *had* been her incentive? Travel to Italy to find Lucienne had not appealed to her. Their parting had been unpleasant to say the least, and she had heard nothing from her in months, and as her circumstances seemed stretched to say the least, Melisende had been unsure of her welcome. It was equally certain that returning to the farm was a bad idea—especially since the soldiers remembered and actively sought her.

But where to go? The night she and Jean-Baptiste had left her uncle's home, sounds of soft chanting had led her to the cathedral. A chance encounter with a pilgrim praying on the steps had given her a new purpose.

"I was accused of aiding an escaped prisoner, but that was not true. He had come to see to my and my sister's safety, for he knew the town would be dangerous as the exchange of power took place. There was no desertion, no treason as was accused. But the acting commander was a man of evil ambitions and considered Kinnon a threat to his goals and so trumped up the charges. When I left *Le Puy* almost a sennight ago, I knew there was still a warrant against me, and returning to our farm was not possible."

Jean-Luc leaned comfortably against the corner of the small shop where he'd insisted on purchasing meat pasties for them to eat. Melisende sat on a small, rough-hewn bench, Jean-Baptiste tucked at her feet.

"What happened to this man?"

Melisende took a deep breath against the sharp pain of loss. "I do not know. 'Twas rumored they held a man in the tower prison at *Châteauneuf* who had committed treason. Very little was said, and I pray it was him and he was eventually ransomed." She lifted her gaze, eyes round with worry. "I know for a fact he was beaten. I hope he was not killed."

"He has a special place in your heart, mademoiselle?" Jean-Luc's question was casual, but his tone betrayed his interest.

"My heart has much to atone for, *chevalier*. Mayhap I can find it at the shrine of St. Jacques."

"'Tis a noble effort. But an indulgence for your sins can be sought at any church along the way. The travel to Santiago de Compostela is long and arduous. And dangerous for a woman alone."

"I must go where I am led. As long as Jean-Baptiste is with me, I will not worry."

Jean-Luc shifted abruptly. "Let me see to his feet. Both of you appear to be tender, unused to the sharp rocks and travel."

He knelt beside the dog who eyed him cautiously as the knight inspected his feet.

"'Tis as I thought. He, at least, needs a couple days' rest and good food." He looked up at Melisende. "As, I suspect, do you." He rose, dusting his hands on his breeches. "Come. I will return you to the *domerie* and the dog will sleep with my horse. I can promise you no greater safety for either of you." He grinned. "*Courageuse* has his own stable lad, and he will be happy to care for the dog tonight as well."

Melisende opened her mouth to protest, but startled at the low growl from Jean-Baptiste at her side. Jean-Luc, his arms open to her, gave her a wry look, his movements checked. "I do not think your protector wishes me to offer you a ride."

Traveling back to the *domerie*—or anywhere—without having to walk was a gift Melisende was loathe to turn away. She placed a quieting hand on the dog's head and offered Jean-Luc an apologetic smile. "He has always been so."

Accepting the knight's help, she grasped the horse's black mane as settled in the saddle as bold muscles rippled beneath the dark red hide. The horse lifted his enormous feet and placed them carefully on the cobbled street, rocking Melisende gently in the saddle. They reached the *domerie* and Jean-Luc slid Melisende to the ground, stepping away before she could remark his closeness.

"Sleep well. The monks are well-used to caring for travelers. I have duty in the morning, but would beg your company for the afternoon. I will bring Jean-Baptiste with me."

Melisende frowned, uncertain how he would entice the dog to part from her. But the big dog's head hung wearily and he only whined briefly as Jean-Luc led him away. He cast a bewildered look over his shoulder before settling beside the tall knight, and they were quickly lost amid the foot traffic.

With unease in her heart, Melisende entered the *domerie* where a monk motioned her to an empty chair. She sat and he removed her boots, placing her feet in a shallow basin of water. Closing her eyes at the heavenly feel of hands washing her worn feet, she waited patiently for the ritual to end. He patted her feet dry and gave her a fresh piece of linen, pointing her to the area where women were allowed to refresh themselves.

She smelled the lingering odor of the smoke and the meal past, and collected a mug of watered ale as she made her way to an empty cot.

* * *

The horses blew tiredly, steam rising from their bodies as the men stripped their saddles away. Kinnon glanced around the area they'd chosen for their camp. He and his men had doubled the size of the group of pilgrims who'd left *Le Puy* that morning, but they seemed grateful for the protection the soldiers provided.

Rory squinted into the distance as the sun framed the mountains in the last of its fiery glow. "'Tis wilder land ahead. The hills arenae so verra tall, but they are verra steep." He glanced at the horses. "They will sleep well tonight."

"As will I," Kinnon noted. "We will set a four-man watch against robbers and beasts, taking it in 2-hour shifts. That shouldnae be taxing and will allow the men a night's rest."

"I will arrange it," Rory said as he turned to the Scotsmen.

A slender man in a white robe, the scallop shell emblem of those who followed the path of St. John embroidered on the left breast, approached Kinnon. Rory sent a questioning look over his shoulder, but Kinnon waved away his concern.

"We are thankful for your protection," the older man said, coming to stand next to Kinnon.

"We will travel with ye as the terrain allows," Kinnon told him. "'Tis slow going now, but we are in a hurry. Once the land levels out, we may move ahead of ye."

"I have traveled this route before. There are dense forests and steep mountains to travel. Once we reach the *Auvergne*, we will face three or four days' travel up and down sharp cliffs and deep valleys. It will be slow going for us and your horses."

"My men and I are used to difficult mountains, but these horses werenae bred for it, I am afraid. We will be careful."

The man nodded. "You do not wish a horse to strain a leg—or worse," he agreed. "Our path will then take us through more forests and fields, as well as pastures and small villages. I would ask you to remain with us through the *Aubrac*. The land there is very wild and rife with bandits—a fearsome place to defenseless pilgrims. Once we reach the plateaus near the village, the Hospitaller knights will provide protection. In the village is a travelers' *domerie*, built by a Flemish nobleman who narrowly escaped death here more than two hundred years ago. It is a good place to rest and restore your focus."

Kinnon considered the man's request then nodded. "I can promise you our protection to *Aubrac*. After that, our paths will likely part."

"Do not mistake me. Villages cling to the sides of steep ravines and travel will not be faster once we depart *Aubrac*. But after the mountains of *Aveyron* there will be plateaus and rolling hills. There, you will find it much smoother going."

"I thank ye, sir, for yer information. We will do well to stick together while we may."

Seeming satisfied with Kinnon's response, the man bowed his head and ambled to the small campfire one of the pilgrims had lit. People clustered around it for the cooking space and for the warmth, as the lowering sun ushered in a cold night.

Kinnon ate a meat pie, bought earlier that day at the market and heated briefly on the Scotsmen's own fire. Too weary to engage in the customary post-supper tales, he rolled himself in his plaide and, facing into the darkness, he plunged instantly into sleep.

They broke camp early the next morning and walked the horses until they were limbered up, then mounted and continued along the trail. Kinnon chaffed at the slow pace, but remembered the pilgrim's words and did not attempt to push faster. They traveled up mountainsides and across icy waterways full of melted snow. All around them was the vast forest until at last they reached a rocky knob overlooking the river *Allier*.

They rested that night in a tiny chapel beneath a statue of St. James. The air blew thin and cold and Kinnon worried about Melisende.

Did the relic merchant tell the truth? Is she ahead on the pilgrim trail? Did she arrive in Aubrac safely? He imagined her adrift, alone, no family and no place to call home. His heart turned grim to think of her fearful, judging every step to ensure Herve's legacy did not follow her.

I will find ye, Melisende. I will do everything within my power to bring joy to the rest of yer days. Dinnae give up, lass. Dinnae give up.

CHAPTER TWENTY-FOUR

The morning tolling of the bell faded. Melisende stared after the departing pilgrims as they set out on the next lap of their journey to Santiago de Compostela. On their heels was a small herd of dark-eyed cattle, their dun hides stretched loosely across jutting hips after their winter in the barns at *Aubrac*. They hurried away, udders swaying pendulously, eager for the tender new grass.

"There will be other groups of pilgrims if you wish to join later." Jean-Luc reassured her. He smiled. "There are *always* pilgrims on the trail."

Melisende turned from the gate. "I know. But there is something about seeing people who have become familiar leave without you." She ruffled Jean-Baptiste's ears. "Your care comes first, *mon ami*," she told the dog. "I will not have you pretending to be sound just to keep up."

She glanced at Jean-Luc. "Thank you for caring for him. I knew when he injured his foot, but it was not until we reached *Aubrac* that he was able to get the care he needed."

"I feel certain he will be able to travel in another day or two." The knight's dark eyes sought hers. "The question is, do you still wish to?"

Heat spread through her as she caught his warm regard. "You have been very attentive to me, *monsieur*—Jean-Luc," she amended as he had begged her over the past two days. "I set out from *Le Puy* with the thought that my life could start anew once I was far enough away to be safe from the soldiers there, and once I came to terms with how my sweet sister could say and do such things." She shrugged, the bitter edge of betrayal souring the years of sheltering Lucienne from harm.

"And yet, along the way, you met me." Jean-Luc nudged her softly, his words prodding a response she wasn't sure she was ready to give.

"You do not know me," she told him. "Since I left *Le Puy* I have become more guarded, less trusting."

"You trust me, do you not?" he pointed out.

"*Oui*, but I am normally bold, self-reliant—and occasionally impertinent," she admitted with a ghost of a smile.

Jean-Luc indicated a stroll about the village with a courteous sweep of his hand. "I would imagine you are in a position in which being self-sufficient is often forced upon you. As for being bold, it is unwise for a young woman such as yourself, traveling alone—albeit with your fierce four-footed protector—to be noticed." He laughed. "I would, however, enjoy seeing your impertinent side."

Some of her melancholy slipped away and Melisende joined his infectious humor. He caught her hand and brought it to his lips, lightly brushing them across her knuckles.

"You must know how I feel about you by now. You captured my heart the moment I saw you emerging from the mists, like a goddess stepping to earth. I wondered then what a poor, earth-bound mortal such as I could possibly offer that would cause you to notice me."

Melisende laughed aloud, feeling more carefree than she could remember in a very long time. "You have given me much, Jean-Luc. I am eternally grateful."

His eyes turned thoughtful and he pulled her aside to a sausage vendor's stall. "Let us break our fast and discuss our plans for the day."

Melisende tilted her head in surprise. "You have all day free?"

His smile was superior, almost secretive. "I have taken the day to woo a beautiful woman."

Melisende nodded, abuzz with happiness. *I have missed the company, the banter of a relationship with someone my own age. I have been too responsible for too long, and missed out on much trying to be a parent to Lucienne.* The easy companionship she had enjoyed with Kinnon came back to her. She slid a look at the tall knight from the corner of her eyes. His stance was full of confidence and a hint of danger, clear warning to all, even without the bold white cross on his black tunic, that he was a man to be reckoned with. And yet, he had shown nothing but kindness to her and Jean-Baptiste. *Even the dog accepts him.* She glanced at Jean-Baptiste fondly.

Thoughts of Kinnon returned, for Jean-Baptiste had accepted—even loved—him as well. The two men were similar, yet different. They both held the self-assurance of a warrior, but she estimated Jean-Luc's blond head would top Kinnon's dark locks by a couple of inches, though Kinnon's broad shoulders had boasted a raw strength Jean-Luc's lighter frame would never have.

Jean-Luc's remark of seeing her in the fog flattered her. A smile crossed her lips to remember Kinnon's attempts to tell her how he felt about her. *I like the way yer hair is neither black nor brown, and how yer eyes pierce my heart—and see my lack of words to tell ye how much I admire ye.*

Had he only admired her? Would it have become more had the war not separated them? *I loved you, Kinnon. I could not admit it, for I did not want my heart to mourn you so much when you left. But you touched me as no one else ever has. Your gentleness, your humor, your love of life. You were so passionate about the wrongs against others, especially against those who could not protect themselves. I longed every day to hear your voice, to talk with you, to soak in your presence. I admit that is now past, but I will not forget.*

She considered Jean-Luc as he accepted the sausages tucked inside fresh baguettes from the vendor with a nod. *I enjoy being with Jean-Luc. I feel protected, cared for. He is kind, but there is a hard core in him that will never be truly gentle. As a knight, it is his sworn duty to be gracious to all—but is it his nature?*

She noted the appreciative glances from the women around them as they admired Jean-Luc, how they preened as he inclined his head in their direction. *Am I jealous? Do I feel superior to have caught his eye? He is courteous to them—do I stake my heart on his fidelity?*

Do I wish to be protected? With Kinnon, I felt his equal. It would be difficult—mayhap impossible—to reach equality in Jean-Luc's world of warfare. It is his life. One I would likely accept, but never enter.

"There appears to be much going on inside that lovely head of yours," Jean-Luc drawled, giving her a patronizing smile. "Here is a bench in the shade. Sit, eat, and tell me what more I can offer you."

* * *

The fog was a fragile thing, drifting in and out of the trees like a seductive ghost, chased by a dawn breeze. Early morning sun gleamed grey and cold, and the camp was already stirring. The sound of hooves on the packed earth prodded Kinnon to battle stance.

A white banner with a red cross appeared out of the mist, snapping against the wind. Thirty men rode abreast, their mantles marked with the same cross. The visors on their helmets were up as they assessed the pilgrims. They slid to a stop, alert to the mounted Scotsmen.

One knight rose in his stirrups, addressing them. "We are sworn to protect the pilgrims along this trail. Speak of your intentions."

Kinnon sent his horse two steps forward, acknowledging himself as their leader. "We have traveled with them since *Le Puy*. We will serve them as long as our paths lie together."

The knight settled in his saddle and conversed briefly with those at his side. He turned to Kinnon. "You and your men are welcome to join us. The pilgrims are our responsibility until they leave *Aubrac*."

Kinnon glanced at the men arrayed behind him. "Well then, lads. Welcome to *Aubrac*."

They rode to one side of the knights across the high plains, passing herds of tan, dark-eyed cattle on their way to summer pasture, with bored lads pacing along behind. Ahead, the town of *Aubrac* appeared, its walls circling protectively.

The commander pulled his horse alongside Kinnon. "The *domerie* is just ahead. The large building there." He nodded to a structure with a square bell tower, surrounded by a nave reinforced with sturdy arches. "You are welcome to stable your horses with ours." He directed Kinnon's gaze to a large, white-walled barn nearby. "And it would be an honor to house you and your men for the duration of your visit as well."

Kinnon started to decline, wishing to forego the welcome in order to more quickly question the monks at the *domerie*, to discover if Melisende had indeed passed through here. But he realized the number of his men would likely stretch the hospitality of the monks, and reluctantly acquiesced to the knight's offer.

They parted from the pilgrims and turned toward the stables. Young lads hurried from the building, each to a different knight and his mount. A few others hustled to claim the new horses, looking at them in awe as their gazes darted from the kilted Scots to the meticulously garbed knights.

"Doesnae appear as if they've ever seen a Scotsman before," Rory muttered to Hamish as a lad sent him a startled look before taking his horse away.

"'Tis the bloody uniform they wear. White and red without a speck of dust. And that eight-pointed star on every one of them."

"'Tis the Maltese Cross," Kinnon informed them. "These are Hospitaller knights. The four arms of the cross represent the four Cardinal virtues of prudence, justice, fortitude, and temperance. The eight points are reminders of the oaths they have sworn, though I dinnae remember them."

"They are to have spiritual joy, to weep over our sins, love justice, and be sincere and pure of heart," the commander supplied as he approached their group. "To live without malice and humble ourselves to those who would cause us injury. To be merciful and be willing to suffer persecution." He smiled broadly, and Kinnon was relieved to see he did not appear offended by Kinnon's lack of knowledge.

He doffed his helmet. "No offense intended, but how is it a Scotsman knows of Hospitaller knights and our creed?"

"None taken. I served for a time in Bertran's army. I saw men of many different creeds on my travels and there was always much opportunity to learn if ye wished it."

"All of France mourned Bertran's passing." The knight paused, a moment of respect for the memory of the man, then turned to his current purpose. "I am Josse D'Aramitz, commander of this tongue of Hospitaller Knights. It is our duty to protect those on pilgrimage, and the hills swarm with bandits."

"I am Kinnon Macrory, of clan Macrory. This is my captain, Rory, with nineteen trusted soldiers. Your men are much appreciated," Kinnon remarked. "One man who had made this pilgrimage more than once mentioned your help to me."

Josse accepted the compliment with a single nod. "Come this way. I will show you to your quarters. You may purchase food in the market or join us as we break our fast. We do not eat before we leave to our morning duty."

"I would leave Hamish to settle the men," Kinnon rejoined, "but I have a personal errand here and wish to see to it immediately."

D'Aramitz's eyebrows rose. "Ah, the *raison* your path may part from the pilgrims's?"

"Aye." Kinnon decided to trust the knight. "I seek a young woman who was unjustly accused of a crime and forced from her home a week or more ago. I had hoped she would find safety, but I seem to be always a few days too late to help."

"A Scotswoman?" the knight asked.

"Nae, French. Her sister saved my life after I was wounded at the siege of *Châteauneuf de Randon*, but the woman I seek was charged after her dog attacked the soldiers who were sent to retrieve me."

The knight turned a quizzical look on Kinnon. "A large dog? One that is her *protecteur*?"

Exitement raced through Kinnon's veins. "Ye know her?"

D'Aramitz shook his head. "Myself, *non*. But one of my knights has a large dog he is tending in the stables for an injury. He says the brute's owner is a beautiful young woman from *Le Puy*."

* * *

Melisende tensed. "I do not know what other kindness you could offer a pilgrim such as myself, *chevalier*," she murmured carefully.

Jean-Luc closed her hand around one of the baguettes and she bit off a small morsel. He finished his own in three large bites and brushed the crumbs from his hands. "I have more than a simple attraction to you and I believe, though you have lapsed back into formality, some attraction exists for me on your part as well, *n'est-ce pas vrai?*"

"I am grateful to you and I enjoy what time we have spent together," she allowed. "Are you insinuating there could be more between us?"

Jean-Luc gave her an amused look. "Have I not said so? I have paid you many compliments—some to lift your spirits—but all because I sincerely meant them."

"Even that I looked like a goddess descending to earth the morning you first saw me?" Melisende could not suppress a grin.

He chucked her beneath her chin. "Especially that one."

She shook her head, her eyes crinkled with amusement. "Then, you should examine either you eyesight or your standards, for I am assuredly no goddess."

Jean-Luc leaned closer, his gaze on her lips. "You are beautiful, Melisende—by any man's standards."

He brushed his lips against hers and she startled. No man had ever been so bold or attempted such a liberty. He immediately drew back, giving her breathing space, but kept his seat on the bench next to her.

"To alarm you is the last thing I wish." He spoke softly, for her ears only. "Whatever you are willing to give—I will not ask you to go beyond what you desire. I can be a patient man, *ma cherie*. You have my heart—and my word."

Melisende set her baguette aside as a sudden chill ran through her. "If your promise is for a short intimacy, *chevalier*," she said, stressing the last word to remind him of his sworn oaths, "then rest assured your patience may be transferred to a woman more suited to your tastes, with no animosity from myself."

Jean-Luc leaned his shoulder casually against the rock wall behind the bench. "I am sure I could change your mind and your hesitancy if you would but remain in *Aubrac* a bit longer."

Melisende rose to her feet in a fluid, angry movement, sweeping her skirt away from contact with the knight. "I am certain you could not. Jean-Baptiste and I—"

The dog surged to his feet, a mighty bark cutting through Melisende's words. She glanced down at him, afraid he was about to launch himself at Jean-Luc, aware what the massive jaws could accomplish on human flesh. To her surprise, Jean-Baptiste did not face the knight, but the crowd on the street. His tail wagged, slowly at first, then faster as he apparently recognized someone in the dense throng of passers-by.

She grasped his collar and he stepped onto the street. The crowd parted around them as people registered the dog's excitement. "*Mauvais chien*," someone mutter darkly.

Jean-Baptiste leapt forward, all but dragging her as she lurched after him. She tripped through a muddy patch of uncobbled street and she lost her grip on his wide leather collar. Barking happily, the dog disappeared into the mass of people. Melisende stretched up on her toes, trying to search above the heads of those around her.

And found herself face-to-face with the one man she thought she'd never see again.

CHAPTER TWENTY-FIVE

The dog bounded out of the crowd, straight for him. Kinnon raised his arm *en guarde* before his chest in an unconscious response as the beast launched himself into the air. People cried out, stumbling over each other to get away as the dog's apparent attack was met with the harsh whisper of steel leaving its sheath. Kinnon recognized Jean-Baptiste a split second before he was spitted on Rory's and Josse's swords.

"No!" he shouted. Stepping quickly forward, he grasped the dog, hands full of furry muscle on either side of the beast's neck, and pulled him close, shielding him from the men's offensive guard. Jean-Baptiste whined, whipping his body around and around, ears creased against his head as he danced his greeting at Kinnon's feet.

"Is this *le chein*?" Josse asked, his sword still in hand as he eyed the massive beast.

"Aye," Kinnon replied happily. And if Jean-Baptiste was *here*, that meant Melisende was . . . *There—*

She stood before him, eyes wide with shock, face drained of color, the hem of her skirt spattered with mud. She stared at him, mouth partly open, and Kinnon had to smile.

"Still siccing yer dog on soldiers, Melisende?" he teased.

She drew in a sudden breath and Kinnon was gratified to see her relax, happiness blooming across her face. He pushed Jean-Baptiste aside and closed the distance between them. He had imagined their meeting dozens of times, and he half-waited for her to fling herself into his arms as he wanted her to. But he hadn't counted on the look of wary hunger in her eyes, or for her arms to remain at her sides, her feet rooted in place.

Something has happened. She doesnae trust me. He mocked himself. *Would ye trust someone who waited nearly four years to come back to ye?* He stepped close and gently kissed her forehead. She tasted of sunshine and fresh air, and he longed to explore her further. But this was neither the time nor place. And he was painfully unsure if she would welcome the intimacy.

Mayhap my place is to see her settled, independent, content. She deserves to have the desires of her heart—not merely accept what I want her to have. He considered this only briefly. *Nae. She will come back to Scotland with me. Whatever the penance, I will do it, but then she will be my wife and I will see she never regrets her decision.*

Unable to part from her, he caught her hand as he gave her space. Her face was now flushed, her eyes sparkling. Her fingers laced with his and he felt a thrill of pleasure.

"You took your time coming back, *monsieur*." Her clear blue eyes were wide, solemn.

Kinnon's grin widened. "My timing hasnae always been my own these past years. Though I do admit to leaving France before my tasks were completed."

"Tasks?" she questioned, drawling the word out as though it tasted unpleasant.

Kinnon grimaced. "Nae, finding ye isnae a task. Blame my poor tongue for not finding a better way to express it." He silently begged her forgiveness as he drank in the details of her face. "And the fact I've been chasing after ye for months. The suddenness of finding ye is overwhelming."

"Does this man have permission to speak with you, Melisende?" An arrogant, hostile voice interrupted their reunion.

She jumped, clearly startled, flinging an apologetic look at Kinnon before facing the man at her shoulder. "This is an old friend, Jean-Luc," she murmured. "I am fine."

Old friend. The words stung. Perhaps there was more to the reticence in her greeting than just their years apart. Kinnon's stare bored into the dark eyes of the Frenchman, a knight by the sight of his black tunic with white Maltese cross on the shoulder. A Hospitaller. The man Josse said cared for Jean-Baptiste. Kinnon instantly hated him.

He turned a soft look on Melisende. "Mayhap we could step out of the busy market and ye could introduce us?" *I can be civil, but `twill take all my willpower. He cannae have known her for more than two days—three at the most. Beyond care for the dog, what claim does he have on her?*

The commander stepped forward. "I will make the introductions. Kinnon, this is Sir Jean-Luc Villeneuve, a knight of good standing with the Hospitallers. He was part of the group that brought this young woman and the pilgrims she traveled with to *Aubrac* three mornings ago."

He turned to the knight. "Jean-Luc, Kinnon and his men are under Hospitaller protection as long as they are in *Aubrac*. He has traveled quite a distance to assure this woman's safety from those who wronged her in *Le Puy*."

Jean-Luc scowled, but quickly hid his annoyance in his commander's presence. He nodded to D'Aramitz, then to Kinnon. "I thank you for your offer of assistance. However, Melisende is quite immune to harm as long as she remains in my protection."

Remains? Kinnon fumed. The Melisende he knew would not sacrifice herself for fleeting protection. She would have gutted any man who propositioned her in such a manner—had she indeed lost everything because of him?

The weight of guilt settled over him like a familiar cloak. Had he not returned to the farm that day, she and Lucienne might have lived there unnoticed by the soldiers, at least for a time. And if they'd had to seek shelter with the butcher or even her reluctant uncle, she would not have had a warrant hanging over her head. The possibility of returning to the farm would have remained open to her, and he would not have found her wandering so far from home.

To his surprise, she tightened her grip on his hand as she tipped her gaze to his. "I would like to speak with you in private if you will allow it."

He nodded to Jean-Luc, trying to keep the challenging tilt from his chin, and failing. "I will see no harm comes to her."

There were no answering words from the knight, but his face darkened and his eyes flashed dangerously. His commander clapped his hand to the knight's shoulder, gesturing that he follow him. The two men retreated through the market crowd which had settled once it was clear the dog was not about to tear Kinnon limb from limb.

Melisende led him through the town gates, Rory keeping pace a discrete distance behind. Jean-Baptiste strolled beside them, tongue lolling to the side. A large tree loomed nearby, solitary and enough distance away to dilute the busy village sounds.

She halted in the shade of the tree's spreading branches and released Kinnon's hand, turning to stare at the land rolling away from the village—the plateau, the dense forests beyond sheltering rivers and steep mountain trails. Everywhere, wild flowers bloomed—albeit a bit sparse along the trail where the cattle made their way to summer pasture.

Sunlight pierced the leaves overhead, catching bits of gold and amber in her dark hair. Kinnon was mesmerized. The pull he'd felt toward her before was back a hundredfold. The knowledge that he could be reassigned—or killed—at any time, had made him cautious whilst attached to Bertran's army. And the uncertainty of taking a French wife back to Scotland where his position all but required he marry a Scotswoman who would bring alliance, money and power to his clan, had kept him from admitting to himself how attracted he was to her.

And now she was under the protection of a Hospitaller knight, on pilgrimage to Santiago de Compostela once she ended her relationship with Jean-Luc. Kinnon clenched his fists then relaxed with a sigh.

"Please accept my most sincere apologies, Melisende, for whatever harm yer association with me has brought ye. 'Twas never my intention to abandon ye, nor see ye forced to flee yer home."

Her back still to him, her words drifted to him over her shoulder on the light breeze. "You did not abandon us. We were in danger already, though we were not yet aware of it." She paused then explained. "Had you not come to us, we may have been able to remain at the farm for another few days, but bandits quickly flooded the area, eager to get whatever crumbs fell from De Ros's table after he abandoned the town. Bertran's death left the struggle for power uncertain, though the *Marechal* de Sancerre did his best to keep order in the town and countryside."

Kinnon shook his head. "I have sought ye for months. There was always another trail to someplace else. I had wanted ye to be safe, not hunted."

She still did not turn to him, and though Kinnon admired the strong curve of her spine and the tumble of night-dark hair down her back, he longed to see her face, to get a glimpse of what she thought.

"Will ye not face me?" he asked. For a moment he was not certain she'd heard him, then she spun about, flinging herself into his arms. Taken off guard, he wrapped his arms about her and buried his face in her hair. He felt her body shake, and he was undone.

She finally drew back a bit, but did not break the circle of his arms. Her clear blue eyes, sparkling with tears, pierced his heart. "You are real, are you not? I am not dreaming?"

"Do ye dream so much of me, ye cannae tell the difference?" he teased.

It earned him a gentle clout to his shoulder, but her fingers lingered, and he relished the contact.

"*Oui*," she said softly. "You have been often in my dreams. But they were bittersweet for I thought I would never see you again. It has been a long time."

One side of his mouth twisted wryly. "I was verra anxious to leave France by the time I escaped the tower prison. I will sometime tell you of it."

"Not now?"

"Only if ye wish, but I would rather speak of you and me."

Her eyebrows rose. "Us? You have found me and I am safe—what more is there?"

Kinnon struggled with the wariness in her eyes. "I wish to do more than assure myself of yer well-being. I wish to bring ye joy and a lifetime of comfort." He changed the last word at the final possible moment. 'Love' he wanted to say. *I want to bring ye a lifetime of love.* But her uncertainty stopped him.

To his relief, she smiled, warming his heart.

They drank in the sight of one another for long minutes, as though parched by their long time apart. Melisende's heart swelled with the joy of being with him again. Kinnon motioned for her to make herself comfortable. His hands were as sturdy as she remembered, strong, gentle, capable. Her entire body felt light, carefree. As simple as it seemed, his very presence chased her worries away.

"Mayhap I should tell ye a bit of what happened after that day." he said.

"Trading information for absolution?" she asked archly.

"If `tis in yer heart to grant it, aye." He leaned toward her, hesitated, then eased back. "I want ye to at least know why I was away so long."

Melisende studied his face, eager for a closer look inside his heart. *Did he seek me out for purely chivalric reasons?* Her mind slid to Jean-Luc's thinly-veiled proposition. *The knight offered safety at the cost of my self-esteem. I cannot believe it of Kinnon. I will not.*

She leaned against the broad trunk of the tree. Kinnon's brow wrinkled.

"I dinnae wish to bore ye with details . . ."

She laughed. "I am so happy to see you, I will gladly listen to you tell me of the number of times you thought of me these past years," she teased him.

His brow leapt upward. "Truly? Ye wish to hear of all the times I wished I'd never left France—because of ye?"

Melisende's chest tightened. "`Twas poor of me to jest. I do not believe for a moment you wished to remain in France."

Kinnon tilted his head. "`Twould be two separate things. By the time I was released from prison, I couldnae see the shores of France behind me soon enough. I was in verra poor health, and angry with Herve and God. In that order."

"I can understand being angry with Herve, but with God?" She was puzzled. Though they had not discussed their personal beliefs, Kinnon had not voiced dissatisfaction with his religion before.

"Herve willingly sent me to a prison where he knew I wouldnae survive." Kinnon scowled. "No one sought to care for my wounds, and my ribs were broken by Herve's louts, giving me a chest ailment that left me frail and near death. I still do not tolerate vigorous activity well, and my leg will never allow me to be a warrior again. But I finally look and feel more like myself and less a scarecrow."

"Did God not heal you?"

"God and the good brothers at the monastery at Iona, an island not too far distant from my home in Scotland. During my time in prison, I felt God had abandoned me. I had not been able to save ye and Lucienne—indeed, I led the soldiers to yer doorstep—and I felt no punishment was too severe for me."

She tried to interrupt, but he touched her cheek, silencing her as his fingertips caressed her skin. He tucked a lock of her hair behind an ear as a smile played about his lips. Self-conscious, she smoothed the strands away from her face.

"It went against all I'd been taught was decent to think the soldiers who had ravaged yer country still roamed the land freely, taking advantage of the innocents and looting at will, whilst I rotted away in a dark, rodent-infested tower room. I am no saint, but where was the justice in allowing this?"

Kinnon rose and stepped a pace away, seeming agitated, and Melisende could only wait, helpless, as he fought his inner demons. "I concluded I had much to atone for, and resolved to spend whatever time I had left in pursuit of leniency, searching for a glimpse of God's grace."

"And did you find it?" she asked softly.

He halted abruptly and faced her, a ghost of a smile on his face. "I found a meddlesome monk who rarely left me time to feel sorry for myself."

Good for him, she thought fiercely. *The long, lonely, and likely terrifying days in prison were enough time to feed your despair.*

"What made you decide to return to France?" she asked.

"Brother Padraig told me that even in times of great turmoil, to think on things of great beauty and I would find peace."

"And did you?" she asked.

"Aye. I thought of ye." His eyes bored into hers, pleading for forgiveness, begging she believe him.

She couldn't stop the smile that tilted her lips. "I think I like your Frère Padraig."

"He was right. Even in the midst of a war that showed me how far men could stray from God and their sworn path, ye brought beauty and peace into my life. Melisende, I have always admired ye. Always found myself a better man for being with ye. I dinnae know what yer place is with Jean-Luc, but I would take ye far from here and explore the two of us without the distractions of war and those who wish to change us."

Caution rose in her. "What precisely are you offering?"

"I am a poor choice for a husband, but `tis all I can offer. We could have a home near my clan, though I turned the lairdship over to my sister's husband when I first returned to Scotland. I dinnae wish to rule, only to serve. Ye first, then wherever I am needed."

Her heart fluttered, so startled by his words. She leapt at accepting his proposal, but her tongue could not speak the words. Kinnon's eyes clouded and she was aware her hesitance stung him. She gave him an encouraging smile and took a breath, the words now whispering all that was in her heart. "You are what I dreamed of when I felt lonely and despaired. Thoughts of you filled the sad corners of my heart and kept me smiling even when I could not see through my tears. But this is all rather sudden. I have so much to atone for. How can I abandon my quest and change my life so completely? There are things I must understand. Only then can I know where I belong."

"I would stay in France with ye as long as ye need," he told her. "Though my memories here—other than ye—arenae fond ones. Making new ones with ye could be a start."

"I thank you, Kinnon. Let me first say that whilst Jean-Luc was prepared to offer me his protection for whatever favors I was willing to give in return, we have only been friends. I've seen much of him these past two days because Jean-Baptiste injured his foot several days ago and needed more healing than I could provide."

Kinnon stared at her and she could not say if his eyes held relief for her or himself. "I believe ye. As a knight he has enough honor to not force ye, though as a man he would have done his best to convince ye to bend to his will." He pulled her to her feet. "Ye are a beautiful woman, Melisende. So beautiful."

He took her hands in his, running his thumbs across the backs of her hands. "I dinnae wish to push ye into this. I understand we should take time to know each other better. Tell me of yer plans. What did ye wish to accomplish by coming on pilgrimage?"

Unease washed over her. "If you spoke with my *oncle*, you know of Lucienne."

"I heard his story, aye. I would now hear yers."

Dismayed with how uncontrollable her sister had become, Melisende made the story brief. "She challenged me whenever possible, but her open flirtations with the men who came to the shop caused unwelcome gossip. I became reluctant to take her with me into the market, and equally reluctant to leave her alone at the shop. But *mon oncle* was away on a trip to Paris and I had no choice."

124

She tried to slip her fingers from his, but he firmed his grip and gave her an understanding look. She took courage from it and continued. "I found her talking intimately with a customer, *en dishabille*, the day she disappeared. She and the young man eloped that day. I am told they settled in Italy." She hesitated to mention Lucienne's daughter. She could still envision the words of Lucienne's letter, telling her she'd convinced Raul the child was premature, and the lingering hurt of Lucienne telling her Kinnon had preferred her over Melisende—she refused to put the two together, to believe Kinnon had fathered Lucienne's babe. Or should he know?

Kinnon placed her palms together, holding her hands in the warmth of his. "I know this weighs heavily on ye, but 'twas not yer fault, Melisende. I see nothing in ye that tells me ye wished her to be anything but sweet and kind and wholesome—like yerself."

The hurt she'd held inside for so long burst forth. "She told me you and she—that you preferred her to me. That you loved her."

He blinked at her in surprise, then his face reddened. "Yer sister was a beautiful lass, and that is the only way I saw her. I loved her for yer sake, but *liking* yer sister was a difficult job."

"Can you please explain that to me?"

"Aye. When I woke in yer house, I was covered with a sheet, but disrobed. Lucienne had taken great pains to sew my wound, but apparently she'd also taken an interest in things she shouldnae. From the verra start, she was a confusing mixture of kindness and seductress, and it was difficult to know which she was from one moment to the next. She tended my wound—saving my life—and taught me to milk the cow. And she invited me more than once into her bed."

Melisende closed her eyes, avoiding Kinnon's gaze. But the image of him wrapped in Lucienne's blonde curls and slender limbs forced her eyes immediately open again. He watched her patiently.

"I dinnae accept. I did, however, scold her for being so forward. When I came back to yer farm, she treated me as her favorite brother—at least 'tis how I saw it."

Memories of Lucienne's squeal of happiness when Kinnon arrived rose to the surface. She was too happy, too excited. *She wished for more from Kinnon than he was willing to give—I see that now.*

"She is very beautiful and men often gawked at her in town," she murmured.

Kinnon nodded. "Aye. But inside that beautiful head, she is confused. When she was abducted years ago, everyone around her was horrified, telling her a 'bad thing' had been averted. She likely accepted that as a child, but as she became a young woman, she was torn between her feelings for this 'bad thing' and normal curiosity."

"Why did she not ask me?" Melisende asked, feelings of failure rolling over her.

"Did she not?" he asked, curious.

Melisende frowned, searching her memory. She sighed. "I once thought to speak with her, but the war interfered and I became too busy. She seemed a troubled child who needed to be protected, not a young woman trying to make sense of herself. It quite surprised me to see her grow up."

Kinnon pulled her close. "Ye wanted to save her. She had to want that, too."

His warmth enveloped her like a blanket and her feelings of inadequacy fled. "I thought mayhap along the pilgrims' path, I would find the answer—what I did wrong. Mayhap seek the answer from St. Jacques, himself."

His hands moved comfortingly up and down her back. "Dearling, ye did nothing wrong."

Melisende sighed. "Why do I feel as though I did?"

He kissed the top of her head. "Let us find out together."

They strolled back through the village and Kinnon led Melisende to the Hospitaller stables. He felt troubled about Lucienne, but certain Melisende would eventually come to terms with her sense of failure. He was prepared to cosset her with love and comfort, giving her the time she needed. But for now, he needed to further his plans.

"See if ye can convince yer beast to stay here with my horse. He's a good sort and doesnae spook easily." He motioned to a stall where a rangy dark chestnut stood.

"Why?" she asked.

"I wish to visit the blacksmith and he willnae want his nags bolting at the sight of Jean-Baptiste."

"Oh." Curiosity laced her voice. She opened the stall door and ushered Jean-Baptiste inside. Kinnon's horse eyed him warily, but remained rooted calmly to the straw to one side of the spacious stall. The dog crossed the space hesitantly and briefly touched noses with the horse. Seemingly satisfied, the two animals turned expectant eyes on Kinnon. He gave a grunt of satisfaction and closed the lower half-door of the stall.

"Good. We will be back anon and take them out for a late evening jaunt." He tugged on Melisende's hand, thrilling to the sensation of her fingers twined with his.

They crossed the village square again and Kinnon couldn't help the joy swelling his chest. Melisende walked amicably beside him, mentioning a few points of interest along the way. He watched her as she spoke, the motion of her hands, the tilt of her head. He had forgotten how the sun brought out vivid shades of copper normally hidden in her hair. He drank in the sight of her, hardly hearing the words she spoke as he soaked up the sound of her voice, happy and content at the same time to be with her at last.

Arriving at the blacksmith's shed, Kinnon dragged his attention away from Melisende and stepped to a lad near the small corral behind the barn. "I need a sturdy mare or gelding with stamina and a soft mouth."

The lad glanced briefly at Melisende and nodded his head. He hurried to the blacksmith, a large man behind a heavy apron, his forehead and neck glistening with sweat from the heat of the forge. The man eyed Kinnon and Melisende, then gave the lad his job with a jerk of his head. He watched the boy for a moment, then stepped to Kinnon.

"You need *un cheval?*" His voice was guttural but placid.

Kinnon tilted his head at Melisende. "For *mademoiselle.*"

The blacksmith pursed his lips. "*J'ai aussi un cheval pour elle. Deux d'entre vous venez avec moi.*"

Kinnon and Melisende followed him, interested to see the horse. He opened a stall door at the rear of the shed and led forth a mare. Her ears pricked forward as she caught sight of Kinnon and Melisende. Her glistening coat was a bright mix of red and white hairs, her mane and tail flaxen.

"Do ye like her?" Kinnon asked.

"She is beautiful, *n'est-elle pas?*" Melisende murmured.

"Tell me about the horse," he directed the blacksmith.

The man began a half-French, half-English report on the mare's bloodlines, naming a price that caused Kinnon to raise an eyebrow as the blacksmith turned her loose in the small corral. She paced the fence with fluid movements, head high. A warning bell went off in Kinnon's head.

He did not feel Melisende slip her hand from his, but saw her approach the corral from the corner of his eye. "Melisende—dinnae—!"

She held out her palm for the horse to sniff. Nostrils wide, the mare flung her head over the top rail, ears pinned back. Melisende flipped her hand over, fingers curled into a fist, and rapped the mare on her nose. Startled, the horse jerked back, but instantly shoved her nose at Melisende's hand, snuffling loudly.

Kinnon flung the blacksmith a disgusted look and the man shrugged. "She bites."

Melisende spoke up. "I like her. I will call her *Ange*."

"*Ange*?" Kinnon asked as they led the mare—at a much reduced price—to the Hospitillar stable. "She isnae an angel. She is mayhap a witch or changeling—definitely fey." He kept one eye on the now deceptively placid horse.

Melisende laughed. "You did not need to purchase her. I told you I can walk."

"Meli, I will help ye with whatever ye need, but I wish to go with ye, and I would prefer to ride."

"What do you mean?"

"Wherever ye go, I want to be there with ye."

Melisende inhaled a sharp breath. "You wish to travel to Santiago with me?"

"If that is where ye are going, then aye."

CHAPTER TWENTY-SIX

"I started the pilgrimage partly because I had nowhere else to go," Melisende said, "and partly to see what God would say to me along the way. Lucienne's behavior left me rather shaken—and sad. Even after all this time."

"I dinnae know what God will tell ye. But I know I want us to find out together."

Warmth bloomed through Melisende, banishing her doubts like the sun after a storm. "I'd like that, *beaucoup*."

The sun's long rays touched the back of the hills, spreading colors of gold and red across the sky. Nearby, the horses cropped the short grass, Kinnon's gelding keeping a distance from Melisende's meddlesome mare. Jean-Baptiste flopped on the ground next to Kinnon, and Melisende couldn't remember a time she felt so content.

"Kinnon?" She turned to him, a question on her lips.

His gaze told her he'd been watching her, and her cheeks heated, unused to his regard.

"Aye, *mo chridhe?*" A flash of passion lit his eyes, the intensity of it startling her. Her heartbeat quickened, wondering what it would be like to feel his lips against hers, the warmth of his skin on hers, his hands . . . Abruptly, she realized her palms splayed at her waist, drifting upward with her thoughts.

She shoved her hands down the sides of her skirt, embarrassment burning her skin—and a spot low in her belly that was both strange and appealing.

She glanced at Kinnon again—completely forgetting what she'd wanted to say, unsure if he noticed her hesitation and uncertain if he would scorn her for these feelings of need, of *want* in her. Though there seemed to be a flicker of understanding in his gaze, he simply took her hand, rubbing his thumb caressingly across her palm.

"Many where I am from speak Gaelic, though many also speak English, or a form of it," he said casually, his tone easing some of her concern. "*Mo chridhe* means *my heart*. That is what ye are, Melisende. The love of my heart."

Her thoughts were a whirlwind. "I do not know how to respond other than to say you stole my heart years ago."

"Then why the hesitation?"

She bit her lip against a smile. "'Twas not because I did not understand your words, though it is true I'd not thought about the differences in our languages." She took a breath to steel her courage. "'Twas because of the look on your face—in your eyes."

He tilted his head at her. "What look?"

"As though you wished to kiss me," she whispered, feeling as though the very depths of her lay exposed, for there was no taking the words back. Kinnon rose, pulling her to her feet with him, and gathered her in his arms.

"I do."

His mouth descended, caressing her lips with gentle pressure that quickly built to an insistence, flaming a hunger in her she'd never known. She leaned against him, her breasts aching as they touched his chest. Her lips parted at his urging as though paired to his, and his tongue mated feverishly with hers.

With the force of a sudden storm, she was no longer plain Melisende. Every fiber of her

felt beautiful and desired. Her world was nothing more than the roughened velvet of his lips, the taste of ale on his breath, and the tender confines of his arms.

She was loved.

A discrete cough broke them apart as Jean-Baptiste shoved his nose between them. Rory stepped closer with an apologetic bob to his head. "'Twill be dark soon and if ye know yer plans, I can finalize them before the morn."

"We will leave with the pilgrims on the morrow," Kinnon replied, his hands sliding reluctantly down Melisende's arms to twine their fingers together.

That was it! Memory struck with clarity. "Kinnon," she murmured, not wishing to counter his order before his man. He lifted his eyebrows in question.

"I do not wish to continue the pilgrimage," she said.

"What *do* ye wish, *mo chridhe?*" he asked. "Name it and it is yours."

Melisende flushed with the pleasure his words piled on top of his actions only a moment ago. "I would prefer to return to *Le Puy en Velay*."

Kinnon canted his head, wishing to hear of her change of heart. "What of yer pilgrimage? Are ye settled on this?"

She nodded. "I have wandered enough. There will be no more of an answer in Santiago de Compostela than anywhere else. Lucienne is her own person and makes her own decisions. I can no longer be responsible for them." With a shrug she added, "Though if she consented to explain herself to me at some point in time, I would welcome the education."

Kinnon chuckled. "And I as well." He turned to his captain. "Get together what ye need for a return trip to *Le Puy*. M'lady wishes to go home."

Rory turned smartly on his heel and strode away to complete his instructions. Kinnon lingered a moment longer, reveling in the feel of his legs compromised by her skirts, her breasts pressed against him, and the memory of her lips on his. He wanted more.

"Marry me, Melisende. Here. Tonight. There are plenty of priests and holy men here." He grinned at her. "We could have a new one for each word of our vows."

A laugh bubbled to her lips, and he fell in love all over again with the merriment in her eyes. He'd appreciated her serious side, calm and unbelievably practical, always the leavening to his frustrations. But to see her truly happy—this was the Melisende he wanted forever.

"So sudden . . ." her voice trailed off, uncertain. But the happiness remained in the tilt of her lips and the shine of her eyes.

"I dinnae wish things to be constrained between us on the trip back. I want to be able to touch ye without checking the propriety of it. We are still learning each other's ways and I want the travel to be exciting and fun, not wishful and unfulfilled if we desire it."

"You truly want to marry me? It still feels like a dream. Only a few hours ago I had no idea we would ever meet again."

"Shall I kiss ye again to prove it?" he growled, half-teasing. "Or should I wrap ye up in nothing but me and my kilt beneath yon tree and show ye how much I mean it?"

Her eyes rounded and her lips parted. "Oh," she whispered, leaning against him, her face tilted up for his kiss. With a hoarse laugh, he kissed the tip of her nose.

"Exactly," he said, pointing out how close they were to consummating their relationship, vows or not.

A light shudder ran through Melisende's frame. "I would marry you this day, Kinnon, were it not for posting the banns."

"Aye, 'tis a problem," Kinnon agreed ruefully. "And I would suppose ye'd like me to ask yer uncle for yer hand?"

She paled. "We cannot post banns there. The soldiers know of me."

"Then what is yer need to return?"

Her face fell, her eyes hollow. "I'd thought to make my peace with my *oncle*. We parted on harsh terms. And I wished to see the farm once more before I leave France." She tried a bright smile that did not quite reach her eyes. "But 'tis merely a passing whim. There is no need to put you and your men in danger. We can leave for Scotland from here."

Kinnon grunted. "While it may be closer to our new home from here, there is no reason we cannae say a farewell to yer home first. Ye have myself and twenty-one braw Scots at yer service, milady. The soldiers in *Le Puy* willnae run afoul of us."

She glanced at him anxiously. "Are you certain? It may also be that my *oncle* has had word of Lucienne. As different as we are, she is still my sister."

For some reason, he found the possibility of making contact with Lucienne distasteful, but there was nothing he would deny Melisende. "Dinnae fash, *mo cridhe*, if there is news of yer sister, we will find it."

She hugged him joyfully, then stepped back. "We depart in the morning?"

"Would ye marry me before we leave if it was possible?"

Her eyes narrowed. "How can we? There is no one here who knows us. Who would stand as witness for us before the priest?"

"Mayhap the Hospitillar commander, D'Aramitz, would help. My men can vouch for me that I am not already married, and ye can answer the same." He eyed her uncertainty. "If 'tis only the protocol that worries ye, we could enter a private marriage, without the priest. Then, when we are settled, we can speak our vows again at the church."

"My decision to marry you is firm, Kinnon. And happily so. Again, you have surprised me so many times today, my head is spinning." She slid her palm down the length of his plaide draped from his shoulder to his waist. "Let us ask the priest what he suggests."

* * *

Candlelight flickered in the chapel. Warmth, intimacy and the heavenly glow surrounded them as they stood before the priest. Outside the church doors, to the glimmer of torchlight, they had satisfied the priest's formal charges. Earlier, he had been convinced to overlook the short notice, giving Kinnon and Melisende permission to wed. Part stemmed from the clink of coin slipped into the offering plate, and part due to the hungry look on the faces of the soon-to-be bride and groom. The tipping point came when Kinnon's man, Rory, assured the priest the pair had been searching for each other for more than three years—since the siege of *Chateauneuf-De-Randon*. With a prayer for Bertran uttered, the priest had welcomed Kinnon and Melisende with open arms.

Now they stood side-by-side, fingers once again laced together. Rory and Hamish stood witness for Kinnon's vows, and D'Aramitz accepted the responsibility for Melisende. In truth, his questioning of Kinnon of his motives for the abrupt wedding had lasted longer than had the priest. With a solemn look of promise, Kinnon faced his bride. Sweet spring flowers, woven into a crown by one of the women at the *domerie*, rested amid Melisende's freshly-washed curls, tendrils escaping to frame her flushed face. Her gown, given to her by another lady who assisted the pilgrims, was a soft green, its belled sleeves lined in cream velvet against the coolness of the evening. He could scarcely believe the moment he waited for was at last here, and he spoke his pledge to her.

"Je, Kinnon Macrory, donne mon corps a toy, Melisende de la Roche, en loyal mari."

"Et je la recoy," she replied. *"Je, Melisende de la Roche, donne mon corps a toy, Kinnon Macrory."*

Happiness spiraled through him. *"Et je le recoy."*

I give my body to you in loyal matrimony.

And I receive it.

The priest beamed at them. Kinnon touched his lips to his bride's in a totally unsatisfying kiss that impatiently promised more. Tucking Melisende against his side, he placed a small bag of coins in the priest's hand.

"The hour is late. Use this to prepare a feast for the pilgrims here, and think of us when ye eat it on the morrow."

Outside the church a crowd gathered. A cheer went up as Kinnon and Melisende appeared in the doorway, and Melisende pulled back.

"Dinnae give them a thought, *mo cridhe*," he murmured, patting her hand reassuringly. They are already half-drunk and willnae follow us."

"How do you know this?" she asked as she stepped through the path opening before her.

Kinnon grinned at her. "Rory has been plying them with wine for some time now. He is a good man."

Melisende returned his smile, relief smoothing the furrowed worry on her brow. "Where are we going?"

"D'Aramitz spoke with a friend who is an innkeeper. He has a private room available for us." He gave her arm a squeeze. "And ye thought all I did was pester the priest whilst I waited for the ladies to help ye prepare for the wedding?"

Melisende's fingers caressed the feather-soft wool of her gown. "They were *très généreux."*

"They tried hard to match yer beauty, Melisende. If it pleases ye, then I am satisfied."

From the edge of the crowd, Hamish approached with Kinnon's horse. A bolt of fabric draped the horse's saddle and rump.

"Ride pillion with me, and we will escape our followers," Kinnon murmured in Melisende's ear. He leapt aboard the horse, pulling Melisende up behind him as Hamish assisted, his hands forming a step for her slippered foot. She wrapped her arms about Kinnon's waist as the people shouted and waved their mugs about in celebration, giggling as a robust man saluted her with his cup and drained the contents in one gulp.

"Are ye settled?" he asked. Melisende nodded against his shoulder and he thumped his heels against his steed's sides. The horse gathered his haunches beneath him and sprang past the last of the gathering, his hooves clattering loudly on the cobbled street.

CHAPTER TWENTY-SEVEN

The room was small but clean and comfortable with a tiny fire behind a metal grate. Melisende glided across the floor, her fingers plucking nervously at the folds of her gown. She felt Kinnon's presence acutely, as though he emptied the room of its air. Her chest grew tight. *Have I done the right thing? So sudden?* She peeked at him over her shoulder as he draped his cloak over a wooden chair. Her skin tingled, blood warming her as her heart doubled its beat. A smile of pleasure spread across her face. *It is like a dream. One I do not wish to wake from.*

It was suddenly imperative she touch him, reassure herself he was real—their marriage was real. A small cry escaped her as she whirled about, throwing herself into his arms.

"Are ye well, *mo chridhe*?" he murmured against her head. "Ye arenae wishing to take back those lovely words, are ye?"

The absurd notion to laugh bubbled at the back of her throat. "You will think me silly, but I am having a difficult time believing this is real."

"Let us take things nice and slow, then, lass, so ye can savor every moment."

A tremor of reality ran through her. "I find myself a bit adrift, Kinnon. I do not know what to expect."

He nibbled her ear and she shivered. "I was hoping ye would show me," he sighed.

Melisende laughed, her tension eased. "Do not lie to me and say you have not done this before," she chided, snuggling closer.

"But this is the first time with ye, and there will never be another woman in my bed. That makes this verra special, aye?"

"I never want to wake again without your arms about me."

"This morning was the last time, *mo chridhe*. The verra last time."

Nervousness stirred tiny whirlpools in her belly. She took a step back and reached behind her to undo the laces of the dress. "I do know I should set this aside," she quipped. Presenting her back to him, she pulled her hair to one side. "Would you help?"

Kinnon kissed her neck, his breath lighting flames along her skin, before plying his nimble fingers to the silken laces. "I willnae be so slow to undress ye again, *mo chridhe*. My mind is addled with the sight of ye, is my only excuse."

His words, and the muttered curse as the laces fouled, made her giggle again, a feeling that was as heady as wine. In moments, she was standing in her thin underdress, slightly dismayed at the tips of her breasts as they puckered visibly beneath the fabric. Kinnon brushed his thumb gently across the peaks, sending a jolt of passion through her. Taking her hands, he guided her to the chair and she sat as he removed her shoes and stockings.

Motioning for her to stay, he filled a wash basin with water. Gathering it along with a piece of linen, he knelt before her and washed her feet. Pure longing filled her as his eyes told her of his love, and his gentle hands promised his service to her.

"I dinnae have much to offer ye, Melisende, but I will never give ye cause to doubt me. Despite the words the priest said over us, tell me again. Will ye love me the rest of our days?"

Leaning forward, she cradled his cheeks in her palms and kissed his lips. "I will love you forever."

Kinnon rose, pulling her to her feet with him. He wrapped his arms about her, his lips claiming hers, slanting his mouth as he deepened the kiss. Hunger and need dissolved her bones, and she clung to him, returning his kiss with fervor. Slipping an arm behind her knees, he lifted her against his chest and carried her to the bed. Swiping the coverlet aside, he followed her onto the softness, stretching beside her.

He toyed with the string at the neckline of her gown. "I want to see ye naked, Melisende."

The idea was not unexpected, but the experience was new, and she hesitated. "Completely?" she asked, a smile playing about her lips.

"'Tis the general idea," he admitted, removing his belt and tossing it aside. His kilt billowed loose and he shoved it to the floor. He pointed from his leine to her gown. "We're a bit more even now. Want to race?"

Melisende dissolved into laughter. Kinnon regarded her with a pained look. "A bit louder and the men will be doubting my ability to please my wife."

She bit her lip. "I am sorry. No one has ever made me laugh as you do."

"'Tis a gift," he agreed. Nodding at her undergarment, he added, "Take all the time ye need."

He'd never meant words less, but he wanted her willing, unafraid, wanting to grow their relationship in every way. He shrugged out of his leine, letting the fabric drop to the floor, and waited for her next move.

Melisende sat, curling her legs beneath her as she loosened the lace at her neck. With a shimmy of her hips and shoulders that nearly pushed Kinnon past the edge of his good intentions, she swept the thin gown from beneath her bottom and over her head. His gaze wandered over her, drinking in the beauty of her breasts, the perfect size to fill his palms, the luminous glow of her skin in the gentle glow of the fire, and the tantalizing view of the shadow at the junction of her thighs.

"Kinnon?" The squeak of doubt in Melisende's voice snapped his attention back to her, and he mentally chastised himself for causing the look of apprehension on her face. He gave a lopsided grin.

"I am a verra lucky man, *mo chridhe.*"

The taut line of her shoulders relaxed. "Tell me," she invited.

Kinnon leaned forward, his lips brushing hers. "Let me show ye."

She fell back onto the bed within the safety of his arms, his mouth trailing over her skin. She tasted of warm honey and smelled of sweet spring flowers. He inhaled deeply, swept away by a wave of need. Burying his face in the valley between her breasts, his hands exploring the softness of her belly, he waited for the fire within him to settle.

"Touch me, Meli," he groaned. "Need me as much as I need ye."

Her palms slid slowly over his sides, then along his flanks, fingers rounding behind his back to splay across his buttocks. He pushed against her, responding to her hands as they kneaded him. He rolled to the side, trailing one hand across her belly then lower, cupping the mounded flesh that had tantalized him earlier. She tensed with a gasp, then relaxed slightly, her knees drifting apart as she offered herself to him. He slid one finger gently between the folds, relishing her warm, wet response. She moaned, lifting her hips, pressing herself against his hand.

"*Mo chridhe*, this time ye may be a bit tight, and I'm told it may likely hurt for a few moments as yer body adjust to the feel of me inside ye. Are ye willing for this?"

Her hand slid between them, her slender finger wrapping about his cock. "It seems we are both ready, *mon amour*," she murmured. She squeezed gently and his ability to think clearly vanished. He pumped himself up and down in her hand, groaning with the sheer pleasure of her touch. With a deliberate attempt at regaining control, he stilled, his breath harsh in his chest.

He covered her mouth with his, his tongue seeking entrance as he rolled atop her and pressed his cock slowly within. His blood ran hot through his veins and pressure built deep inside. Her small cry was like a dash of cold water and he waited to feel her move beneath him again.

The need for her roared through him, and as she stroked herself against him, he gave in. Her fingers dug into his shoulders, and she shook hard as a different cry tore from her. With a groan of satisfaction, Kinnon followed her over the edge.

* * *

Morning was a faint glow on the horizon when Kinnon eased from the bed. He fed a few pieces of wood to the small grated fire and the resulting flames shot their amber light about the small room. Melisende sighed softly and reached for him. He stepped back to the bed and gathered her hands, kissing both palms before settling a lingering kiss on her lips.

"We have a journey to begin, *mo chridhe*."

"Last night was a good beginning," she remarked, stretching languidly beneath the sheets.

"I am verra glad we had last night to ourselves, and a proper bed."

She slanted him a sultry gaze. "Every night will be like this?"

He grinned. "Och, I am fair certain we will sleep one night or two. But the days will be long and my arms will ache to have ye in them again."

"More like your cock will ache," she chuckled, eyeing him as he pulled his leine over his cock as it stretched eagerly toward her.

Heat rushed to his cheeks, surprising him. He paused, kilt in hand. "We could satisfy that ache now—for a time at least. My hunger for ye is no secret."

Melisende sat up, waving him off as she pulled the linen sheet over her breasts. "Be off with you," she laughed. "I am not sure how I will sit a horse this day as it is."

Kinnon was instantly contrite. "I am sorry, *mo chridhe*. We can wait until tomorrow to leave, or even the next day if ye wish."

She blew him a kiss. "I will be fine. Give me a few moments to wash and dress without you tempting me to take you up on your generous offer."

"Are ye certain?" he asked, not sure how he, with his cock growing harder by the second, would sit a horse, either.

"*Oui.*" She waved him toward the door. "And see that there is food to break our fast. I am famished!"

Kinnon snagged another kiss from his bride and gave her a salute as he opened the door. "'Tis my wish to fill yer every hunger. I will rouse the kitchen."

Her laughter followed him down the hall.

Kinnon stepped into the great room, gratified to see two of his men seated at a table closest to the stairway leading to the room he and Melisende shared. Two more eyed him from their spot near the door as they tucked away the morning fare. Rory crossed the floor.

"We can be ready in a few moments," he said. "When shall we expect yer wife to be down?"

"My wife," Kinnon said, liking the way the words tripped off his tongue, "will be down in a few moments." He grinned at his friend. "At least 'tis what she said. My guess is she will be a bit longer than that, and she did mention a good breakfast." His stomach rumbled.

Rory's eyebrow rose. "Worked up an appetite, aye?" He did not flinch as Kinnon clouted his shoulder in mock reprimand. "I can have a wagon arranged if ye are too weak to ride."

"Save yer cheek for someone else," Kinnon growled, his crinkled eyes denying any antagonism. "I wouldnae ask my worst enemy to sit a wagon on some of the trails we crossed getting here." He shuddered in memory. "I will see to the horses. Wait for Melisende and see she is fed. I will break my fast on the trail."

Rory nodded and Kinnon left the inn, enduring the men's good-natured ribbing about leaving his bride so early in the morning.

He hurried along the cobbled road to the Hospitaller stables, eager to start the journey, to see Melisende and himself settled in Scotland. As he passed through the stable gates, horse heads shoved through open half-doors here and there along the edge of the U-shaped building. Stable lads stumbled sleepily into the courtyard. A few knights strode past. One broke away and made his way somewhat unsteadily back toward Kinnon. He halted before him, blocking the path. Hands fisted at his sides, his chin jutted out, he glared at Kinnon.

"Bloody Scot. You think you are better than me."

Kinnon eyed the man, recognizing the knight of Melisende's acquaintance. "Get some rest," he said dismissively. "Ye are drunk."

Jean-Luc jabbed a finger at Kinnon's chest. "Not so drunk I do not know who the better man is. I would have had her in my bed had you not shown up. She would have been grateful to have me for her protector."

Kinnon's light-hearted mood darkened. "Ye can shut yer mouth now, or I can do it for ye." He paused a moment as a wave of anger swept over him. "I would be happy to do it for ye."

The Hospitaller knight searched him up and down with a disdainful look. "You are not man enough." He drew his arm back, hand fisted, and threw a punch at Kinnon's head.

Rocking slightly to one side, Kinnon easily avoided the strike and grabbed the other man's wrist as it passed. Taking one step away, he dropped his weight and turned, snaring Jean-Luc's arm behind his back. Straightening, he shoved the knight's fist up between his shoulder blades and Jean-Luc grimaced, sagging a bit to counter the painful arm lock.

Kinnon leaned forward, his mouth close to Jean-Luc's ear. "This would be where ye apologize for being a fool and challenging me. Even sober, ye wouldnae stand a chance."

Rage purpled Jean-Luc's face and his mouth worked as he assembled adequate words. "I apologize."

Kinnon shook his head, aware he would likely not get a further admission from the knight unless he took the time to teach him some manners. An ache in his leg reminded him he was not as agile as he once was, and he was a married man now. He did not need to be acting like a hot-headed youth.

Giving Jean-Luc a shove forward, he released him. The knight stumbled several steps, catching himself against a wooden rail used to tie horses. Kinnon wiped his hand down the length of his kilt, disgust tugging his lips down. He turned to the stalls given over to his horses.

With a roar, Jean-Luc surged to his feet and rushed Kinnon. Half-expecting something of the sort, Kinnon swung around mid-stride, catching the glint of steel in the knight's hand and the glare of deadly intent in his eyes. Kinnon's blade slipped effortlessly from its scabbard and he pivoted, forcing Jean-Luc to stare into the rising sun.

* * *

Melisende greeted the Scotsmen as she entered the small gathering room of the inn. Rory stepped immediately to her side, smoothly taking her cloak and leather satchel of belongings from her. With a solicitous hand at her elbow, he motioned for her to have a seat at a nearby table. A single place had been set, a platter with mug at its side, and a covered basket from which wafted the tantalizing aroma of fresh bread. She glanced at Rory.

"*Merci*, but can you tell me where Kinnon is? It would be nice to eat with him."

"He has gone to see about the horses, *Madame*. He said he would eat along the way."

Melisende laid her palm against Rory's sleeve. "Then I will do so as well." She snuck a speculative look at the table. "Mayhap a sip whilst this is wrapped up."

"As ye wish. 'Twill take no more than a moment." Rory summoned a serving lass with a jerk of his head. Melisende swallowed a mouthful of watered ale and a bite of bread against the rumble in her belly.

"Do ye have other belongings?" he asked.

Melisende shook her head. "My belongings are in my satchel," she replied. "As a pilgrim, I carried only what I needed."

"Smart lass," he grinned. His smile of approval vanished into a look of mild horror. "*Milady*," he corrected himself.

"Do not call me *milady*," Melisende laughed. "For I am certain I will never learn to answer to it. *Madame* if you must, Melisende if you would."

Clearly discomfited, Rory gave a short nod. "I will see what I can do. Though the men willnae call ye by yer given name, no matter how charmingly ye ask."

Melisende stepped into the cloak as he held it for her. "I shall endeavor to remember this," she answered. "We have many days of travel together ahead. Let us not trip ourselves up on protocol."

He motioned her to join him, then led her to the door of the inn. Four braw Scotsmen fell into step behind them. Their boots clattered on the cobbles of the street, the sound mixing with the scattered calls from merchants opening their shops for the day. Not too far ahead, a murmur rose, and heads turned at the noise.

Rory stepped round in front of Melisende, pointing a rigid finger at her nose. "Stay put." He glanced at the Scotsmen who had gathered close. "Watch her," he commanded and broke into a jog through the gathering crowd.

Melisende hesitated only a second before darting after him, her guard in tow. Ignoring their protests, she wound through the throng, pulling up short just inside the Hospitaller stable where two men circled each other, swords drawn.

Kinnon! She recognized her husband's form immediately. Her gaze flew to the other man. *Jean-Luc!* Her stomach clenched around its meager breakfast as she realized the men had little to dispute except her.

Horses whinnied, sensing danger in the air, but the people about her remained silent, anticipation apparent in the lines of their bodies and the expressions on their faces. To her left, a man eased forward. She glanced quickly to the side, recognizing his Hospitaller colors of white cross on a black tunic. A furtive look on his face, his hand drifted to the sword at his belt.

Slipping her dagger from the pocket in her cloak, Melisende turned toward the man, hand fisted on the knife's hilt, angled just below belt level. "This is their fight, not yours, *monsieur* knight," she admonished softly. His head turned at her words, distaste on the sneer of his lips as he saw who gave him challenge.

Melisende nudged him with the tip of her dagger, glancing down as she did, offering him a chance to reconsider. "Should you wish to assist, you will do so as a eunuch." The knight blanched and stepped a pace away. Giving her an angry look, he disappeared into the crowd.

A quick look around showed kilted men scattered at the perimeter of the crowd, and Melisende took a deep breath, satisfied Kinnon's men would do their best to keep the people from interfering. The ring of steel shifted her attention back to the combatants.

Jean-Luc circled Kinnon. Melisende cringed to see the subtle shift in Kinnon's balance as he favored his injured leg. His gaze bore into Jean-Luc as he deflected the knight's half-hearted attacks. Melisende fumed. *Fall, Jean-Luc. Trip over your overwhelming ego and be done with this nonsense.* Furious barking sounded from within the stables. *Jean-Baptiste!*

Jean-Luc lunged again, just inside Kinnon's defensive circle. Kinnon parried the thrust, but did not advance. "Fight me!" Jean-Luc roared. "Let us see who the better man is."

For a heartbeat, nothing happened. Jean-Luc's guard relaxed, the line of his shoulders drooped slightly, allowing the tip of his sword to dip down. "Coward."

Kinnon's attack was a blur of motion, and Melisende gasped, waiting for his leg to betray him. He beat Jean-Luc back, his sword hammering against the knight's, the ring of the blows nearly one continuous flurry of sound. In an instant, Kinnon was inside Jean-Luc's guard. Holding the knight's sword to the side, braced against his own, he rammed Jean-Luc with an uppercut from his left fist that sent the knight sprawling. He landed on the ground amid the dust, sliding a few feet from the force of Kinnon's blow. Still clutching his sword, Jean-Luc thrust it tip-down into the earth, using the hilt to brace himself as he tried to rise.

A crash sounded from the stable as the upper half of a stall door burst open, slamming against the wall. Jean-Baptiste leapt through the opening, landing on the ground at a hard run. He skidded to a halt before Jean-Luc, teeth flashing in the early light as he fought against Kinnon's sharp command to hold.

"Get up," Kinnon barked at Jean-Luc.

Clearly addled from the blow, the man levered himself up, but slipped, falling to one knee. Kinnon kicked the sword from Jean-Luc's hand and stood one foot on the blade to keep him from picking it up again. Using the tip of his sword, he forced Jean-Luc's chin up.

"I can finish this now, or ye can admit ye are an arrogant prick and hie yerself away to yer barracks. Either way, it ends now." He slid the blade a bit forward, toward the tempting pulse in the knight's throat.

Jean-Luc spat in the dirt. "Keep *la prostituée*," he snarled.

With a forceful kick to the man's chin, Kinnon laid Jean-Luc in the dirt. "I dinnae call that an apology."

He turned with a slight wince, and strode to the edge of the crowd, snapping his fingers for the dog to follow. With a last sniff at the prone knight, Jean-Baptiste bounded after Kinnon as he pushed through the throng, a dark scowl on his face.

Melisende gathered her skirts and ran after him, catching him as the Scots converged on him. "You are injured!" she exclaimed, half questioning him, half chiding him for fighting on a leg that was a possible liability.

His furious gaze stopped her. "He was drunk!" He stopped and snapped at his men over his shoulder. "Get the horses." Half of them barreled their way through the crowd, the rest formed a guard about him and Melisende. Jean-Baptiste eyed them warily, still on the defense.

"Forgive me," he said to Melisende. "I am not angry with ye. I dinnae provoke him, and he was rather uncomplimentary about ye." He cast a look at the knight's form still sprawled on the ground. "Mayhap he will wake a better man."

"I am sorry," Melisende replied. "I was full of worry about you, knowing your leg bothers you. I should not have spoken so sharply."

"And I was still angry with a knight with more balls than brains." He shook his head. "My leg willnae allow me to go to war again, but I can do battle should the need arise." His face finally softened and he touched her cheek. "Thank ye for yer concern. Does it mean ye love me?"

"More every day," she answered, warmed by his gaze.

They glanced up as Kinnon's men approached with the horses. Hamish led Melisende's mare forward, a wary look on his face, a frayed edge to his plaide. Kinnon helped her mount, then climbed aboard his own horse. Moments later, the entire group was mounted, and the crowd dispersed, leaving the stable courtyard nearly empty.

As one, they reined their horses toward the double gate, but a man striding through the gates ahead of them, cape billowing at his back, guards four deep on his flanks, halted their progress.

Commander D'Aramitz stopped a few feet from Jean-Luc's body. The downed knight began to stir, his moan clearly audible. Jean-Baptiste bounded over to Jean-Luc, barking his challenge. Melisende directed him back to her side and he reluctantly abandoned the knight. D'Aramitz turned his back on Jean-Luc's attempt to sit, and addressed Kinnon.

"I apologize for the poor hospitality. You have my utmost regard, and I assure you this man will be punished. There were plenty here who saw his actions—and yours. I can thank you for sparing his life, though he may wish otherwise before it is over."

Kinnon cocked his head. "Dinnae torture the lad. The blow I gave him will have his head swimming for a day or two. A few days cleaning the *privee* in his condition should do nicely."

D'Aramitz cut his gaze to Jean-Luc then back to Kinnon. "As I said, he will wish he had rethought his words and actions of this morning, and have reason to be grateful you do not press charges."

"I have said all I will on the subject," Kinnon replied. "And your personal hospitality was beyond what was necessary. I am eternally thankful to ye."

D'Aramitz bowed to Melisende. "May you and *la belle femme* have a safe, uneventful trip. Godspeed to you both."

He stepped aside, and Kinnon, his bride, and their men-at-arms, rode from *Aubrac* as the sun rose above the mountains.

CHAPTER TWENTY-EIGHT

They allowed the horses to gallop whenever possible, enjoying the heady sense of freedom, but the terrain often had them picking their way carefully down a steep rocky trail, or fording an icy river. The countryside was now littered with herds of cattle at last out of their barns as the new grass promised full bellies. Their bells could be heard of an evening as young boys guided their charges home for milking, full udders swaying as they lumbered to their stalls.

Melisende wrapped her arms about her legs and rested her chin on her knees, watching as the camp prepared for the night. Her belly was pleasantly full with hare captured earlier in the afternoon, and the last of the bread they'd brought with them from the innkeeper's kitchen in *Aubrac*. But that was three days ago, and it had only been fit for sopping the stewed rabbit from her trencher.

Two days more, if they could keep their pace up, and they would be back in *Le Puy en Velay*. She wondered what awaited her there. She wished to make peace with her uncle. Other than Lucienne and her baby daughter, she knew of no other family living. It was exciting to be starting out on a life she'd never dreamed could be hers, but a bit sad to think she may never see France again.

Her thoughts turned to Kinnon. He crouched next to the small fire, only a few feet away, prodding the embers as the flames died down. She admired the play of muscles across his shoulders beneath the leine stretched tight across his back, and longed to run her hands across their smooth cords. Her blood ran hot to think of pressing herself against his back, wrapping her arms about his waist. She knew if she trailed her hands downward, they would find the evidence of the passion he had for her. Passion she returned to him whole-heartedly. Humming to herself, she considered the night ahead. Their intimacy had grown tremendously from their time together, and the presence of others on the trail only challenged them to find what privacy they could.

Tossing his stick onto the fire, Kinnon rose, dusting the crumbling bark from his hands. His gaze met hers and a lazy smile played across his lips. Melisende found herself licking her lips as she stared hungrily at him, and his grin widened. He settled beside her and took her hand, drawing lazy trails of pleasure across her palm and up the inside of her forearm. Sparks flashed across her skin and she shivered.

"Cold?" he drawled.

"*Non*. And even if I was, I could count on you to warm me," she replied. "Even watching you from a distance fills me with longing."

Kinnon's eyes lit. "And I would deny ye nothing." He pulled her to him, settling her across his lap.

"The others," she murmured an instant before his lips claimed hers. He wrapped his arms about her, his palms rubbing up and down her back, her sides, her breasts. Melisende's breath came short and fast. Kinnon ended the kiss and pressed his forehead against hers.

"My men will be discrete, and there are no pilgrims on the trail with us tonight," he reassured her. "There is a lovely view overlooking the river *Allier* where we could linger the night alone." His scorching gaze raked over her. "Though not as beautiful as what I see before me, and interesting to me only for the privacy it would afford us."

Melisende nodded and he helped her to her feet. Giddy, she strolled from the campsite to the overlook, then to a small secluded area nearby. Moonlight filtered through the trees as Kinnon removed her gown, and sounds of the river rose to her ears as he whispered endearments to her alone.

His fingers traced lines of fire across her skin, his lips following in their wake. Passion blossomed deep inside her and she arched against him, eager to feel his body on hers.

Kinnon stretched out beside her. "Ride me, *mo chridhe*." He pulled her to his side. "I want to feel the weight of ye, feel ye take charge of yer passion."

Melisende splayed a palm against his chest, uncertain. His hands on her arms, he urged her, and she found herself astride him, his cock nestled against her already throbbing mound. Jolts of pleasure shot through her, and she sucked in her breath, amazed at the sensation.

Kinnon chuckled lightly. "'Tis a great position, aye? Let's give ye something to reflect on during our ride tomorrow."

Melisende closed her eyes and breathed deeply—the aroma of Kinnon's heat, the smell of the forest and river, and the heady scent of arousal. She lit wherever he touched her, and the fire within as she took him deep inside quickly overtook her, tearing a cry of completeness from her lips. She shuddered as he reached his own climax.

He pulled her down to his chest, nestling her head against his shoulder. "I love ye, Melisende Macrory. I dinnae believe I can ever get enough of ye."

A tiny, sated smile played about her lips. "I love who I have become when I am with you," she replied. "You make my world a beautiful place with your love."

She lay curled atop him in contentment, listening to the beat of his heart until the sound of it combined with hers and she drifted to sleep.

The sunrise lit the sky with streaks of pink and yellow far too early the next day. With the lingering blush of loving warming her skin, Melisende rose and dressed as Kinnon belted his kilt about his waist. He pulled her into his arms for a thorough good-morning kiss.

"Does this ever become old?" she wondered aloud as he ended the kiss and tucked her against his chest. His answering rumble tickled her ear and she grinned.

"Nae, lass. It only gets better."

* * *

Crowds thronged the streets along the market. The lace shops were doing a brisk business, judging by the number of people elbowing in and out the doorways. The Rue St. Jacques leading from the cathedral was barely passable for the pilgrims and icon merchants clogging the way. The horses pressed through the crowds, Jean-Baptiste following at their heels.

"'Tis the evening trade," Melisende informed Kinnon, a fond smile of remembrance on her face. "I shopped for food for the table early in the morning, but occasionally enjoyed a leisurely stroll in the late evening, shopping for laces, which they are famous for here, sweets and other extravagances—when *mon oncle* could spare me, that is."

"It appears yer uncle is closed for the evening," Kinnon pointed out as they arrived at the shop. Melisende stared, puzzled, at the closed door, curtain drawn over the glazed window. She dismounted, scarcely noticing Kinnon's help as she wondered anxiously about the closed shop.

Dusting off her skirts, she hurried to the door and rapped loudly on the wooden frame.

There was no response, but she could hear voices within. Just as Kinnon grasped her elbow, signaling caution, she laid her hand on the latch. The door clicked open, and with a quick glance at Kinnon, she stepped inside.

Three heads turned at her entrance, Kinnon at her side. The balding pate belonged to her uncle, and the lavish gold curls bounced around Lucienne's pretty face. But Melisende's gaze was drawn to the little girl dressed in exact miniature of Lucienne's costume. *Could this be my niece?* Small and delicate, she was the image of Lucienne, but instead of having her mother's golden curls, her gently waving locks were a deep brown, nearly black, with hints of red and gold.

Lucienne was the first to speak. "There you are! *Uncle* swore he did not know where you had hared off to." She gave Kinnon a flirtatious tilt of her head. "But at least it appears your prayers were answered as I see you found this one whole and looking quite well. It is good to see you again, Kinnon."

Melisende waved a hand in Kinnon's direction, encountering his shoulder. Grateful for the anchor, she laid her palm against his arm. "Kinnon and I were wed a week ago in *Aubrac*."

"You always did land on your feet, Melisende," Lucienne remarked. "I might have stuck around if I had known he was coming back." When neither Melisende nor Kinnon commented, she gripped the small girl's shoulder, pivoting her to face them. "I have fallen upon rather difficult times, it seems, and I have brought the child here."

Stunned by her sister's demeanor, Melisende hesitated in confusion. "Here? Why?"

Lucienne's rouged lips tilted upward in a sly smile. "It seems appropriate, somehow. Raul has divorced me. Apparently marrying his wealthy heiress was better than living in poverty with me." She scowled. "I can no longer feed myself and the child."

"Why not send her to live with her father?" Kinnon asked.

Lucienne shrugged. "He does not want her, and neither does his new wife."

"We will finish this discussion later," Melisende said firmly, raising her hands between Kinnon and Lucienne. She nodded toward Arielle. "This is not something she needs to hear."

Uncle Ramon rolled his gaze to the ceiling. "I believe I need a drink."

CHAPTER TWENTY-NINE

"Come with me to settle the child," Lucienne ordered as she lifted her daughter to her hip. With misgivings, Melisende followed her sister up the narrow stairs. Arielle's large dark eyes stared at her over her mother's shoulder and Melisende wrinkled her nose at her in a friendly way. Arielle ducked her head.

A valise lay atop the narrow bed in the room Lucienne had briefly occupied when they first came to live with their uncle. It was open and clothes spilled from it onto the floor. Lucienne set Arielle down and ushered her inside the room with a small push of her hand. The little girl stepped inside the room, fingers fisted tight in her mother's skirt. Lucienne brushed her hand away. "You are wrinkling my gown, *ma petite*. Haven't I told you not to muss my clothes?"

Arielle dropped her gaze then lifted it slightly to stare at Melisende. Feeling as though her heart would break to see the results of her sister's callous behavior, Melisende gave the child a tender smile. An answering one tugged at Arielle's lips.

"She is not *muette*, she is shy," Lucienne declared, irritation coloring her voice. "Say *bonjour* to *Tante* Melisende, Arielle."

"*Bonjour*," the little girl whispered with a quick glance to her mother.

"*Bonjour*, Arielle," Melisende replied. "*Comment êtes-vous?*"

"She speaks Italian more fluently than French," Lucienne informed her. She rifled through the pile of clothes, snatching a tiny gown from the jumble.

"Oh, I see," Melisende said, thoughtfully. She turned back to Arielle. "I suppose if I'd been born in Italy, I would, too."

Arielle's gaze slid away and Melisende stepped closer to the bed and picked up a small gown to fold. "How bad is it, Lucienne?" she murmured.

"I brought her back for you to raise."

Melisende cast her a startled look. "You cannot be serious."

Lucienne bent to unlace Arielle's gown. "You mean, why would I trust you with my child after you failed so miserably with me?"

"Lucienne! That is not what I mean at all. How can you think of giving up your child?"

Tugging the travel gown over the little girl's head, Lucienne quickly replaced it with a thin undergarment with a plain drawstring at the neck. "There. Hop into bed. It is time you were asleep."

Obediently, Arielle climbed onto the thin mattress as her mother pulled back the blanket. Lucienne tucked her in and placed a quick kiss to her forehead. "Someone will come for you in the morning."

Melisende could scarcely believe her ears. There had always been stories or nursery songs for Lucienne as a child. Did Lucienne not remember? *She acts as though she can scarcely be bothered by her daughter.*

Lucienne motioned her to the far side of the room near an open window. "I am not a good mother. I want to go to parties and wear pretty dresses. Not read bedtime stories and worry about stains on my gowns."

"But, Lucienne, if you are in such dire straits, you will not have these things to worry over as you cannot afford them. You can stay here and—"

"With *Oncle* Ramon?" Lucienne gave a harsh laugh. "He barely tolerated me the last time I was here."

"He is family. He will not turn you away," Melisende declared, though she rather doubted the extent of his goodwill.

"You think not?" Lucienne waved a hand dismissively. "No matter. I have grown accustomed to court life, and I intend to return."

"But how? If you have no money . . ."

"There is a system. I do not linger long after a party, but the houses are large and an extra guest or two is rarely noticed for a few days. There is always the next weekend retreat."

"How will you receive invitations as a divorced woman?"

"That is hardly a problem," Lucienne drawled, her world-weary voice sending chills along Melisende's spine. Her sister's eyebrows lifted and a deprecating half-smile pulled at one side of her mouth.

"As poor a mother as I may be, I do not wish to raise my daughter in such a world as I live in. She is old enough to interest some men who are fascinated by young girls. In my position, I would not be able to deny them."

Melisende's eyes widened in horror. "She is but three years old! Please tell me . . ." She could not say the words, and her hand flew to her throat, attempting to relieve a choking sensation.

Lucienne shook her head. "*Non.* But it would be only a matter of time. I have seen the looks."

"Lucienne, you do not have to go back."

"*Eh bien?* And where would I live? With you and your new husband?" She scowled. "You are such a saint, Melisende. Everyone likes you, everyone has a kind word for you. Do you know what it is like to depend on the next person's grace for an invitation to their home for a few days, for you do not have one of your own? To laugh and pretend 'tis a new stain on your gown so your hostess would offer something of hers? To know if no invitations arrive, you will sleep on the street?"

Melisende raised her hands to embrace her sister. "Lucienne, stop! You can live with us." Lucienne waved her away. "*Non.*"

Melisende's arms fell by her side. "Why would you go back to such a life?"

"To the parties," Lucienne answered, "and the gowns of fabrics so fantastic they make you cry from the sheer pleasure of them. Laces so delicate they can scarcely withstand the needle. Embroidery so fine it takes four seamstresses a week just to produce one sleeve." Her eyes closed and rapture lit her face. "The men so courteous, so eager to woo me. Dancing, stealing kisses behind the fountain. They tell me how beautiful I am, how much they desire me." She opened her eyes, settling her gaze on Melisende's shocked face.

"Once Raul began divorce proceedings, their interest increased a hundredfold. I will have no lack of sponsors once I return."

"That is a shameful way to live, and you know it, Lucienne." Tears burned in Melisende's eyes. "How can you do this to yourself?" She swept a hand toward the bed. "To her?"

The scorn returned to Lucienne's face, casting ugly shadows beneath her high cheeks.

"You think you know what is right for me. That I should be exactly like you, drowning behind your polite façade. You believe everything is perfect in your little world with your adorable new husband who loves you?" Her eyes narrowed as she slid her gaze to Arielle. "Have you not wondered why she looks like him?"

Melisende immediately turned to the child asleep on the bed. Her dark hair spilled across the pillow like a shadow in the dimly lit room. She glanced back at her sister. "Why do you say that? I think she looks just like you."

"She has my nose and eyes, *oui*. But her dark hair comes from her father."

"Raul."

"*Non*. From your oh-so-sweet husband."

Melisende's gaze bounced from Lucienne back to the child. Lucienne's parting words so many years ago loosed themselves from the depths of her mind. *What do you think went on whilst he slept in our house—only me and him? He would be unable to look you in the eye if you knew everything that happened.*

She shook her head. *No! It is impossible to think of it! He has already assured me there was nothing between himself and Lucienne.* But her heart turned cold in her breast.

Lucienne strolled to the bed and stroked her daughter's hair. "She looks so much like me. But she has Kinnon's hair." Her smile set an arrow in Melisende's heart.

Brushing aside her doubts, Melisende stepped forward. "Do not be absurd, Lucienne. Her hair is much like mine, and Raul's is dark as well."

Lucienne tossed her head. "You do not seem to recall Arielle was born early—or so I told Raul."

"Lucienne, did you have relations with someone whilst we lived in *Randon*?" Melisende demanded. "Did you marry Raul knowing you were already *enceinte*?"

Lucienne sent her a mocking look. "You would love to believe that, wouldn't you? To keep your lover innocent of the deed."

"I do not believe you," Melisende replied firmly, against the reservations that gnawed at her.

Lucienne's eyes narrowed, a lofty smile taunting Melisende. "Yet you see the resemblance, *non*? No matter what you tell yourself, you will always know there is the possibility. We spent an entire week together, unchaperoned. You know how insatiable he is, *ai-je raison*?" She turned away. "No matter what you try to believe, you will always wonder if he shared his body with me first."

Melisende fled the room, Lucienne's mocking laughter at her heels. She burst through the back door of the shop into the small courtyard used for deliveries and discrete transactions. Rory glanced up from cleaning his saddle, surprise on his face.

"May I help ye, *Madame*?" he asked.

Melisende waved a hand in the air, battling back the words and emotions that threatened to choke her. "I am fine," she lied, her throat tight with unshed tears. "My sister—I needed some air."

Rory nodded as though he understood. "Yer husband is inside with yer uncle," he offered.

Melisende nodded, gulping great gasps of air as she battled back the scream building inside. She leaned against the door frame behind her, gripping the wooden post as though a great wind threatened to sweep her away.

I can NOT doubt Kinnon. Lucienne is not the sweet child I knew and loved. She has become hateful, manipulative. Would she brazenly lie about this? Again, Lucienne's words from long ago surfaced. *What do you think went on*—No! She pushed the heels of her hands against her temples, forcing the sound of Lucienne's voice from her head. *I will not believe what she said. I believe Kinnon's words above hers.* She stared overhead as stars pricked the darkening sky. *But can I forget it?*

* * *

Kinnon glanced up from his seat at the table as Melisende entered the small room that served both kitchen and living area. Her face was white, two spots of color high on her cheeks. She gave him a haunted smile that barely lifted the corners of her mouth. Alarmed, Kinnon rose to his feet.

"Is aught amiss?" he asked, reaching for her hand. She flinched and caught her skirt in one hand, avoiding his gesture. On purpose? His eyes narrowed. What had her sister been up to? Melisende pulled a chair from the table and Kinnon stepped behind her to settle it beneath her. He reclaimed his seat and scooted it close. She gave his arm a quick pat and turned to her uncle.

"Can your head bear a bit of conversation, *Oncle*, or should we wait until morning?" she asked with a nod to the nearly empty jug of wine at his elbow.

He gave the flask a bleary look then turned his gaze to Melisende. "It depends on the conversation."

"Yer uncle has been telling me about the town," Kinnon interjected.

She gave him a startled look. "You have talked about *Le Puy*?"

"About the soldiers and their interest in ye."

Her nostrils flared briefly. She had apparently forgotten them. "Do they still seek me?" she asked, nudging her uncle's arm from across the table.

He shook his head. "I have not heard from them in the past several days. I do not know if they still watch the shop or not."

"For nearly a sennight they camped on his doorstep," Kinnon told her.

"Stood inside my shop, they did!" Ramon slurred, reaching for the jug. Melisende snared his wrist, denying him the wine.

"I am sorry, *Oncle*. Kinnon and I will leave in the morning."

"We are in no danger, Melisende," Kinnon soothed. "My men will alert us if there is trouble."

"They will continue to harass my *oncle* even after we are gone," Melisende pointed out. "Please let us be gone quickly."

A sharpness he'd not heard before edged her voice. "Are ye well?" he asked again. She flashed him a quick smile, meant to reassure him, but it fell flat and he found it disconcerting. He hesitated, not willing to confront her in front of her uncle about something she clearly did not wish to discuss. It would wait until they were alone.

"Rory has enough food for all of us for dinner—those of us who dinnae wish to drink their meal," he added with a glance at Ramon. The goldsmith grunted and slouched in his chair like a chastened child. "Where are yer sister and her wee lass?"

"Arielle is abed, and I do not know where my sister is." Her words sounded as lofty as those of a priest denying absolution.

It was clear there was a rift between the two again. Kinnon sighed. He'd hoped they could smooth things over between them before leaving for Scotland.

"Then eat a wee bite, *mo chridhe*. It has been a long day."

Melisende rose to her feet. "*Pardon*, but I am too tired. I beg your indulgence and an early evening." Giving him a nod, she slipped out the door.

Jean-Baptiste lifted his head and stared after her, a whine in his throat.

Hell in a basket! She willnae get off so easily. If she is angry with me, she will give me something to refute or ask forgiveness for.

Ignoring the snores issuing from Ramon's slack lips as he slipped the leash of consciousness, Kinnon stood and stomped across the floor. He looked through the doorway, but did not see Melisende. Steeling himself, he bounded up the stairs. Half-way up, the stairway turned sharply to the right, and he came face-to-face with Lucienne.

Hell's bells a'jinglin'. He flattened himself against the wall to allow her to pass, but the space was narrow and Lucienne halted a step above his. She allowed her gaze to slide leisurely up and down his body, lingering speculatively just below his belt. The tip of her tongue poked between her lips. His cock jerked to attention.

Damn! "I am headed upstairs to join my wife," he said, his voice rough and low.

"That would explain the bulge beneath your kilt, *ne serait-il pas*?" She jerked her eyes back to his, a mocking smile threading her lips. "How is your leg?"

"I am grateful for yer healing. I am sorry for yer troubles. How can yer sister and I help ye?"

Lucienne slouched against the wall, lowering the line of her breasts on level with Kinnon's eyes. "I am sure we could come to some arrangement." Her eyes danced, sparkling in the dim light.

He could smell the arousal on her, dark, cloying, mysterious. The young, inquisitive siren had matured into a soulless seductress, and his stomach churned, shutting down his cock's interest. "Ye should have better care for yerself, Lucienne. Ye sell yerself too cheaply."

She sighed. "Without a noble lineage, I think I have done as well as I could. I have *accesso* to most *case nobili* in Italy. I serve a very useful purpose."

"What of being a mother? Of caring for yer wee lass upstairs?"

Lucienne looked down her nose at him. "And lock myself away for the next ten to fifteen years? Without a husband, we would be destitute, and Arielle would have no future—unless she captured the eye of some jaded *nobiluomo* who wished her for himself."

Kinnon clenched his teeth, trying to rein in his temper at her casual words. "Then she is better off without ye for a mother."

"Exactly. But you do not have to go to your wife so soon." She lifted her hand to the plaide across Kinnon's chest, long delicate fingers playing with the folds. "We could finish what we started so long ago, and you could tell me if I am a good learner or not."

Kinnon grasped her wrist, halting her play. "This stops here. We had nothing more than friendship between us then, and I am sorry to say that is now finished. Get some sleep. We will discuss Arielle in the morning—with Melisende present."

Disappointment twisted her mouth. "I rather enjoyed our encounter on the stairs. A man such as yourself shouldn't waste himself on a simple woman such as my sister. I have far more to offer, I assure you. I yearn to show you the many ways I could love you. But my proposition is for tonight only."

"I can live with that," Kinnon responded dryly. "The answer is no."

"Then I bid you *buona notte*." She stepped lightly to the landing and slipped past him with excruciating slowness. Her breasts pressed firmly against him and her hand dipped low to cup his manhood as she passed. Eyebrows raised in silent invitation, she gave him a firm squeeze before she finally descended the stairs. Kinnon took a deep breath and counted to ten before he continued to his wife's room.

There was no fire in the grate, and Melisende lay with her back to the doorway beneath a mound of blankets. Kinnon quickly unlaced his leggings and slipped out of his kilt and leine. He slid into bed next to Melisende, spooning against her back. He ran his hand lightly from her shoulder to her hip, the soft fabric of her undergown catching on his callused palm. She shifted, but did not pull away.

"I would be happy to keep ye warm if ye'd care to slip out of yer gown. I've grown fond of feeling yer skin against mine."

After a brief hesitation he may have imagined, Melisende rolled to her back and pulled her gown over her head. Kinnon tossed it to the floor and drew his wife to his chest. "Can ye tell me what is wrong, *mo chridhe*?" he asked gently.

Melisende's soft sigh barely reached his ears. "'Tis an old argument between myself and Lucienne. She quite vexes me."

"I can understand that. Are ye vexed with *me*?"

"I am angry with my sister and confused by the woman she has become and the things she says. I am not angry with you."

"Good. It seemed ye were, and I would rather answer for my sins—real or imagined—than see ye upset."

"Could we talk about this tomorrow?" she asked. "I am overwhelmed enough for today."

"Aye, then. *Corrie doon, mo chridhe*. Snuggle close and sleep. I will keep ye safe."

Melisende nestled against his side, and Kinnon stayed awake long into the night wondering just what Lucienne had said.

CHAPTER THIRTY

Melisende jerked awake, startled to find a pair of large smoky gray eyes staring at her over the edge of the bed. Kinnon's spot beside her was empty, and she pulled herself onto one elbow, clutching the bedsheet to her neck.

"*Bonjour,* Arielle. How are you this morning?"

The child looked down at her feet before meeting Melisende's gaze again. "I cannot find *mia madre.*"

"Do not worry, *ma petite.* We will find her," Melisende reassured her.

Arielle shook her head. "She did not come to sleep last night." Her eyes rounded with concern. "Do you know where she is?"

Mère Marie! What has my sister done? "If you would give me a moment to dress, I will help you." Melisende motioned to the door. "Only to the door—no further," she added.

With an obedient nod, Arielle stepped through the open door and closed it behind her, leaving Melisende to wonder what she was used to seeing in her mother's bedroom. She leapt to her feet and snatched up her discarded shift, shivering as the fabric, cold from its night on the floor, made contact with her warm skin. She grabbed her travel gown from its peg and yanked it over her head, twisting to settle it about her. Opening the door, she ushered her niece back into the room.

"Give me a moment more," she told her as she washed her face and did up the laces on her dress. She hurriedly rebraided her hair, smoothing it with a comb from her satchel. Stepping into her slippers, she gave Arielle a bright smile. "*Fini!* Let us find your *maman.*"

The child's hesitant nod melted Melisende's heart, and she gently took the little girl by the hand. Leading her down the stairs, she discovered Kinnon entering the back door.

"Good morning, *mo chridhe,*" he said, giving her a kiss. He dropped to his haunches. "And who do we have here? A faerie princess?"

Arielle gave him a shy grin and buried her face in Melisende's skirts.

"She says she cannot find *sa mère.* I am certain she is here." She cast a look around the small room that was empty except for the three of them. "Or mayhap she has gone to market." She looked at Kinnon. "Have you seen her?"

"I have been seeing to the horses. She was not at the stable."

"Kinnon, you and I must talk. I am not comfortable staying here much longer, and we need to discuss our plans."

He stood to his feet and hooked his thumbs in his belt. "Aye. Feed the lass and we can talk."

Melisende quickly gathered some bread and cheese and a glass of watered ale and sat Arielle at the table. "I will need a milk-goat," she murmured.

"Pardon?" Kinnon asked. "What about a goat?"

Melisende motioned him to the far side of the room. "Lucienne wants me to raise the child," she said with a quick look to Arielle.

Kinnon grunted. "I cannae say that is a bad decision on her part, but do ye wish to?"

"Oh, Kinnon, you do not know what would happen to her if she returned to Italy with my sister! Lucienne is not in her room, and I fear she has already left."

"Leaving the lass with ye?"

Melisende dropped her gaze. "I know we have only just wed, and neither of us anticipated bringing a three-year-old into the marriage. But I cannot turn her away." She stared at him, begging him to understand. "Please, Kinnon. She will be no trouble."

He rubbed his fingers over the stubble on his chin. "No trouble? How could such a sweet lass be trouble?"

* * *

A thorough search of Lucienne's room confirmed she was no longer there, leaving her daughter behind. *Such a sad legacy for your child, Lucienne. I will do my best to raise her, to see that she is loved and cared for.* She glanced at Arielle, busily placing her few belongings into a small bag donated by *Oncle* Ramon. *And happy.*

She brushed aside the doubts plaguing her. *What makes you think you can raise her to be a better person than Lucienne? Spending the time necessary to make her feel welcome will take away much time from your new husband. Will Lucienne succeed in driving a wedge between you and Kinnon?*

I have already denied him the chance to defend himself against Lucienne's charges— again. And denied him the true words in my heart, as well as my affections. Her cheeks burned. *I must make amends.*

She helped Arielle finish packing and led her to the courtyard. The sun was bright overhead, and the men stood in the yard and beyond, checking their saddles and bags as they readied for the next part of the journey. Kinnon stepped forward, leading a shaggy pony.

"Rory found this wee beastie for ye, Arielle. Do ye know how to ride?"

The child nodded solemnly, her eyes wide. "It is mine?" she breathed.

"Only until we get to our ship." Kinnon chucked her under her chin. "Once we are in Scotland, we will get ye yer very own pony, and ye can help pick it out." He held out his hands to her and she reached up, allowing him to place her in the saddle.

She grinned, happiness lighting her elfin face. "I like him."

"He is a good lad. Ye look like a princess up there."

Melisende caught his gaze. "You are very good with her. *Merci.*"

"High praise from milady. I am humbled." He sketched her a salute and offered his hand to help her mount. "I see no reason we cannae go to the farm in *Chateauneuf-De-Randon,* if that is still yer wish."

She begged him with her eyes to not be so formal with her. "I would like that very much. I know 'tis silly, when there is likely nothing there but deserted buildings, or mayhap someone else lives there now, but it was my home for a while."

Kinnon smiled, but it was not the jaunty, heart-stopping smile she longed to see, and she doubled her resolve to mend things between them as soon as they had a few moments alone.

Jean-Baptiste gamboled into the courtyard on Hamish's heels. The dog spied Melisende and headed directly to her, halting at her pony's feet. Arielle gave a small cry.

"Do not worry, *ma petite.* He will protect you, not harm you."

"I want to pet him," the child declared.

Pleased to see her emerge further from her shyness, Melisende placed a hand on Kinnon's sleeve. "Would you please help her down so she can meet Jean-Baptiste properly?" she asked. Kinnon set the little girl on the ground, and she stared at the dog, one hand gripping the edge of Kinnon's kilt.

"Put your hand out like this for him to smell so he knows you," Melisende instructed, showing Arielle a fist. "Please sit, Jean-Baptiste, and show her your manners."

The big dog lowered his haunches to the ground and offered the child a paw. Arielle flashed an excited grin to Kinnon and Melisende then took a step forward. Jean-Baptiste leaned forward and sniffed her tiny knuckles, then gave them a quick swipe with his tongue. Sitting back, he seemed satisfied with their meeting, tongue lolling to the side, a grin on his face.

Arielle laughed and clapped her hands. "*Egli è mio amico!*"

"Yes, *ma petite,*" Melisende agreed with a smile for the little girl's happiness. "He is now your friend."

* * *

They rode through the streets of *Le Puy* and past the Chapel Saint-Michel d'Aiguilhe perched on a rocky pinnacle near the edge of town. A bit south of town, they entered a wooded valley and stopped beside a waterfall.

"I wished to be quit of town and the eyes of the soldiers there as quickly as possible. We will eat a bite and refresh ourselves here." Kinnon assisted Melisende from her horse as Rory lifted Arielle from her pony, before vanishing into the woods without a backward glance.

Biting her lip in frustration, Melisende fed Arielle from the stores in the saddle bags, nibbling on a piece of hard cheese as she waited for Kinnon to return. Jean-Baptiste drank from the foot of the waterfall then collapsed to the ground, panting softly as the day warmed.

The men were ready to leave again when Kinnon slipped through the trees into their midst. With a nod of thanks, he took the bread and cheese Rory handed him downing it in several hasty bites before turning to Melisende. She sat, her back against a tree, Arielle sound asleep in her lap.

"I will wake her," she said, ducking her head to whisper in the little girl's ear.

"Nae. She can ride with me." Kinnon mounted his horse then motioned for Hamish to hand the lass up to him. Arielle blinked owlishly at this change, but settled herself against Kinnon and dropped back off to sleep. Rory handed Melisende onto her mare.

Melisende tried not to feel slighted, but she could see no reason for him to share his thoughts when she had been less than forthcoming with her own. She rode amidst the men-at-arms, struggling to keep her thoughts on her new home and life ahead and off the remembrance of her treacherous sister—and Kinnon.

"Are ye tired?" Kinnon asked, reining his horse to her side. Arielle draped across his lap, but he did not seem to mind.

"A bit," she admitted.

"We have a long journey ahead. We will take a day's break at Bordeaux and again at Brest before crossing to Ireland."

"Ireland?" she asked, her interest piqued.

"Aye. North by northwest from Brest to Ireland, then up the coast a bit before crossing to Scotland. My clan has a holding along the Firth of Clyde. Depending on the ship, we can land there, and 'tis only a short ride to the castle."

"Mayhap I should hear more about your clan," she encouraged him, warmth from his attention flooding her.

"My sister's husband, Ranald, is laird at Scaurness Castle, overlooking the firth."

"What is a firth?" she asked.

"'Tis the opening of a river from the sea. The River Clyde goes inland to the Bishopric of Glasgow, a major shipping town, and our castle controls the traffic on the river."

"Are you much at war? It sounds like a military post."

"Pirates from time to time, or an ambitious man who would wrest control of the firth for himself. Ranald is a strong leader." Kinnon stared at her. "How is it we have not discussed this before now?"

Melisende's lips curved. "We spoke of other things in *Aubrac*, and our travel along the pilgrims' trail was often too swift and treacherous for casual talk. And our nights were spent making love," she added.

Kinnon nodded slowly. "Aye. Hard travel doesnae make for much talk. And I expect ye will need yer sleep at night. As will the lass."

Unmindful of the men around her, Melisende replied, "I want to spend my nights with you." His eyebrows lifted as though surprised, cutting her to the quick. "I wish to speak with you later," she said. He nodded and they rode the wooded trail side-by-side.

* * *

Kinnon sank to the ground beside Melisende. "Is the lass abed?"

Melisende looked up from her spot on the plaide she'd spread out for sleeping. Her hair was loose and spilled about her like a dark cloud. "*Oui*. I am sorry we were so late leaving my *oncle's* house. I know we could have made this trip in a day had we left earlier."

"Och, it would have been a verra hard day's travel. We've plenty of those ahead." He tucked a lock of hair behind her ear, tamping down a surge of desire. "Ye said ye wished to discuss something with me?"

"*Oui*. It is about Lucienne and me. And you."

A curious combination of relief and apprehension twisted in his chest. "Tell me."

Melisende rose to her feet and he reached for her arm to help her, rising with her. Warmth sparked through his hand and higher, then pooled low in his belly. *I wish to clear this up between us, Melisende. But talking is not what I want right now.*

He released her and followed her a few feet away. She halted, twisting her hands at her waist.

"It cannae be as bad as that," he remarked.

She faced him. "It has worsened throughout the day."

"Aye, problems have a way of doing that the longer we put off confronting them."

She tilted her head. "Why are you being so agreeable? I have treated you horribly—"

"Nae," he drawled. "But I have withstood battle and imminent death better."

She released her hands, letting them drop to her sides. "Last night, I went with Lucienne to her room. She told me of her life in Italy, going from house to house since she and Raul had none of their own. Then, after he divorced her, going from bed to bed."

Leaning back against a tree, she closed her eyes briefly, pain and regret etched on her pretty face. "It was then she told me she wanted me to raise Arielle. Not only is she unable to provide for her, but men—perverted men—had cast their gazes on the child. It was not nice of

151

me, but I told her what a shameless life she led, and she became hateful, telling me how perfect I must be, how little I understood her."

She stepped closer, taking his hands in hers. Kinnon's heart missed a beat. "It was then she told me Arielle is your daughter."

Heat of a different sort surged through him. Anger blinded him and instead of Melisende, he saw Lucienne's smug face, her sly smile and covetous eyes.

"Be damned!"

He gripped her hands, noting the chill of her flesh. Regret tightened his chest. "I never touched yer sister. She was scarcely older than a child. A flirtatious lass, aye, but I would never betray her or ye in that way." He demanded her attention. "I have told ye this before."

Tears glistened in her eyes. "I believe you."

The unspoken words hung in the air. "But, what, Melisende?"

"But it has hit me hard. I did not want to believe her when she told me the first time—when she ran away with Raul. I could not believe it of you. I knew she was angry and capable of saying anything that day." She slipped her hands from his and his blood froze as she turned away.

"She was angry yesterday, too. Why is this different?" But he knew. Only a few feet away slept a little girl who had been born too early for her mother's husband to claim her as his. And instead of having her mother's coloring, she had those of her aunt—and his.

Melisende's voice sounded soft in the night. "She was such a sweet child. So eager to please." She gave a wistful laugh. "She did not always like her *légumes*, and was often lost in daydreams, but she always had a pretty flower for me or a witty song she made up."

She faced Kinnon, hands twisting at her waist. "Why is she trying to destroy me?"

* * *

He held her as tight as he could through the night, long after her silent, shuddering cries eased and she drifted off to sleep. *Damn Lucienne for wreaking havoc wherever she goes, feeding her own pleasures without care to the cost. And damn the need for her to ruin her sister's happiness.* The stars twinkled above them through the leafy canopy and the moon sent its filtered light through the glen. Melisende's head lay tucked beneath his chin, her body curved against his. Arielle was a small bundle of plaid only an arm's reach away, Jean-Baptiste curled at her feet.

Poor lass needs a mother who can protect her, love her, teach her. He recalled Melisende's earlier words. *Neither of us thought of bringing a child into the family so soon—or at such an age. I am not against raising the lass. But now I wonder if her daily presence will tarnish the trust Melisende and I should be building.*

He thoroughly disliked the turn his thoughts were taking. Firmly, he schooled his mind away from such things and imagined Scaurness Castle and the firth beyond. The breeze in the trees became the sound of waves on the beach. When he woke, it was morning, the smell of breakfast was in the air, and Melisende was gone.

CHAPTER THIRTY-ONE

He scrambled to his feet, tossing the blanket aside as he scanned the area for signs of his wife. The plaide Arielle had slept on was no longer on the ground, and neither was Jean-Baptiste. Hamish squatted beside the campfire, prodding the embers.

"Where are they?" Kinnon demanded.

Hamish gave him a startled look then relaxed. "Yer wife and the wee lass have been up for an hour or more. She said they wished to get an early start."

"An early start? They've left?" Kinnon shook his head to clear his mind.

"Nae," Hamish replied easily. "But they are likely to call ye a slug-a-bed."

Feminine voices reached his ears and he looked up sharply. Melisende and Arielle strolled into camp, the lass skipping beside Melisende's skirts, the pair hand-in-hand.

"Where have ye been, and why are ye alone?" He wasn't sure what vexed him more. That he'd though she'd left him, that she had no guard, or that she looked so right with Arielle at her side.

Melisende's eyebrows drew upward. "Good morning. We have been completing our morning ritual, if put so bluntly." She tossed a glance over her shoulder. "And six of your most trusted soldiers came with us and Jean-Baptiste to keep us quite safe."

Kinnon felt it entirely too early in the morning to take criticism well. Especially since she was right and he was wrong. She hadn't left him, and an adequate guard which included her dog had accompanied her. She and Arielle did look well together. If only they'd taken an aversion to each other . . . Nae, that was uncharitable. The wee lass needed to be with family.

His cheeks warmed. "My apologies. I only just woke to find ye gone and Hamish entirely too flippant with yer whereabouts," he added unfairly. "I agree we could use an early start."

"Arielle and I have already eaten. Since you have a penchant for eating in the saddle, we only await your pleasure."

Kinnon bowed. "As ye wish." He stalked into the trees to begin his own morning ritual, splashing his face with water from the cold pool at the base of the waterfall. When he arrived back at camp, he found it cleared and the horses saddled and ready to go. He grabbed a chunk of bread from the small bundle Hamish handed him and crammed it into his mouth before climbing into his saddle. Melisende reined her mare next to him.

"Might I have a good morning kiss, or does sleeping late always disagree with you?"

He chewed twice and swallowed before turning to her upturned face. A mixture of gentle teasing and wariness lurked in her eyes. Drawing one arm about her waist, he lifted her from her horse and set her across his lap. He lowered his head, and amid laughter and cheers, he kissed his wife as though the words the night before had never been spoken.

His hurt and pain appeased, he returned her to her saddle. It healed his heart to see the love in her gaze, and he smiled at her as he urged his horse to a walk.

* * *

The early evening stars were out before they arrived at the old farm house. They had taken pains to skirt the small town of *Chateauneuf-De-Randon* where Kinnon feared they might run into the same trouble with the soldiers as they had in *Le Puy*. Memories of the area assaulted him. Bertran's army had camped just beyond that ridge. He recalled the white canvas tent where Bertran had died and an entire city had paid him homage. Such an enigmatic man. He accomplished so much for France and was a shining hero to the people, and yet the darker side of war lived within his camp.

Kinnon emerged from his memories into the reality of the abandoned farm. Melisende had dismounted at the opening to the yard. The gate hung by one hinge, its frame weathered and worn. A chicken squawked, chased by a ragged rooster. Jean-Baptiste bounded past Melisende and stopped in the middle of the overgrown area, a puzzled look on his face. Arielle ran after him, squealing as she caught him by his heavy collar. He licked her face.

"Only two chickens, no goats. Not even a cow left," Melisende mourned.

"It has been a few years," he reminded her.

She sent him an apologetic look and picked up her skirt as she stepped slowly up the path to the house. Stepping through the doorway, she vanished from his sight.

The sun beat down on him much as it had the first day he'd urged the horses and wagon up the winding, rocky trail almost four years ago. The air had the same sweetness, rising from the sun-warmed grass. It was quieter, though, with the farm animals gone, and this time Jean-Baptiste would not question his right to step onto the property.

He watched Arielle as she played with the big dog. She laughed as she ran from one side of the yard to the other, Jean-Baptiste's long strides keeping pace with her easily. She slipped and fell, her hands splayed forward as she caught herself against his sturdy frame. The dog licked her face and stood firm as she grasped his collar and righted herself.

The men stood about, talking quietly among themselves. Kinnon knew the journey ahead would be long and arduous, and the men were, for the most part, eager to be home. But the south of France was nowhere near the Scottish Highlands, and weeks of travel lay before them. Weeks that would test the strength of his and Melisende's new bond as the close confines of a ship and each night in a different spot would soon wear at even the most placid demeanor.

And what of Arielle? Like it or not, the child would come between them, even if only in the simplest manner. She could not be turned loose to wander the ship, and certainly would not be allowed to sleep anywhere except with Melisende. There would be limited space on the ship, and too many dangers for a three-year-old to encounter.

Movement to his right caught his attention. Melisende had left the house and made her way down the path to the spot overlooking the hillside. The trail was almost non-existent and cluttered with weeds and leaves and other debris, but her track was true. He followed her to her favorite spot and found her leaning against one of the boulders. He eased next to another large stone.

"Mind the snake," she murmured. With a start, Kinnon glanced down at the rock in time to see the flash of a whip-like tail as its owner vanished over the far edge.

"It was harmless, but I remember how much you dislike them," she added.

Kinnon abandoned his position next to the boulder and approached Melisende, staring out over the field with her.

"Do the Highlands look thus?" she asked.

"A bit. But wilder. Great glens or clearings that sweep into the mountains and hide amid vast forests."

"Is it cold?"

"Often. But my clan lives on the sea, and the weather there is milder than in the Highlands."

Melisende was silent and Kinnon was not sure if she found that agreeable or not. He stepped closer. "Is this what ye want? To remain here? Will ye be terribly homesick if you come to Scotland?"

She took a deep breath. "I cannot say. There is the desire to rebuild the farm, to make it prosperous again. It is so very sad to see it thus. But there would always be the fear of someone who remembered me—and Jean-Baptiste." She shook her head. "And I am now your wife. Being with you is the most important thing—more than this could ever be," she added, motioning around her with her hand. "I will take my memories with me to my new home and try not to think on them over much."

"I could stay here with ye," he offered carefully, trying to judge her heart. "Mayhap a few of my men would consider living here and marrying a pretty French lass—like I have. We could protect ye."

At last she faced him. "And I would look for Lucienne around every corner, in every room and walkway." Her lips twisted to one side. "I cannot do that."

"Then come with me to Scotland and raise Arielle with that overgrown dog of yers. We could start a small monastery and support young widows who have no family, and orphans who need a home. A *domerie* such as the one in *Aubrac* where none are turned away. Everyone would work together to be clothed and fed."

"And feel needed?" she asked.

"That is curious," Kinnon replied. "Why do you ask that?"

"I think Lucienne is searching for something that makes her feel needed—complete. For whatever reason, she seeks it in her encounters where she believes she has power and it makes her feel good. It is my hope that someday she will find someone who will care for her, make her feel needed and loved so that she abandons the life she has now."

He saw the same need in Melisende's eyes. Unlike Lucienne, she had been content to wait, to fill her life with other things until love bloomed. But the same emptiness demanded to be filled in her. The hunger to meet that for her grew inside him.

He tenderly touched his fingertips to her cheek. "I need ye, Melisende. I need your warmth, your laughter, your wisdom to fill my life. I loved ye the first time I saw ye with dirt on yer face and yer great dog at yer side. And I crave yer touch like I need the air to breathe."

Flinging her arms wide, she threw herself against him. Tilting her face up, she demanded his kiss, and he happily obliged her. He crushed her to him, slanting his mouth across hers as he deepened the kiss, coaxing, urging, demanding she admit she belonged to him. Her arms slid around his neck, her breasts pushed against his chest as she pressed closer to him. Her mouth opened and her tongue played feverishly with his. His cock grew instantly hard, pressing against the folds of fabric between them.

She struggled against him, and he loosened his arms, breaking the kiss with a moan of disappointment. Reaching behind, she grabbed at the laces of her gown. With a rumble of laughter, Kinnon reached down and jerked her skirt up, running his hands up the length of her legs. She shuddered and gasped, leaning against him so the vee of her legs pressed against the head of his cock. He scooted backward until he sat upon one of the boulders, dragging her into his lap.

Bracing her knees on either side of him, she leaned forward, giving him a chance to rake his kilt up, and their bodies finally came together. Her shoulders hunched forward and he feasted on the sight of her breasts pouring over the top of her gown. She wiggled her hips and his attention snapped immediately to her velvet warmth as it enveloped his cock. He shuddered as he penetrated her depths. Her head arched back as she stroked him faster and harder until her breath caught and she teetered on the edge of passion. With a powerful thrust, he spent himself as she spasmed around him, the sweet sound of his name on her lips.

His palms splayed across her bottom as he held her in his lap, savoring the last tremors of her body. Her forehead rested on his, escaped tendrils of her hair forming a curtain about their faces. He kissed the tip of her nose.

"I cannot live without you, Kinnon," she breathed.

"Nor I without ye, *mo chridhe*. But there is still the matter of yer sister's words between us. I know ye dinnae believe her, but once heard, 'tis hard to un-hear them."

Melisende nodded. "*Oui*, but my heart knows the truth. 'Tis my hope that when I look at Arielle, I will believe I see both you and me in her, as our daughter. And mayhap, from time-to-time, I will see Lucienne as well."

"I will endeavor to forgive her for trying to cause a rift between us. And pray for her." Kinnon shifted, suddenly feeling the hard stone beneath his bare buttocks.

Melisende gave him her sweetest smile. "Are you ready to get up, *mon amour*?"

He grinned. "My bum is, though the rest of me could stay like this forever."

She laughed as he lowered her to her feet. "We have a long voyage ahead of us. I am eager to see the charms of Scotland."

Kinnon jerked his kilt back into place and placed his lips against her ear. "And I am eager to show them to you."

EPILOGUE

Rain beat steadily on the roof of the small cottage, damping down the sharp scent of burning peat. Melisende breathed deeply, aware the odor, so strange at first, had become a symbol of her new home—and her new life. She smiled contentedly. Kinnon drowsed in a nearby chair, his feet propped on the hearth. Arielle sat on the floor beside him, playing with a doll he had crafted for her a few months earlier. Jean-Baptiste lay sprawled on his rug on the far side of the hearth, his job of protecting Arielle suspended pending a nap.

Her little family, though outside the walls of their snug house, there were many others she considered the same. They'd found the perfect site for Kinnon's vision close to the Bishopric of Glasgow, an abandoned monastery whose walls were still in good order, though they'd begun replacing roofs and clearing gardens for the next year. And though she knew it was further from his home than he would like, his face glowed with the contentment of being able to help others in need. His family had welcomed them warmly, smoothing her and Arielle's entrance to Scotland, and she missed seeing them almost as much as he did. But this was where they were meant to be.

She'd even met Brother Padraig when he'd visited only a month or so after they'd arrived. He shared a few stories of Kinnon's time on Iona, earning him some pained looks from Kinnon, and laughter from her. And he'd brought Kinnon's wee cat, Angus, now quite grown and eager to claim the house for himself and keep the rats and mice at bay. For which she was very grateful. And perhaps even as grateful that Jean-Baptiste seemed to take little notice of the cat, as Arielle had taken quite a liking to him, though Jean-Baptiste remained her ever-present companion.

It was even possible Brother Padraig would return and take over the monastic side of their mission, for it was clear the need for a place of sanctuary for widows and orphans exceeded the work she and Kinnon could do alone. He'd promised a setting much like the *domerie* at *Aubrac,* and to do so, they would need many more dedicated hands.

She hoped they would arrive soon. She ran a hand slowly across her belly, still hiding the secret she was anxious to share with Kinnon. After months of love-making and no sign she was *enceinte*, she had feared she was too old to conceive a child. She had shared this once with Kinnon, and he'd assured her she and Arielle were all he needed in his life. And then loved her so thoroughly it took her breath away. For a time, she'd been content. But now she knew for certain their babe would arrive next winter just before Yule, and she waited for the perfect time to tell Kinnon.

Kinnon stirred and glanced at her from beneath hooded eyes. Arielle yawned and hugged her doll as she climbed into Kinnon's lap. With an enormous sigh, the child fell asleep. Kinnon rose carefully and tucked her into her bed behind a curtain on the far side of the hearth.

He crossed the room to Melisende and wrapped his arms about her waist. "How is *ma petite* French bride?" he asked, nuzzling her neck.

Shivers of longing shot through her and she arched against him, feeling his arousal against her buttocks. "She is ever in love with the Scot who swept her off her feet," she replied.

His hands splayed across her belly as he swept his palms up her ribs and cupped her breasts.

"Mayhap she would care to show how much she loves him," he murmured huskily.

Melisende inhaled a long, deep breath. She turned in his arms and nibbled his lower lip. Her heart filled so much she thought she could not contain it. A year ago, she had faced life as her uncle's assistant, with no other family to care for and love. Joy welled up in her and she stared into her husband's adoring eyes. It was time. She had news to share.

ACKNOWLEDGEMENTS

To begin, Kinnon would not have his story were it not for the readers who asked for it. He was the hinge-point in The Highlander's Reluctant Bride—would he show up at some point and change the course of the book? Though he only appeared briefly in that story, he was apparently a sympathetic character, and people wanted to know what happened to him. My readers are a wonderful well of inspiration, and I enjoy hearing from them.

As mentioned earlier, as I began my research, Kinnon's story became entwined with that of Bertran du Guesclin, Constable of France. I wish to thank a generous lady at Murray State College, Dr. Rebecca Jacobs-Pollez, who has a doctorate in Medieval France, who helped me with several references on this great man. One particularly helpful source was *Bertran du Guesclin: the hero of chivalry* by H.D.T. (Harriett Diane Thompson), publisher – London: Burns & Lambert, [1859].

I'd like to also thank my critique partners, Dawn Marie Hamilton and Derek Dodson for their hard work. And my editors, Liette Bougie and Simone Seguin for their invaluable help. And a warm thanks to Dar Albert for creating the new covers for the series

Other books by Cathy MacRae

The Hardy Heroines series
(with DD MacRae)

Highland Escape (book 1)
The Highlander's Viking Bride (book 2)
The Highlander's Crusader Bride (book 3)
The Highlander's Norse Bride (book 4)
The Highlander's Welsh Bride (book 5)
The Prince's Highland Bride (book 6, available 2020)

* * *

The Ghosts of Culloden Moor series

(Please read The Gathering by LL Muir first to avoid confusion)

Adam
Malcolm
MacLeod
Patrick

* * *

De Wolfe Pack Connected World series
(published by Wolfbane Publishing)
The Saint
The Penitent
The Cursed

About the author: Cathy MacRae enjoys writing stories of strong Highland heroes and feisty women on their way to their happy-ever-afters. She loves hearing from her readers, and you can sign up for her newsletter and learn more about her and her books—and the occasional dog or gardening story—on her website, www.cathymacraeauthor.com. You can also look her up on facebook or follow her on Twitter @CMacRaeAuthor.

Author's note about the Highlander's Bride series: Each book can be read as a complete story on its own, but characters tend to show up in other books from time-to-time, so reading them in order is preferable, though not necessary.

www.ingramcontent.com/pod-product-compliance
Lightning Source LLC
Chambersburg PA
CBHW061241170626

46809CB00007B/2770